# COALBROOKDALE

# Coalbrookdale

## *The Bangham Family Story*

MARILYN FREEMAN

Spellbrooktales

First Printing, 2022
Published by: Spellbrooktales

Cover photo: Part of the picture 'Morning View of Coalbrookdale' by William Williams, displayed at the
Shrewsbury Museum and Art Gallery.

DEDICATION


This book is dedicated to my father,

Herbert Bangham (1915 – 1995)
and also to his great grandson

Herbie Ray Bangham (10th March 2021-)

# Acknowledgements

In the course of researching the background for this book, I have been assisted by several authors who have written extensively about the Severn Gorge and its history, particularly relating to the 18th Century.

The monumental work 'The Industrial Revolution in Shropshire' by Barrie Trinder has been my 'bible' throughout my journey of discovery. It is a mine of information about the ironmasters, mine owners, and other employers in the district, as well as describing in great detail how their employees lived, worked and worshipped.

'Pitmen, Poachers and Preachers' by Ken Jones was invaluable as I learnt about the precariousness of the lives of the poor, and how any unfortunate occurrence could easily result in destitution, and their being returned to their home district, often to live 'on the parish' in the local poorhouse.

'Abiah Darby' by Rachel Labouchere provided me with some insights from the perspective of the employers, in this case, the Darby family and was very helpful as I placed the Bangham family within that context.

In addition, I must express my gratitude to the clerks of the Coalbrookdale Company, whose detailed records relating to the early 1700's, which have miraculously survived and are kept in the Shropshire Archives, enabled me to discover that Joseph and William Bangham were both employed by the Darby family.

It would be remiss of me not to mention the wonderful Ironbridge Gorge Museum Trust. I have visited all of the museums in the Gorge often over the years. It was here that I began to build the picture of the people who lived and worked in this amazing district. I hope I have done it justice within the pages of this book. It is rightly designated a World Heritage Site

Finally, I want to thank my husband Barry for his encouragement and support during the gestation period of this book, and to my wider family for believing in me.

Marilyn Freeman
2021

# Prologue

It was 1956 and I was ten years old, sitting on the hearthrug by Grandad's chair. As I leant my head against his knee, the smell of cotton mill and Woodbine enveloped me, and I knew I was in my favourite place. The light outside was fading fast and every now and then a spurt of gas from the coal fire would ignite and flare into life, illuminating the room. I looked up at Grandad and asked a question that had been bothering me for some time, 'Where had our family come from?' As he smiled down at me, the firelight twinkling in his eyes, in his broad Lancashire accent, he told me he understood that two hundred years ago our family lived in Shropshire, in a place called Coalbrookdale.

At the time, I had never heard of Coalbrookdale, and found the name confusing. Was this a place like Oldham, where I was growing up, where the smoke from the coal fires and mill chimneys hung in the air, diluting the sunshine, even in the middle of summer? Or was it a beautiful place, in a green valley with a brook running through?

I asked him how we got from Shropshire to Oldham,

but he didn't know when or why the family had left that place, to move to the industrial towns of the north of England. All he knew, was that his father Edwin had always told him the family was from Coalbrookdale. I determined that one day, I would find the answers.

Some years later I did become seriously interested in researching the family tree, eventually tracing the Bangham line back to 1652 and Walter Bangome, living in the Severn Gorge area of Shropshire. In the course of my research, I was fascinated to learn that one of Walter's sons, Joseph, my fifth great grandfather, had worked for Abraham Darby, at his ironworks in Coalbrookdale. I was even able to locate references to Joseph and his brother William in the surviving accounts books of the Darby works.

Abraham Darby and his descendants were responsible for developing a way of making iron using coke made from coal, rather than charcoal made from wood. Unlike wood, coal was plentiful. With a ready supply of the other raw materials in the area, namely limestone and ironstone, there was virtually no limit to the amount of iron which could be smelted in the Coalbrookdale furnaces. As the process was adopted across the country the unlimited supply of iron fuelled the Industrial Revolution, by providing the raw material for building machinery and engines for the mills and railways of Great Britain and beyond. Over the $18^{th}$ and $19^{th}$ centuries, the first iron rails were cast in the Coalbrookdale works, as were cylinders for the first Newcomen steam engines, parts for the first iron ship, the SS Great Britain, now restored and sitting alongside the docks in Bristol, and the World's first bridge made of iron, which still stands today at Ironbridge in the Severn Gorge, now a World Heritage Site.

Over the years I have often imagined what life may have been like for Joseph and his family. Did he realise as he worked at the furnace, that he was involved in events that were to change the world? I have visited the Severn Gorge many times and it never fails to move me just as strongly as it did on the first day I stood in the churchyard of Holy Trinity on the steep slopes of the Coalbrookdale valley, gazing to the south, across the Gorge towards Banghams Wood.

Is there such a thing as 'folk memory?' That, I cannot tell, I only know that as I surveyed the valley I felt a connection with the place. It felt like home. This was in the 1970's and the name Coalbrookdale still confused me. This was certainly a beautiful dale, with steep sided, thickly wooded slopes, and a brook running along the valley floor toward the River Severn. There was just a hint as to the origin of the reference to 'coal', in the partially derelict industrial buildings standing beside a railway viaduct.

So, this is where my story begins, Banghams Wood, over three hundred years ago. Now in my seventh decade I am able to add the perspective of my own life to that of the Bangham family. I can see and understand more fully the impact of those changes witnessed, and, yes, implemented by Joseph Bangham and his workmates.

Over this period, their lives in the peaceful rural hamlet in Banghams Wood, must have changed fundamentally as industry came to the Gorge. Working in the fields and coppicing in the woods, would have given way to days and nights of toil, in the hot dirty and dangerous world of the smelting and forging of iron. The fresh air and sweet scent of wildflowers and woodsmoke was to be replaced by acrid fumes from the blast furnaces. Soot and dust must have eventually covered everything, and the sound of birdsong would have been drowned out by the roar of the fire and the hammering of metal on metal at the forges.

When Joseph started out at the Darby Works, I have imagined that he was probably excited at the prospect of change coming to the Gorge. I wonder, when he looked back on his life, whether he felt the changes had been for the better, or whether something of the old life had been lost? These are the kind of thoughts many of us have as we look at the world today and contemplate whether our civilisation will survive the effects of industrialisation and the resultant climatic changes it has brought about.

However, I see the story of our family as a microcosm of so many family stories, as the agricultural gave way to the industrial way of life. Whatever the final outcome for humanity and the planet itself, I do feel it's a story worth telling. This then, is a fictional story based on the life of Joseph Bangham and his family.

# The Banghams

Walter Bangome
Abt 1650
**Joseph Bangham**
1695 - 1759
Nathaniel Bangham
1729 - ?
Thomas Bangham
1809 - 1850
Edwin Bangham
1848 - ~1920
Wilfred Bangham
1886 - 1968
**Herbert Bangham**
1915 - 1995
David Bangham
1944 -
Nicholas Mark Bangham
1980 -
**Herbie Ray Bangham**
10th March 2021 -

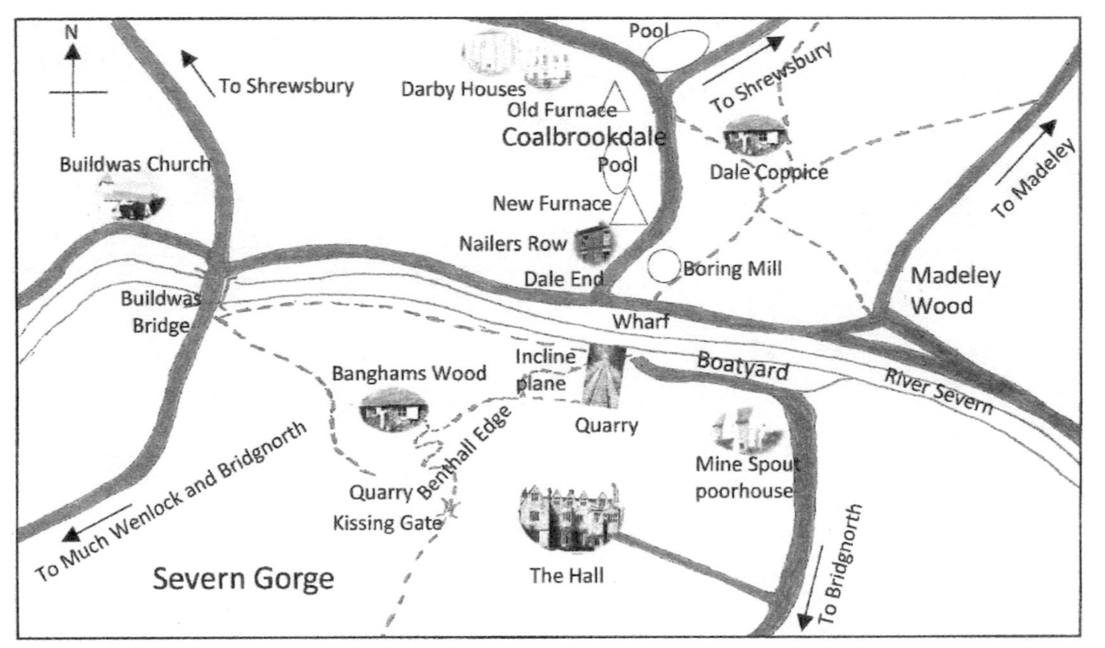

N
To Shrewsbury
Darby Houses
Old Furnace
Coalbrookdale
Pool
Pool
To Shrewsbury
Dale Coppice
To Madeley
New Furnace
Nailers Row
Dale End
Boring Mill
Madeley Wood
Buildwas Church
Buildwas Bridge
Wharf
Boatyard
River Severn
Incline plane
Banghams Wood
Quarry
To Much Wenlock and Bridgnorth
Quarry Benthall Edge
Kissing Gate
Mine Spout
poorhouse
The Hall
To Bridgnorth
Severn Gorge

# Chapter 1

1713: Spring had arrived early in the Severn Gorge and the hedgerows were bursting with birdsong. Joe Bangham strode along the track from his home in Banghams Wood at the bottom of Benthall Edge, down to the bridge over the River Severn at Buildwas. He noticed the river was high, after the rain which had swept along the Gorge yesterday. Crossing the river, he turned right, along the north bank, then after a mile or so, took the track running beside the Coalbrookdale stream. He had heard the ironworks were taking on new men. Sustaining the family on agricultural labourers' wages was impossible. Even with the charcoal burning, it didn't bring in enough to feed and clothe the family. Times were hard at home after his mother's death, with eight children, the youngest being just one year old. Walter, his father, had done his best, but losing his wife had hit him hard. Two of Joe's sisters had to go into service up at the Hall, and as the boys grew up, they each, in their turn, were apprenticed for seven years to the Benthall farm and then eventually helped Walter with the coppicing and charcoal burning.

On visits to Madeley Wood on market days, there had been talk of Mr Darby building another furnace at his works in Coalbrookdale and that he would need more workers. Apparently, he was paying eight shillings a week, which was more than Joe could earn as a farm labourer even when there was work, which was intermittent. It was said that the jobs at the works weren't permanent and couldn't be guaranteed, but Joe felt that even if he could do a few weeks in the year, it would be a great boost to the family's finances. So, he was determined to try his luck, and as he walked along the track towards the works, was feeling hopeful. He was eighteen years old, strong and ambitious. He was at an age when anything seems possible, and he exuded an air of optimism that was infectious. He was certain Mr Darby would take him on.

For decades, the family had been supplying furnaces up and down the Gorge with charcoal for smelting iron. From what he'd heard about the events at the Darby Works, the demand for their charcoal may well be about to decline. Apparently, Mr Darby had much improved his way of making iron for casting, and new ways of working were coming to the Gorge. The making of iron would no longer rely on coppicing and producing charcoal. Joe had long since realised the limits of this endeavour, which relied on growing trees, of necessity a slow business. Mr Darby used coal instead of charcoal to make his iron. Joe instinctively knew that the family's reliance on making and selling charcoal was going to have to change, and he could be an instrument of that change, rather than resisting it. To a young man such as he, it felt exciting. This was the future. As we can imagine, his father was not too pleased with the prospect of his eldest son going to work for Darby, the man who was showing the world that charcoal was no longer needed in the production of iron.

Of course, Joe understood his father's reluctance. To produce a clamp of charcoal needed two people to camp out in the woods for five days and nights on end, to tend the fire. If the fire got out of control, becoming too hot, the product was ruined. If he went to work at the Darby works, it would mean that Will, his younger brother would have to work with his father during the 'burn', leaving only the youngest brother Richard available for a second clamp, which without him, would be impossible, and the family would be limited to producing one clamp at a time.

As he walked along the track up the steep sided valley, the sound of industry grew louder. He passed the forges and the foundries, which were surrounded by stacks of iron pigs, the raw material from which they produced their various wares. Here, was all noise of metal on metal and the shouts of men trying to make themselves heard above the din. As he walked further on, the bulk of the furnace came into view. He could smell the smoke and fumes and hear the sound of the stone being tipped into the mouth of the furnace, and the rumble of another load being wheeled across the bridge to be next in line. He stood for some moments, transfixed by the noise and the smell and the sight of the bright golden red light issuing from the mouth at the base of the structure, with sparks flying in all directions. He was used to the sounds and sights of the woodlands and meadows where he had lived and toiled all his life. Obviously, he had seen many small furnaces over the years, but this was something completely different. As he watched and listened, he began to understand more fully, the extent of the change that was coming.

He noticed a gentleman, full bearded and rather better dressed than the rest of the men, standing to one side, also observing the scene. He immediately recognised him as Mr Darby. He had seen him several times in Madeley, on market days. Taking a deep breath and standing tall, Joe strode up to him and, removing his cap, asked if he could speak with him. Mr Darby smiled, and Joe introduced himself, offering his hand. Mr Darby seemed a little taken aback but nonetheless, shook Joe's hand warmly.

'What can I do for you, Joe Bangham,' he asked, with a wry smile.

'Well sir,' said Joe, 'I wonder if you might have any work? I had heard you were taking on more men.'

'Oh, you did, did you? Well, I might be. What work have you done before?'

'I've worked the land since I was eight-years old, and my family make charcoal in the wood under Benthall

Edge.' Joe replied, 'But I'm strong an' fit, an' willing to do what's needed Sir.'

Mr Darby asked him what he knew about making iron. Joe replied that at the moment he didn't know very much, although his family had supplied several furnaces in the area with charcoal for producing brass and iron over the years. He assured Mr Darby he was willing to learn and wasn't afraid of hard work.

'Well Joe,' Mr Darby explained, 'I am minded to give you a try, but as I'm sure you know, this work is not guaranteed. Some weeks, particularly in the summer, we produce no iron, maybe because there is no rain to fill the pool, or maybe because we just don't have the orders.'

'I understand sir, but I believe this to be the future of making iron and I want to be a part on it.'

Mr Darby nodded thoughtfully, then smiled and agreed he could start the following Monday. The work was to be from six in the morning, until six in the evening when the furnace was blowing. He would also be expected to work night shifts as needed. He would start on six shillings a week until he had gained some experience and then Mr Darby said he would look at it again. The usual rate for an experienced worker was eight shillings a week. Joe was happy and grateful to be given the chance to prove himself.

'I won't let you down, Mr Darby,' he said, offering his hand, which Mr Darby took, once again with a wry smile, thinking that there was something appealing about this young man. Of course, time will tell he thought, let's see how he performs when his real work begins.

Joe turned and walked briskly away down the valley. He was excited. For the first time in his life, he could see horizons opening up before him. For as long as he could remember, all that was ahead of him were days of toil in the fields, interspersed with long nights camping by a clamp in the woods. Now he had the opportunity to become part of a bigger future, part of the change he was certain was coming to the world.

Joe arrived home half an hour later. Home was a stone-built house with a turf roof. It had originally been built as a squatter's cottage by his grandparents many decades earlier. At the time, in order to claim squatters' rights, it had to be constructed within one night, with four walls and a roof, to qualify as being finished. Since then, the Bangham family had been coppicing in this wood, and over the years it had become known as 'Banghams Wood.' In the beginning, the house had just one room, but over the years, the family had added another two rooms above, a wash house, a hog pen, and a separate privvy. Other families had arrived and built their squatter cottages, and it became a hamlet, and a water pump was installed, to be shared by all the families.

The Banghams cottage was sparsely furnished with little beyond the beds, a table, several stools, an old trunk, and a few rustic chairs. Years ago, his mother had made bedspreads and rugs out of old rags which gave it a cosy feel. The log fire blazing brightly in the hearth was the main source of light. Candles were expensive and only lit when the last of the daylight had gone. His sister Elizabeth had a stew-pot cooking above the fire, which was emitting a wonderful aroma as Joe entered, reminding him just how hungry he was.

No one spoke as he came in. There was an awkward silence. They all knew where he'd been of course, and they also knew what their father, Walter, who was sitting in one of the chairs by the fire, felt about that. Joe took off his coat and cap and hung them behind the door.

'Well,' he said, 'Is none of ye going to ask 'ow I got on?'

'We can see how ye got on,' Walter retorted, 'by that look on thy face.'

'In case any of thee wants to know, I start next Monday.'

Still, no one spoke, all eyes now on Walter.

'Look father, I know ye aren't happy about this, but 'tis the future tha knows, an' we need to be part on it. With this new way of making iron, a big part of our market for charcoal will go, I'm sure on it.'

'And in the meantime?!' Walter shouted, 'How are we supposed to feed ourselves? Did Darby say thee'd have work every week?'

'Well, nay, it might be a bit up and down like,' Joe replied.

'There ye are then, what are we meant to do when 'ee can't give thee work? Stop eatin' fer a week or two?'

'Well, we can carry on with the charcoal as well, there's still a market for it at the moment.'

'Tha means me and father can, while ye goes off chasing dreams,' interjected Will, who was becoming irritated by Joe's assumption that the charcoal burning could go on as before, trapping him even further in his life of toil.

'An' how are we meant to do that when we won't know from week to week whether ye'll be around to 'elp?' Walter went on loudly, 'me Will 'n Dick'll never run two clamps when yer called away to thy precious Darby's!'

Joe looked crestfallen and the others all kept quiet for fear of making Walter even more angry.

'Look father,' Joe said finally, 'I'll work harder than I ever worked afore. I'll make sure I bring in enough to top up what we might lose from cutting back on the farming an' charcoal. I just want a chance to give us all a better future.'

'So, the past ain't good enough for thee now, I suppose!' Walter responded angrily.

'Please, father, that's not what I meant. I know you've always done yer best for us. You and ma, when she was here, God rest her soul, but times are changing, an' we need to be part on it. I can do this, father. I can make life better for all on us. Just trust me.'

'Well, I don't seem to have much option, do I?' said Walter now. He felt and looked visibly smaller. He knew that some of his authority was ebbing away to the next generation. Joe was young and capable, and deep-down Walter knew he was right. The family had to move on if it was going to survive and Joe was the one who would lead the way. He would still have Will to help him carry on with the charcoal, unless, that is, he decided to desert him too. Will, for his part, sat broodingly gazing into the fire. He would have liked to carry on with the conversation, but Walter's capitulation cut the ground from under him and he too had no option but to accept it, albeit grudgingly. He couldn't help feeling that Joe was somehow deserting the family, leaving him to carry the greater part of the burden.

Still, no one else spoke. They were all aware that something important just happened. After a few minutes Elizabeth got up and laid the table for supper. She lit the candles and then ladled the stew from the pot into each bowl, placed the loaf of bread she'd made earlier in the middle of the table and told them all to sit down for their supper. It was eaten largely in silence.

The family was somewhat depleted now that both Margaret and Abigail were away in service at the Hall. Walter sat at one end of the table, and Elizabeth, his eldest daughter at the other, where her mother had once been seated. Elizabeth was well past the first flush of youth, being thirty-two last birthday. After her mother died, she realised she would have to take on the roles of mother to the little ones and housekeeper for her father. Her own dreams of getting married and having a home of her own had to be sacrificed on the altar of keeping the family together. Joe's brother Will sat next to his father. The genetic connection was obvious. They both had broad shoulders, heavy brows and a large nose. Still brooding, he knew, once Joe had left, he would have to assume responsibility for the family should anything happen to Walter, who wasn't getting any younger. His future would be tied to this family come what may, and he couldn't afford the luxury of dreaming of a different one, unlike his older brother.

Martha sat next to Elizabeth. Dear Martha, Joe thought, glancing at her now. Martha was one of those people blessed with a sunny disposition, but not much in the way of reasoning power. She was thirty years old but never seemed to grow up somehow. Of course, she was always willing to help Elizabeth with the chores, particularly looking after their old horse, Ned. Her favourite jobs though, were feeding the hog and cleaning out the pen, which was just as well, as no one else seemed keen. Often she could be found searching the woods for snails to give the hog as a special treat, and which the beast always crunched with gusto. Service would never be for Martha though, and she would remain in the family home. All the family loved her dearly and were very protective of her.

Dorothy was a pretty, bright, eleven-year old. Like Joe, she was always ready for something new. Margaret had brought a few books discarded by the family up at the Hall, and Dorothy would spend hours pouring over the pictures and trying to understand the lettering that went with them. By the time she was eight, she had grasped the concept of reading. If only she could get some schooling, thought Joe, she could go far in the world. Maybe he could do something about that if all went well at the Darby works. He had heard that soon there might be a Charity School in Buildwas. Maybe he could help to send her there.

Sitting opposite Joe was Richard, the youngest of the boys. At fifteen he was still half man, half boy. He was as bright as Dorothy and had never had the chance of an education either. However, he was strong and willing, and maybe, thought Joe, he'll be able to follow in my footsteps in Coalbrookdale.

Elizabeth broke the silence to tell them all that she had seen Margaret at the market today and she had said she would be coming home for a visit on Sunday. Margaret was twenty-eight and had been in service up at the Hall for twelve years, working her way up to chambermaid. When Abigail was fourteen, Margaret had secured her a position as a scullery maid. They were both allowed to come home to visit the family on one Sunday a month, but of course, hardly ever on the same day. Walter beamed at the news. Margaret had always been the apple of his eye, being the spitting image of her mother.

Thus, the mood in the Bangham household lifted and when the table had been cleared, Martha popped out to the pig pen to feed the scraps to Archie, this year's pig. The family settled down to an hour or two in front of the fire until it was time for bed. After taking turns to visit the privvy and having a quick swill in the bowl of water brought from the pump, they all prepared for bed. Will, Joe and Richard slept with Walter in the main bedroom. Martha and Dorothy shared the smaller room with Elizabeth.

# Chapter 2

Sunday was the one day the whole family tried to avoid work if possible. Of course, if they were in the middle of a 'burn', whoever was tending it had to stay in the temporary shelter erected in the woods beside the clamp, and couldn't join the rest of the family. This Sunday, however, they were all there and excited at the prospect of Margaret's visit. She always brought news of the comings and goings at the Hall, and from the wider world. They had many visitors from further afield, and the news of the day always managed to percolate down to the servants, and thence to the Banghams. There were often a few sweet treats that Cook gave Margaret for the family and she herself often brought a little something from the market or tobacco for her father, who enjoyed a pipe beside the fire when the day's work was done.

She arrived in the early afternoon, with a basket full of various titbits as usual. Everyone gave her a great welcome of course, and then they all settled down around the fire to hear her news. She soon picked up the rather strained atmosphere and asked her father what was wrong.

'You'd better ask Joe,' he snapped.

Margaret turned to look at her brother.

'What have you been up to now our Joe?' she quizzed.

'Nothing! I haven't been 'up to' anything. It's just that father's none too pleased that I've got a job working at the Darby Works. I start tomorrow.'

'Well, that's good isn't it?' Margaret said, 'The family could do with the money, after all.'

'Father doesn't seem to think so.'

'Father?' Margaret said quizzically.

'Well, I'm sorry if I'm bein' daft, but I don't like the idea of one of us workin' with the Darbys, making iron by burnin' coke instead of our charcoal!'

'Oh I know father, but it is said, this new way of iron-making will bring great change, and surely it's better to be part of it than be left behind by it?'

Realising that he was outnumbered on this issue, he changed the subject, asking Margaret what had been going on at the Hall. She told them that things had settled down now, with the new master. It had all been a bit difficult after the old man died a year or so ago, but things were much better now. The new master and his wife liked to entertain, which obviously meant a lot more work for the servants, but she had to admit, it was a much happier place. The mistress was considerate of the servants, was a good manager, and things were running smoothly, which was more than could be said for matters further afield. There was news of riots in the streets and mobs attacking chapels up and down the land. Everyone was grateful she reported, that this unrest hadn't reached the Severn Gorge as yet. She wasn't quite sure what it was all about, but she did know it concerned religion, and people called 'dissenters'.

Dorothy, who had been quiet until now, piped up

'What are we, father?'

'We aren't much of anythin' right now,' Walter responded. 'Mind, way back we was known as Hoogenots or some such. I remember my father tellin' us that 'is father, my grandfather, had crossed the sea from France.'

'Why?' asked Dorothy, as always, in pursuit of the whole story.

'Because, so he said, they weren't allowed to go to a church accordin' to what they believed like.'

'So does that make us the same as these 'dissenters' then. Does that mean they'll attack us too?'

'Enough!' exclaimed Will, 'Your imagination's far too active our Dotty. No one's going to attack us!'

'How's our Abigail doin',' Elizabeth enquired. Elizabeth had a soft spot for Abigail. They had become very close after their mother died. Abigail was easy to understand, always being an uncomplicated, obedient child, unlike Dorothy, who had much more definite ideas of her own and was often challenging of Elizabeth's authority.

Margaret assured her that Abigail seemed to have

settled in well and was doing a good job. She hoped to be home for a visit in two weeks' time, but in the meantime sent them all her love. They chatted on, while Elizabeth prepared the Sunday tea. She had asked Walter to slaughter one of the older chickens as a special treat to cook along with the rabbit he'd caught, as Margaret was coming home. They had been boiling in the pot over the fire along with vegetables from the plot outside. Elizabeth jointed and shared out the meat, serving it up with vegetables piled high and they all enjoyed a hearty meal.

When they had finished, Walter settled down in front of the fire, filling his pipe from the twist of tobacco Margaret had brought for him, feeling content with most of his family around him for once. Soon, Margaret noticed the light was fading outside and announced she must be getting back to the Hall. Joe immediately offered to walk back with her. He was grateful that she at least, hadn't dismissed his decision to work for the Darby's as a 'daft idea', as his father had called it. He was eager to talk to her about it all, and the excitement he felt at this chance to change his future. She had done it, after all. Working in service had its advantages as well as the drawbacks, and at least she had escaped the fate which loomed for Elizabeth and Martha.

She was happy to accept his offer and after she had said her farewells to the rest of the family they set off for the Hall. Joe took the lantern as it was now getting quite dark. They strolled arm in arm down the track then clambered up the steep slope of Benthall Edge, chatting easily about this and that. Eventually Joe asked,

'Margaret, do you really think I'm doing the right thing, workin' for Darby?'

'I do Joe,' she reassured him. 'There are big changes afoot, and I see and hear about them all the time, but you have to understand that father doesn't see it. He's spent all these years farm-working, coppicing and making charcoal, and probably thought it would go on this way forever.'

'I know. it's hard for him to understand, but I thought Will would.'

'Will can't allow himself to, Joe. He knows that father will need him for the charcoal as long as he's able to carry on with it. He probably resents that you're free to choose your own path.'

'Aye, you're probably right, I hadn't thought of it like that. Well, I'll just have to make sure I make a success of it then, for all us sakes,' Joe asserted.

'I know you will, our Joe. Come 'ere and give your big sister a hug.'

They had arrived at the gate to the Estate and now they hugged each other, Joe saying,

'Thanks our Margaret, I knew you'd understand if anyone would.'

With that, they reluctantly parted and went their own ways and holding the lantern high, Joe made his way back down through the woods then along the track, thinking about tomorrow and the new path his life was about to take.

Joe arrived early in Coalbrookdale the next morning. He had woken early, eager to get started on this new life. As he approached the works, he joined several workmen also walking up the lane towards the furnace. Some said 'Mornin' and others just nodded in greeting. The thought crossed Joe's mind that he would soon know these men. They would become part of his life.

The furnace now loomed up ahead of them and he noticed a man who had an air of authority standing to the side of it and assumed this might be the person who would be his 'maister' here. He was obviously right in this assumption, as the man suddenly raised his voice, so that all could hear him and said,

'Mornin' all! First of all, Bangham here is having a try with us. I want you Bamforth, to show him the ropes. Understood?'

'Aye sir, that I will, Mr Newton sir' replied Bamforth, touching the peak of his cap.

Joe nodded at Bamforth and moved to stand nearer to him. He knew Bamforth vaguely. He assumed he lived in the cottage down at the end of the track, where it joined the road up to Madeley. He had seen him a few times, coming or going along the road when making his way up to market. They exchanged nods but spoke no words as Mr Newton had continued to give the day's instructions to the men.

Some of them were told to go and tend the lime-kilns which were ranged at the other side of the site, beyond the furnace. Joe and Bamforth, along with two others were given the job of charging the furnace, one man was to deal with the bellows, and the last two were to deal with running off the iron. Joe wasn't sure what any of this meant as yet, but knew that he soon would.

When Mr Newton had finished speaking, the men dispersed across the site. Bamforth introduced himself as Fred and motioned to Joe to follow him up the steps to the platform behind the furnace. Joe noticed three piles, one of limestone, one of coke and one of ironstone. Bamforth said,

'Right lad, let's see what you're made on.'

So began the Banghams' long association with the Darby's of Coalbrookdale. The work was hard, and the days were long, but as they passed, Joe grew in strength and over time it became easier. The hardest part of his day was the long walk home at its ending, and he promised himself that one day he would build his own cottage in Dale Coppice so as to be near to his work.

Life in the Bangham household settled down to its new routine. When there was no farm work, Walter and Will worked at the coppicing and when they had gathered enough fuel would set a clamp. As the burning process took around five days during the night, they took turns at sleeping in their makeshift shelter or watching the clamp. In the daytime one of them might go home for food or a bit of rest. Once the charcoal was ready and nicely cooled, they would load up the cart and with Ned between the shafts would take it to sell at the market or deliver to their various regular customers up and down the Gorge. Without Joe's involvement, all this kept the two men pretty busy.

Richard, having no one to partner him in setting a second clamp, had taken to doing more work on the home farm at the Hall. This suited him well. He enjoyed being out in the fields and whenever he had the chance, loved to get involved with the horses. Moses, the horseman, had noticed Richard's affinity to them and the way they responded well to him. Thinking that he might make a good horseman with a bit of instruction, he had taken it upon himself to encourage Richard's interest. He let him help with the grooming and bedding down whenever other duties allowed.

Elizabeth, helped by Martha, had her hands full with the cooking, washing, cleaning and tending the vegetable plot, which is where most of their food came from, supplemented by the odd chicken, rabbits and the hog when it was slaughtered once a year. Of course, there was always something to darn or repair. Margaret often brought discarded clothes from the Hall which Elizabeth repaired or refashioned into clothes for the family.

Washing took a whole day by the time she'd fired up the tub in the scullery, filled it with buckets of water from the pump and got it hot enough to make a difference to the state of the men's clothes. Joe's were always full of limestone and coke dust, Walter's and Will's were covered in charcoal and Richard's in horse muck. Thankfully, they didn't change them too often. Still, it was always satisfying to peg them out on the clothesline and see them flapping in the breeze. She would often see Rose from the next cottage doing the same on washday which was usually on a Monday. They would have a chat, mostly about family news or what was going on up at the Hall.

There were four more cottages in this small woodland community, arranged in a rough semi-circle and Rose and Alf Bottoms with their three youngsters, Alf, Tommy and Jess, lived next door. Alf worked at the quarry on Benthall Edge. Next to them were the old couple Mary and Eddie Grove. They'd lived here all their married life and raised their four children in their little cottage. They had all flown the coop now. Eddie did a bit of gardening for the Hall, which along with the odd rabbit he managed to snare, just about kept them fed. The neighbours helped them out whenever they could. Elizabeth always made sure they got a few joints each time the hog was butchered.

Next to the Groves were the Foresters. Tom also worked up at the limestone quarry, and Ella was kept busy with her two little ones, Charlie and Freddie, and with the housekeeping. They were a nice young couple in their twenties. Ella loved to grow vegetables and their little plot always had something ready to harvest. She would also share a crop with Mary and Eddie if she had anything to spare. She was pregnant with their third child, so there would soon be another resident in their little community.

At the end of the row lived Arthur Green, on his own now, since his wife Jane had died a couple of years ago in childbirth, along with their third child. It was so sad. They had been a devoted couple with two children aged four and six, far too young to lose their mother. Arthur was a labourer on the farm and was finding it hard to be father and mother to Freddie and Eliza, who were now six and eight. Of course, he had to work to bring in the food, and so the children were left alone most of the day. Elizabeth and the other women looked out for them when their father was at work, particularly old Mary, who was always ready to share whatever she had with them if they were hungry. She would take them foraging in the woods for blackberries or elderberries whenever they were in season, or hunt for mushrooms or wild onions. The children loved her dearly.

So this is how, like so many others in the Gorge, this tiny community rubbed along together, just helping each other to get by.

# Chapter 3

Harvest time came early to Benthall Edge that year. There had been plenty of rain to grow the crop and plenty of sun to ripen it. There was much work available for the few weeks of harvest. Joe was still largely laid off from the works because the furnace was closed down for the summer. He had been given some labouring work on the construction of the new furnace, which the Company was building further down the valley towards the Severn. However, the work was intermittent, and he was glad to make up his wages by working at the Hall farm along with Dick, Will, and Walter, scything the wheat, and then stacking and tying the sheaves.

Once the harvest was in, the women and children of the hamlet went to work gleaning any ears of wheat that had been missed by the men. They did well that year, and when they had pooled all their gleanings together were amazed to see they had several sacks full. Elizabeth and the other women spent several days threshing the wheat to extract the grain and then grinding it into flour, which was divided up between the households according to the number of mouths to be fed.

During the first week of September, the furnace at the Works was charged and blown in, and Joe settled down to regular day shifts once more. Mr Darby had told Mr Newton that he was pleased with how Joe was doing, and instructed him to pay him the full eight shillings a week he had promised. This was great news and even Walter had to admit that the extra money would come in handy. Mr Newton told Joe the new furnace would soon be ready for blowing in, when it might be necessary to introduce a night shift. There would be extra money for anyone willing to take it on, and he asked Joe if he would be interested. Joe didn't hesitate, and readily agreed.

In October, Walter judged that the hog was fattened up enough for slaughter, and Old Ted, the pig killer, was sent for. He had been performing this job, up and down the Gorge for decades. Martha of course was upset at the prospect of Archie being killed, but she had known it would happen, as it always did. Pork was, after all, the family's main source of meat.

Old Ted was a blacksmith during the day, so the slaughtering had to be done at night. He arrived at dusk and erected a tripod of poles about eight feet high from which Archie would be suspended once it had been cleanly and skilfully despatched. The animal was hung by its hind legs and the blood allowed to drain away to improve the quality of the meat. The scene was illuminated by several torches and presented quite a spectacle, enjoyed by all the adult residents of the hamlet and also by any of the children who could peer unnoticed from their bedroom windows. Martha had grown fond of Archie and couldn't bear to watch.

Once the blood had drained away and the carcass singed using the torches, Old Ted butchered the beast into joints. Nothing was wasted and the next day, Elizabeth set about placing the hams and sides of bacon in salted water, set the lard to dry out and thoroughly rinsed the chitterlings before frying them up for tea. The day after that, the joints were hung against the wall at the side of the fire to dry.

On the following Sunday, Margaret and Abigail got special permission to come home for the 'pig feast', and for once, the whole family were together. After waking early, Walter had lit the bread oven and Elizabeth and Martha had prepared cakes and pork pies which went in, along with a huge joint of pork, and the potatoes. It was a happy day in the Bangham household and for once, there were no arguments. It was good to have everyone together. One of those memorable days for any family.

Joe noticed that Abigail, now sixteen, was growing into a pretty young woman. She had a ready smile and a kind nature and Joe worried that she might easily be taken advantage of. After tea, he and Dick took the lanterns and walked Margaret and Abigail back to the Hall. Walking ahead with Margaret, Joe quietly mentioned his concerns to her, and she assured him that she would keep an eye on Abigail, who was walking some ten paces behind with Dick.

Returning to the hamlet, Dick and Joe took advantage of a rare opportunity to enjoy some conversation. Joe asked if Dick would like to come to work for the Darby's, as if he fancied it, he was sure he could get him on, as the new furnace was soon to be blown in. Much to Joe's disappointment, Dick told him there was no way on earth he would leave working on the land to work in that noisy, hot, dirty and smelly place. Besides, he said, he hoped to be the horseman at the farm one day.

'But there's more money to be had up at the works than ye'll ever get on the farm,' Joe said.

'Well our Joe,' Dick replied, 'money ain't everything.'

Joe couldn't really argue with that, and they continued their walk home in silence.

When they arrived at the cottage, Elizabeth had made some possett, and they all sat down to enjoy a piece of the cake brought by Margaret and spent a companiable hour in reflection on the day. The larder and their bellies were full. Life for the Banghams seemed good and they took a moment to enjoy it. However, as so often happens in life, things were about to change.

When Joe got home from the works the next day, he could see that Elizabeth was upset about something.

'What's to do our Liz?' he asked.

'I just bin round to Arthur's,' she said, 'an I don't like what I just seen.'

'Why, what's wrong?'

'It's the little uns. Oh Joe, I think it's measles! They've got terrible fevers, both on 'em, and that red rash our Abigail had, d'ye remember?' she went on.

'Oh I do, an' she was so poorly with it. We nearly lost 'er! Is there owt we can do to help poor Arthur, him being on his own, an all.'

'Well, I've just made some basil and ginger tea with a bit of honey in it, fer the fever, and I've said I'll go over after tea an' see what I can do.'

'Right, well tell 'im, if there's owt he needs, just to let on.'

Elizabeth had boiled some bacon in the pot with vegetables for tea, and as soon as Will and Walter came in, served it up. They were all shocked at the news, Dorothy of course wanting to know what measles was.

'Well, I 'ope you don't find out,' Joe told her 'it's none too pleasant if you catch it.'

'Have you 'ad it?' Dorothy went on.

'We all have, apart from you, so you keep well away from that cottage, d'ye 'ear me!' Walter interjected sharply.

As soon as she had served up the supper for the family, Elizabeth threw her shawl around her shoulders and picked up the jug of basil tea. Telling them she didn't know how long she'd be, so not to wait up for her, she strode out into the night.

Matters at the Green's house were not at all good. Eliza, the eldest at eight years old seemed the worse of the two. She had a raging fever and bright red spots all over her body and even on her face. Elizabeth was very worried about her. Her brother Jimmy didn't seem quite so bad, but he was definitely hot, and the spots were redder than they had been when she'd called in earlier.

Poor Arthur was in a terrible state. When he saw the look on Elizabeth's face as she checked Eliza, he said quietly, his eyes full of fear,

'Ah can't lose 'em Liz, Not after, you know ....'

'And nor shall you,' Elizabeth replied earnestly, 'not if I have 'owt to do with it!'

She set about sponging the children down with calamine lotion. The room was hot, and she told Arthur to damp down the fire a bit. She poured two cups of the basil infusion and handed one to Arthur to give to Jimmy, while she propped Eliza up against her arm and coaxed her to take some. Then she gave both children a cupful of water and settled them back down.

'Have you eaten anythin' Arthur?' she asked him.

'Nay, I couldn't fancy anythin',' he replied.

'Well I'll fix you some bread and drippin', and then ye should try an' get some rest. You've still got to work tomorrow.'

'I con't leave 'em Liz,' he retorted.

'I'll stay fer a few hours, they're all fed an' watered back 'ome, so they'll do fer awhile and I told 'em not to wait up.'

Elizabeth made some supper and they both sat by the fire, just talking quietly for an hour or so, then after kissing the children, Arthur went to his bed, asking her to wake him in a few hours. After dozing for about an hour, Elizabeth woke with a start. Eliza had cried out and as Elizabeth felt her forehead she was very concerned. The calamine and the basil brew hadn't seemed to do much to cool her down. She gave her some more of the infusion and sponged her down again, but she continued to be restless, tossing her head around and then she seemed to be hallucinating. Her eyes were wide open, but she didn't seem to recognise Elizabeth. She was calling out for her mother, reaching out her arms and pleading for her help.

'Hush child,' Elizabeth said, and stroked her hair, as maybe her mother had once done, and that seemed to calm her a little. Jimmy, meanwhile, was sleeping peacefully, and he wasn't quite so hot.

It must have been about two in the morning when things reached a climax. Eliza's fever had worsened, and she grew more and more restless. She was pouring in sweat and looked white, although the spots seemed redder than ever. Elizabeth woke Arthur, telling him that it looked like things were coming to a head. He ran down the stairs and fell down beside Eliza, grasping her hand and putting it to his lips.

'Thee cannat leave me, Eliza,' he whispered, with tears now coursing down his face.

'Father,' she whispered, suddenly lucid. 'Ma's come fer me,' she said, with a sweet smile on her lips, and then her face relaxed, her eyes glazed over, and she was gone.

Arthur was distraught. He let out such an unearthly moan, the whole hamlet must have heard it, and anyone who did, would have known what it meant. Young Jimmy had woken up and was crying now. Elizabeth went to him and 'clipped him up' to her breast to comfort him.

'Hush now little man,' she said.

'Why is father mekkin' that noise,' he asked, 'why is he cryin'? Is Eliza alright?'

'I'm so sorry,' Elizabeth replied to him, 'Eliza has gone to be with yer Ma.'

'Noo!,' he cried, 'I want to go too! Father, I want to go too!'

Arthur dragged himself away from his daughter and turned to Jimmy.

'Nay lad,' he told him 'I need thee 'ere,' and took him from Elizabeth's arms, hugging him as if he might break him.

Elizabeth tended gently to the little body, carefully washing her, brushing her hair and placing her in a clean nightdress. Then she covered her with a sheet and turned her attention to the living. Jimmy was a little better and seemed to be over the worst. He was sitting on Arthur's knee and hugging him tightly. They were both rung out and Elizabeth persuaded Arthur to go to his bed, suggesting that he take Jimmy with him. They both needed the comfort each would bring to the other.

Elizabeth told Arthur she would come over at first light to check on Jimmy again, and to help him with the arrangements. He knew what she meant but gave no comment. She made sure the fire was damped down and then quietly left the sad little home.

She crossed the clearing to her own home, thinking how sad it was for Arthur, losing not only his wife but his beloved daughter too. Life could be so cruel she thought to herself. He didn't deserve such grief. She also realised how lucky they had been as a family, that they had managed to raise all their young ones to adulthood, all except Dorothy, who wasn't yet an adult, but was nearly so.

Rather than wake the others, she took a drink of ale, then rested in the chair for what was left of the night. After dozing for what seemed like half an hour or so, she heard Joe moving around upstairs, getting ready to go to work. She roused herself and poured him some ale and made him some bread and dripping. Joe clattered down the stairs and swung round the door jamb into the room. He was surprised to see his sister up at this hour, but then he remembered where she had gone to, last night.

"Have ye bin up all night our Liz?' he asked, "Ow are things over at Arthur's?'

'Oh Joe,' Elizabeth replied, fighting back the tears, 'It's young Eliza. The measles took 'er in the early hours.'

'Oh no!' Joe cried, 'Not young Eliza! She be such a sweet child.'

'Arthur's distraught Joe. First Jane and now Eliza. Tis so sad!'

'D'ye think he'd want me to call in at Johnson's on my way to the works?'

As she refilled his cup, she replied,

'Well, I don't want to rush things our Joe, thanks anyway, but he'll need to move at 'is own pace. Anyhow, I'd best get over there, I said I'd help 'im get on with the arrangements.'

'Aye, of course. Well, tell 'im if there's owt' I can do, just let us know.'

'Aye, that I will, our Joe,' Elizabeth replied then picking up her shawl went out into the chilly October morning.

As Elizabeth made her way across the clearing, the thought occurred to her that she would need to let Rose know what had happened as soon as she could, they would need to keep an eye on their little ones, and keep them inside, away from Jimmy. She knew how quickly measles could rip through a community and it wasn't fussed who it took as it passed by. She just hoped to God that it wasn't already too late.

It was cold inside Arthur's cottage. He obviously couldn't have much of a fire for the moment and there was just a small one in the hearth. Just big enough to boil a kettle.  Once the undertaker had been and little Eliza had been dealt with, they would take her upstairs until it was time for the funeral. Elizabeth made a pot of herb tea and then called up the narrow stairs to see if Arthur was awake. After a few minutes he came down. He looked terrible. His eyes were red-rimmed and his face white. He had obviously not been able to get much sleep.

'Mornin' Liz,' he said, 'I can't believe my little Eliza's gone.'

He went over to where Eliza was lying beneath the sheet and lifted the topmost edge. At the sight of her sweet little face, he broke into heaving sobs once more. Elizabeth went over to him and put her arm across his shoulders to offer him some comfort. They stood like that for some minutes until his sobbing subsided. Elizabeth led him gently over to the chair in front of the fire, then poured him a cup of the herb tea. Then without a word, she went quietly up the stairs to check on Jimmy and was relieved to find him sleeping peacefully. His fever had abated, and he had obviously passed the climax. He would survive.

'When you're ready Arthur, we'll need to get in touch with Johnson,' she said quietly.

'Aye I know,' Arthur replied.

Johnson was the carpenter who lived down in Buildwas. He also doubled as the local undertaker and he would come up to measure the body and then make the coffin, which would be a plain deal wood affair but adequate to the task.

'D'ye want me to ask Will to pop down fer ye? He's just in the wood building a clamp with Walter, but I know he could spare an hour to nip down to Buildwas.'

'Aye,' Arthur responded quietly, like a man in a dream, 'if thee thinks he wouldn't mind.'

'Right, well I'll pop o'er to our house, I might just catch Dick afore he leaves, an' he can take a message to Will straight away.'

Arthur just nodded and carried on staring at the fire.

Elizabeth walked home quickly and was glad to see that Dick was still there. He already knew what had happened because he'd seen Joe before he left for work.

'It's a bad do Liz,' he said sadly.

'Aye, it is so,' she replied, and then asked him if he would find Will in the coppice and ask him to fetch Johnson.

He readily agreed and left shortly afterwards. Elizabeth decided she'd better do the rounds with the news and was soon knocking on Rose's door. Of course, she was shocked to hear about Eliza and immediately checked her little ones, but for the moment all seemed well. Then Elizabeth thought she had better let the Groves know. Mary and Eddie had treated the children as their own since Jane had died. They were devastated, Mary bursting into tears. Eddie put his arms around her in comfort and Elizabeth left them like that, to continue on her sad mission. Next door she found that Tom had already left for his work at the quarry, but Ella was devastated as well as desperately worried for her own two, Charlie and Freddie. She told Elizabeth Freddie had seemed a bit under the weather for a day or two, and when she checked him, he did seem a little bit hot.

'Well, best they both stay inside where ye can keep

a close eye on 'em,' Elizabeth told her, 'Ye can't be too careful with measles.'

'Aye, I will that,' Ella replied.

Elizabeth went back into Arthur's cottage to find him sitting exactly as she'd left him.

She was full of fear now. If Ella's two came down with it, it would be more than likely Rose's would as well. After all, they would have all been playing together nearly every day. She was fervently hoping that all the adults would have already had it. She had seen what it could do to adults who had never caught it as children. Of course, she realised, Dorothy was very much at risk as well, and that terrified her.

'I've sent our Will to fetch Johnson, Arthur. 'E should be 'ere pretty soon. Will ye have her buried with Jane,' she asked gently.

Arthur dropped his head into his hands, saying,

'Oh God, I cannat bear it.'

'Ye can and ye will,' Elizabeth assured him quietly, placing a hand on his shoulder.

Just then there was a knock on the door. It was Johnson, and Elizabeth invited him in.

He took his cap off, then said to Arthur,

'I'm right sorry for thy loss, this is a bad do.'

He asked Arthur if he could carry Eliza upstairs where it was cooler, or would he like him to do it? Arthur suddenly sprung up, saying

'If anyone's goin' to carry 'er it'll be me,' and proceeded to pick her up. With tears streaming down his face he made his way upstairs and laid her gently on the bed. He picked Jimmy up out of the other bed and took him downstairs. Elizabeth helped Johnson to lay Ella out properly. Then Johnson set about his work, which basically just meant wrapping her in a woollen shroud then measuring little Eliza's body so that he could make a coffin. When he went downstairs, he asked Arthur if she was to be buried with her mother. Arthur could do no more than nod.

'Right, well, you leave it to me. I'll be back tomorrow with the coffin and in the meantime, I'll arrange for the funeral to be the day after, if that's alright with thee.'

Again, Arthur nodded in agreement and Johnson left.

The next few days were busy ones for Elizabeth. She took it upon herself to look after Arthur and Jimmy, feeding them as well as her own. Ella's Freddie did go down with it, and then Charlie. Somehow, Rose's three managed to avoid catching it and she kept them inside the house for weeks, just in case.

Young Eliza's funeral was a sad affair. As the autumn winds swirled the fallen leaves around them, Will, Joe, Walter and Alf carried the little coffin down the hill, with Arthur, Jimmy, Mary and Eddie, herself, and Martha walking behind. Tom and Ella were busy caring for Freddie and Charlie, and Rose and Alf didn't go for fear of passing something on to their youngsters. Elizabeth felt that Dorothy would be safer at home as well, much to her annoyance because she'd never been to a funeral and was desperate to go.

The little procession slowly made its way to the bridge over the Severn, turning left towards Buildwas and the burial ground at the ancient church. The vicar said a few words and a prayer or two and everyone threw a handful of dirt on the coffin. Elizabeth stood beside Arthur and steadied him as he leant so far over the grave, she was afraid he was going to throw himself in with his little girl. It was heart-breaking to see and hear his grief.

The next couple of weeks were touch and go with Charlie and Freddie, but eventually they recovered, apart from some loss of hearing in Freddie's right ear. Thankfully, none of Rose's three got it and nor did Dorothy.

# Chapter 4

The hamlet slowly returned to its usual routine, but Elizabeth continued to look out for Arthur and Jimmy, making sure they were eating properly, and along with Mary, seeing to their washing. She had to admit she was quite drawn to Arthur. He often wore a helpless expression, as if he had no idea how he had ended up in the situation in which he now found himself. This had awakened her mothering instincts, and she couldn't do enough for him, or Jimmy for that matter. This wasn't lost on her menfolk back home. Walter in particular sometimes seemed a little impatient with her when his meal wasn't ready because she'd been distracted by helping Arthur and Jimmy out. Elizabeth never rose to the bait. I've done enough for that lot over the years, she would say to herself, it won't do them any harm to wait a bit now and then. December brought the first snows of winter to the hamlet, but no more than a dusting, just a hint of what was to come. More of a problem was the icy wind which seemed to find its way through every nook and cranny in the old cottages. Rags were pushed into gaps round windows and doors, in a vain attempt to keep it out.

Joe had settled in well to the work at the Company. He was a good worker and was earning the respect of his workmates and bosses alike. He had agreed to move over to the new furnace when it was blown in, which would be in the New Year. For months there had been a lot of talk among the men about the riots taking place up and down the country against the new protestant King George and the Whigs. Rioters were attacking the homes and businesses of anyone who was not High Church. They were aware that the Darby's were Quakers of course, as were quite a few of the men themselves and there was much apprehension in case the Shrewsbury mob who had been attacking dissenters, as they called them, might find their way into the Gorge. Joe himself wasn't religious although he knew that his family was descended from the Huguenots of France and had affiliated to the Church of England when they arrived in the country. He wasn't quite sure where all this left him as far as religion was concerned but he knew very well that if it came to a test, his loyalties would be with his employer, Mr Darby, who he knew to be a good and fair man.

Winter arrived in earnest a couple of weeks before Christmas. A blizzard had blown along the Gorge from the east overnight, and when the hamlet dwellers opened their doors in the morning, the world was white and silent. The snow had formed into huge drifts sweeping up from the ground and reaching to the roof of the privvy. It was laying several feet deep, right across the clearing.

There would be no coppicing for Will and Walter today, thought Elizabeth, which would be just as well as there would be plenty of work to do around the hamlet. Joe set out for work as usual, hoping he would be able to get through the snow drifts. However, when he reached the track leading down to the bridge, he realised it was going to be impossible for him to get through. The snow had drifted across the track from hedge to hedge. It was completely impassable. He retraced his steps to the hamlet and then decided to try another route. If he cut through the copse under Benthall Edge, maybe he could take the track down beside the incline plane the quarrymen used to send their limestone down to the wharf. When he arrived back at the cottage, Arthur was just delivering Jimmy for Elizabeth to look after while he made his way over to the quarry to see whether they had any work for him, as farm work would be impossible in the snow.

As the two men walked together they were fairly silent as they negotiated their way along the track which was cloaked in snow and difficult to make out. As they went along, Joe was thinking how much he liked Arthur.

'How are ye doin'?' he asked Arthur.

'Oh ye know, it's hard, being father and mother too. I often think, if Janey had still bin around she would have seen that summat was up with our Eliza, afore she got properly poorly like.'

'You mustn't blame yourself, Arthur. Everyone knows you did your best.'

'Well, it just don't feel like it, an' that's the truth Joe. But I dunna know what I'd have done without Liz these past months. She's bin me rock!'

'Aye, I know man, she's a good lass, our Liz.'

Arthur was a decent sort, thought Joe. He'd had so much tragedy to deal with and yet it hadn't made him bitter. He had noticed that Elizabeth rather liked Arthur too. Well, she deserved some love and happiness and a life of her own. She'd spent every waking hour since his mother died, caring for others. It would give him great pleasure to see her settled with a family of her own, and it sounded like Arthur was pretty keen as well.

They emerged from the coppice and in front of them was the incline plane, not that they could actually see it, as it was covered in snow. However, the track which ran down the lee side of it had been sheltered from the wind somewhat and the snow hadn't drifted across it. Joe decided he would be able to make his way down to the river this way and said goodbye to Arthur as he set off down the track. Once down at the river, he turned left and made his way to the bridge.

The snow on the north side of the Gorge didn't seem anywhere near as deep. It must be the way the wind was blowing, thought Joe, grateful that he could now stride out up the valley and he would still only be a few minutes late for work. When he arrived at the furnace, he could see there seemed to be fewer men than usual. Obviously, some of them had not been able to get through the snow. However, the furnace still needed to be loaded, even though there were few men to do the work and Joe got straight to it.

The snow lay around for a week or so, and then just as it was beginning to thaw, a hard frost set in, freezing the wet surface solid, making walking treacherous. Icicles began to form, hanging down from the cottage eaves like daggers, threatening to fall on anyone who banged the door shut. The children of the hamlet had a wonderful time of course, sliding around and playing with a 'sledge' old Eddie had made for them. A week later the thaw set in.

Christmas 1714, brought a couple of days respite from work and on Christmas Day, Elizabeth prepared a veritable feast of pork, apple sauce, potatoes and vegetables. Everyone brought something to the feast as well, and Eddie brought a flagon of beer he'd been brewing for weeks. Ella, now heavily pregnant, had made some tiny pink sugar mice for the children, Arthur brought a bag of apples he'd been storing since harvest time, and Rose had made some ginger biscuits. Of course, everyone had to bring their own stool or chair to sit on and it was quite a crush to fit everyone inside Walter's living room, but it was all the merrier for that. Eddie had brought his old fiddle and to the delight of all, the day was rounded off with singing.

It was late when they all reluctantly decided it was

time to leave. They had full bellies for once and were happy to be part of this little community in Banghams Wood. They felt content to look forward to the year ahead, with the exception of Arthur of course, who had found the day particularly hard, watching the other children playing around and wishing his Eliza had been there with them.

Elizabeth was up early the next morning. There was a lot of clearing up to do after the previous day's revelry. It had been good though, she reflected, to see everyone enjoying themselves together for once. Of course, it had been hard for Arthur and she had felt for him. Young Jimmy as well, seemed very quiet at times, obviously unsure where he fitted in to things without his big sister around.

Margaret and Abigail would be coming down from the hall in the afternoon. This was one of the rare days when they were allowed to visit their own family after the busy Christmas Day at the Hall. They arrived about midday with a box of sweetmeats for the family to enjoy and cook had been generous with the left-overs from the Christmas Day feast at the Hall, and had given Margaret enough food to provide the Bangham family with a hearty meal, which they thorougly enjoyed, particularly the rich fruit cake, not being something they saw very often. It was lovely for Walter to have all his children around him for once.

Margaret entertained them all by telling them about the Christmas festivities up at the Hall, the mountains of food, the house full of guests, and the music and dancing. Dorothy sat at her feet, eyes shining as her imagination ran riot. The rest of the family showed varying degrees of interest. Will wasn't interested in the least. The way he saw it, he could never aspire to such a life of luxury, so why would he want to hear about it? It only made him even more discontented with his lot.

Finally, it was time for Abigail and Margaret to leave, and as always, Joe was the first to volunteer to walk them home. There was still quite a bit of frozen snow around and it took them longer than usual to reach the gate into the estate. Joe said how great it had been to see them both together, for once. They all embraced warmly and went their separate ways. By the time Joe got home, the family were all preparing for bed and as he had an early start the next day, he did the same.

The following day, as she did every day, Elizabeth was crossing the clearing to Arthur's to check whether they needed anything, she noticed Ella going out to the privvy. From the look of her, she thought, Ella won't be long now, her time must be coming up. Elizabeth would need to be ready to help deliver her baby as she had done with so many of the others. Mary would help too, of course. She had seen many babies brought into the world and had had four of her own, so unlike Elizabeth had personal experience of the pain that must inevitably precede every birth.

So it was, that three days later Elizabeth was

preparing for bed when there was a loud knocking on the door. It was Tom, as she expected.

'Liz, can you come? Ella's waters have broken. 'Tis time.'

Grabbing her shawl and throwing it around her shoulders, she picked up the bag she had already prepared, containing the things she might need.

'Aye lad, c'mon, let's go,' she quickly replied.

She told the rest of the family not to wait up for her then followed Tom out into the darkness. Ella was upstairs and Elizabeth could hear that the pain must be getting bad. She was wailing loudly and Elizabeth immediately went up to her after instructing Tom to bring some hot water from the pan on the tricket. Ella was standing, bent almost double and holding on to the bed. Every couple of minutes she tensed, and cried out in pain. Elizabeth managed to persuade her to get on to the bed so that she could see where things had got to. At that minute Mary turned up. She had heard Ella's cries across the clearing and knew what it meant. As Elizabeth checked the progress of the baby, Mary held Ella's hand and between contractions, wiped her brow with a damp cloth.

The baby was taking quite a while to emerge, and Elizabeth was getting rather worried. Ella was tiring now and she was worried she wouldn't have the strength to push when the time was right. Then, after one particularly strong contraction, she could see the baby's head. With the next contraction she told Ella to push as hard as she could, and the baby flopped out into her waiting hands. It was a little boy.. She was concerned he wasn't breathing and started to rub his little body and flick the soles of his feet to stimulate him. After a minute or so, she was relieved to see him open his eyes and start to cry loudly. Having tied the birth cord in two places with string, Elizabeth quickly cut the cord with her scissors. Mary had been tending to matters while Elizabeth had been dealing with the baby and was awaiting the arrival of the afterbirth, which appeared after another contraction. Elizabeth sponged the little one clean then wrapped him in his blanket and offered him to Ella.

'It's a grand lad,' Elizabeth told her, and Ella reached out her arms to receive her son, with tears streaming down her face. Tom ran into the room and dropped down beside his wife and child, and mother and father beamed with happiness, heads together, gazing down on this tiny soul that would share their lives.

Elizabeth tidied up, then she and Mary left them in peace as Ella put the child to her breast. As they came out of the bedroom, two little heads were poking out of the doorway to the other room wanting to know if they had a brother or sister. Elizabeth said that they'd better go and ask their mother and father, and held the door open for them to join their parents. Charlie and Freddie burst through the doorway and gathered round their mother, staring in wonder at their little brother, who was to be called Benjamin.

Downstairs, Mary made a jug of herb tea, took cups

up to Tom and Ella and then poured drinks for Elizabeth and herself. They put another log on the fire then settled down to enjoy their well earned drinks. So, another life had successfully made its entrance into their little community and as they sat, they wondered aloud what kind of a life the little one would have. Mary hoped it would be an easier one than she and Eddie had lived.

# Chapter 5

Winter dragged on through January and February, with more snow and frost making life harder than ever in the little community in Banghams wood. There was little farm work to be had and Walter and Will had no choice but to carry on with the coppicing and charcoal burning to bring some money in, but camping out in the woods for five days and nights in the middle of winter took its toll, particularly on Walter. At the end of February he had a particularly bad bout of bronchitis, which they were all afraid might be consumption as they called it, but which today we would call tuberculosis. As it was, after a few days rest in bed, and a week or so in front of the fire, he slowly recovered, much to the relief of all.

Joe managed to keep working all through the bad weather, bringing in much needed money for the family. He observed that things were changing rapidly in Coalbrookdale. The new furnace was now working at full capacity and the workforce had more than doubled. Carts were coming and going when the snow allowed, bringing raw materials and taking away the pig iron to various foundries and finished goods down to the wharf to be shipped down the Severn to Bristol and beyond. It was bustling with activity and Joe enjoyed being part of it. It was hard work, of course, but it was exciting, especially when, on rare occasions, when they were a man short, he was asked to help out with drawing off the iron from the furnace.

Joe could see that the business was prospering as he admired the grand new house Mr Darby was building a little further up the valley. He was a good man though, and he worked hard, even alongside his men when needed. He was constantly experimenting with different mixes of raw materials to improve the quality of the iron they were producing. He was greatly respected by the men and whenever there was talk in the ale houses about 'dissenters' his workmen would always speak out in his defence. So far, the Gorge had escaped the riots that were still raging around the country, although there had been talk about trouble in Shrewsbury, when a mob had attacked a dissenters' chapel.

One morning when Joe arrived at the works, Fred Bamforth was in an agitated state and told him that a riotous mob had been seen by Tom, one of the men who came from a small hamlet to the north of Coalbrookdale, making its way down from Shrewsbury, intent on attacking Mr Darby's works. Tom said he had seen their torches in the distance and heard their angry cries. He had hurried down to the works to warn them.

Mr Newton had sent a message to the Justice of the Peace in Much Wenlock to come to read the riot act. Mr Darby was sent for and was soon standing on the steps of the furnace, calling to the men to use restraint. He wanted no violence, he told them. However, he realised that the mob had to be confronted if the works was to be saved.

Mr Newton told him they would try to hold up the mob until the Justice of the Peace arrived. He quickly called all the men from the forge, the foundry and the furnaces together and told them to gather in the lane to block the way, to prevent the mob from reaching the works. No one dissented, as they all knew that by defending the works, they were defending their own livelihoods. If the works was destroyed, they would all be destitute.

Each man picked up whatever he could use to defend himself, then they formed up in a line four deep across the lane and awaited the arrival of the mob. It was still fairly dark, being around seven o'clock in the morning, and they could see the lights of the torches approaching as the mob made its way down the hill towards them. The shouts of 'Down with George!' and 'Down with Dissenters!' rang out.

Joe had picked up an iron bar. Predictably he planted himself firmly in the front row of the Coalbrookdale men and waited for the onslaught. As it happened, the 'mob' turned out to be rather fewer in number than the men defending the works. There were maybe twenty or so, with at least sixty Darby men standing their ground, armed with iron bars and hammers and anything else that they had been able to pick up along the way, and making rather more noise than the rioters.

The mob halted about thirty yards from the Coalbrookdale men. Several of their number, seeing that they were so obviously outnumbered, and by a crowd of men considerably stronger and probably tougher than they were, first faltered and then began to turn around and start running back the way they had come. When Joe saw this he shouted, 'Come on men!' and led the charge to chase the mob away. It was a rout, and in minutes the rioters had disappeared over the brow of the hill, heading back towards Shrewsbury. The men who had chased them off strode back towards the works and as they approached, a cheer went up. As he had led the charge, Joe became the hero of the hour, and Mr Darby thanked him personally for his loyalty and his courage at seeing off the mob. A message was sent to tell the Justice of the Peace that his services were not needed on this occasion and the men returned to their work, relieved that violence had been avoided.

As often happens in a close community such as this, word of the events spread around the district, from one neighbour to the next, growing more notable with each telling. By the time word reached the Hall, the story was that Joe Bangham had led the charge to see off the mob, and when Margaret arrived at the Banghams house the following Sunday she was full of it. Joe wasn't at home, as he was working an extra shift at the furnace as they were short-handed.

Even before she took her coat and hat off, she said to Elizabeth,

'Our Joe's the talk of the valley, who'd have thought it?!'

She proceeded to relate the current version of the story, of how Joe Bangham had charged the mob single-handedly and saved the Darby works, and how he was now famous for his heroic stand against the rioters.

Joe himself hadn't said much about it during the week, so what Margaret had to say came as a bit of a surprise to them all. Everyone was greatly impressed, particularly Dorothy, and proud of their brother. Everyone, except Will of course, who, jealous as ever of Joe, said he didn't believe a word of it and that it was all an exaggeration. He was right, of course, but no one chose to believe him, as they would rather bask in the reflected glory of Joe's considerably enhanced reputation.

The next week, twelve hour shifts were brought in. Joe was asked if he still wanted to work night shifts at the new furnace as it was now fully functional and producing good quality pig iron. He knew it would be hard, and not easy to fit in with the rest of the family's routine, but the money was better and he welcomed the chance to take on more responsibility. He would be in charge of loading up the furnace and would have an assistant working under him. The pay would be twelve shillings a week. He gladly accepted and started the following week. The shift was from six in the evening to six in the morning.

He was right that this proved rather inconvenient for the rest of the family, particularly at meal times, which didn't please Elizabeth, who liked to keep to a routine. Still, they all realised that the extra money Joe would be bringing in would certainly be a boost to the family finances, and so they began to work around it. Actually, once she got into the rhythm of it, Elizabeth decided that she quite liked having Joe around in the afternoons. She made tea for the family for about four thirty so that they could all eat together before Joe set off to the works. Will was a bit resentful because it meant that if he was working on the farm, whereas before they would all have waited for him to get home, now he had to eat his meal on his own, later in the evening. Typical, he thought, everything has to revolve around Joe, the hero of the Valley, these days. This just added to his brooding resentment of his older brother.

Although Joe settled in to his night shift pattern, he was thinking more and more that he ought to start planning to build his own house in Dale Coppice. It would be so much more convenient. Of course, he would still help out with the family's finances. He began to think how he could broach the subject with Walter, who he knew would see it as just one more betrayal of the family, and goodness knows what Will would think of the idea. He thought he would speak to Margaret first, the next time she came to visit. She would understand and would perhaps give him some support when he told the rest of them. So he filed the idea at the back of his mind for the moment.

Meanwhile, Elizabeth was spending more and more time with Arthur and Jimmy. Whenever her work was done at home, and everyone was fed, she would go over to Arthur's and once Jimmy was in bed, they would spend a pleasant evening in front of the fire, just talking quietly. They discovered they had a lot in common in the way they felt about things. They were both kind and gentle souls, always ready to help anyone. Neither of them was particularly ambitious. They were just content to live as comfortably as possible, without extravagance, which was just as well, as there wasn't much of that in Banghams Wood. It was perhaps inevitable that their relationship fairly soon developed into more than just friendship and it became apparent to them both that they needed to be married, and one day in April, Arthur quietly proposed to Elizabeth. She was delighted. She had long since abandoned the idea that she would ever get married, but Arthur had changed all that. She wanted this more than anything in the world. She had fallen deeply in love with Arthur and had grown very fond of Jimmy too. The next evening after tea, Arthur crossed the clearing to speak to Walter. He knew it would be difficult for him. He supposed that he had thought Elizabeth would always be around to keep house for him. How would he react to the thought that she would be leaving?

Actually, when he asked Walter if he would give them his blessing, he didn't seem shocked at all. Arthur guessed correctly that it had been pretty obvious to everyone the way things were going. Elizabeth had been spending so much time with him that they would all have been more surprised if it had come to nothing. No one was sure how things were going to work out though. They doubted whether Martha would be up to keeping house and cooking and so on. Of course, although Dorothy was still young, she would be able to help Martha out with many of the chores. In any case, they reasoned, Elizabeth would be just across the clearing if she was needed.

Of course, at this point, they had no idea of Joe's plans to build his own house on the other side of the Gorge. When he came home the next morning, Elizabeth was full of her news. Joe wasn't unduly surprised, but he did realise that perhaps he would have to postpone his plans for a while, until things at home had settled down and they could all see how things worked out with Martha. They would all undoubtedly need some support with Elizabeth no longer living in the house.

It was a beautiful day in May, when Arthur and Elizabeth made their way down to the Holy Trinity Church in Buildwas to make their vows. The apple and may blossoms and pussy willows were out on the trees and the track was lined with bluebells, daisies and wild violets. Margaret had brought a lovely yellow dress which was surplus to requirements from the Hall, and Elizabeth had altered it until it fitted her perfectly. She wore a headdress of wild flowers and carried a posy of the same in her hands. With help from Martha and Dorothy, Joe had decked out the cart, even securing a few flowers to old Ned's bridle. Elizabeth and Walter sat on the cart arm in arm, and with Will holding the reins they led the procession down the track. It was a proud day for Walter and he only wished Elizabeth's mother could have been there to see their eldest daughter married to Arthur. He was a good man and Walter knew he would look after her, as best as he could. They would never be rich, but Walter was sure they would be happy together.

Arthur and the rest of the family and neighbours followed them down to Buildwas. The sun sparkled on the river as they crossed the bridge, and the whole Gorge looked particularly lovely in the sunshine. The service in the church was short but adequate to the task in hand, and the couple emerged as happy as any couple should be on their wedding day. A wedding breakfast had been prepared by the women of the hamlet and was laid out in Walter's living room for when they returned from the church. All agreed that it had been a wonderful day and finally, Arthur and Elizabeth left to return to the Green's house to begin their life together.

Young Jimmy stayed with Mary and Eddie for a

couple of days, while the newly weds enjoyed a short honeymoon. Elizabeth moved her things into Arthur's cottage the next day and their married life began. Things in the Bangham house seemed very strange to everyone without Elizabeth organising them all. It took a few weeks to get into some sort of routine. Martha did her best, but did need quite a bit of support from the others. Dorothy was good at reminding her what needed doing and when, particularly with regard to the cooking. Of course, Elizabeth was literally only yards away if anyone was in any doubt about anything. For her part Elizabeth threw herself into organising their own cottage, which had been without a woman in it for three years. It needed a good 'bottoming' as she told Arthur. She soon had everything clean and ship-shape. Then she started on the vegetable patch which had also been rather neglected. Having Elizabeth around certainly suited Arthur. Everyone remarked how cheerful he now was, which, given the tragedies he'd had to endure was a tribute to Elizabeth's good care.

Will and Walter found extra work on the farm with the lambing and spring planting, and after that was over, went back to the coppicing and charcoal burning. Dick was getting more involved with the horses. Old Moses was finding things harder these days. He was plagued with rheumatism caused by a lifetime spent out doors in all weathers, and was only too happy for Dick to give him a hand. Alf and Tom were very busy at the limestone quarry. It seemed that the

Coalbrookdale Ironworks had an insatiable appetite for the stuff, and there always seemed to be another cart at the bottom of the incline plane, waiting to be filled.

Over at the Works, Joe was in his element, organising his shift at the new furnace. There had been a few teething troubles with the furnace but by April 1716 it was going well. He found he was good at making sure that all went as it should, and he kept the furnace topped up and blowing well. As well as doing his own job, he was always ready to help his workmates out, and he had earned their respect as well as that of his employer. Of course, things didn't always go smoothly. As in any industrial environment at that time, there were accidents, particularly when the commodity being produced was molten metal. Joe was just finishing his shift one day when, as the men down at the mouth of the furnace were pulling the plug to run off the first batch of the day, there was a sudden surge of energy and molten iron shot out and struck Bill, one of the workmen, on his arm. He screamed out in agony and Joe was the first man to reach him. He was horrified to see that the metal had gone clean through the man's left arm. Bill continued to scream as Joe picked him up bodily and removed him to a safe distance where Mr Newton was calling out for someone to fetch the surgeon.

They carried him out of the furnace building and over to the clerk's office, where he was placed on a blanket on the floor awaiting the arrival of the surgeon from Madeley. Joe was shocked to see the extent of damage inflicted by the molten metal and he understood more clearly than ever, how it had to be treated with the utmost respect. The next evening when Joe came on for his shift he learned that Bill had had the lower part of his arm amputated as the wound was too extensive for it to heal safely. It would be a long recovery and of course, he would no longer be able to work at the furnace, but it was said that Mr Darby would find him a job that he could do, once he was well enough.

The spring and early summer of 1716 were quite dry and the furnaces had to be blown out in June as the water in the pools became dangerously low. They couldn't risk it being so low that it couldn't turn the water wheels to work the bellows at the furnaces. This meant that Joe was without work for three months. He helped Will and Walter with the coppicing and with Dick's help when he wasn't at the farm, they were able to burn a couple of extra clamps and build up their charcoal stocks. Walter was very pleased to have Joe around more often, particularly as he was feeling rather tired these days. The bronchitis he'd suffered in the winter had taken more out of him than he liked to admit.

Arthur and Elizabeth had settled into married life. Young Jimmy adored Elizabeth, who gave him plenty of love and affection, which he had sorely missed since the death of his mother. It was no surprise to anyone when, in September, Elizabeth joyfully announced that she was expecting a child. Another new life was soon to make its appearance in Banghams Wood.

Will's resentment at what he perceived as Joe's desertion in going off to work for Darby, hadn't diminished over the months. In fact, if anything, it had grown. Even though Joe was able to help out during the summer, Will knew that come the autumn, he would be off again, working nights for Darby, leaving him to toil in the woods with his father who seemed to be growing weaker with every passing year. He would have to bear the increased load alone, whereas he had always expected that he and Joe would take over once Walter was no longer able to do the work. He was worried what would happen, when that time came. He couldn't work the charcoal burns alone, and Dick was getting more and more involved with the horses up at the estate. He knew that he would never leave his beloved horses to join him in the charcoal business. In any case, even though he would never admit it to Joe, Will knew that the demand for the product would be diminishing over time. There was no guarantee that it would be a viable business in the future.

Would he, could he, contemplate crossing the valley to work for Darby? He thought not, after all he'd said to Joe about that. There was always the quarry, but that was back-breaking work, even harder than what he was doing now, and the pay was poor. The thought occurred to him that perhaps he could seek work on one of the Severn Trows that carried goods and people to and from Gloucester. This was an altogether more exciting prospect and he determined to explore the possibilities when the time came.

In the meantime, he and Walter carried on as usual, coppicing and then burning when there was no farm work to be had. This year there had been plenty of that, as the harvest had been good and the wet weather held off until all the crops were safely gathered in. Grudgingly, he had to admit that Joe had pulled his weight in that direction, and it had been good to be working with him again. He wished he would give up the Works and come back permanently, but sadly, he knew that wasn't going to happen.

Ella's baby, Benjamin, was thriving and in fact, all the children in the hamlet seemed to be enjoying a healthy spell after the traumatic events of the previous year. However, everyone had noticed that Eddie was in declining health. He was looking older. He was stooping slightly and walking more slowly with each month that passed. Mary mentioned it to Elizabeth one day when they were hanging out the washing. She could see the decline in him. Nothing she could put her finger on, just a general 'gooin doon 'ill', as she said. Of course, she knew that if anything happened to Eddie, without any income at all, she couldn't survive on her own. She supposed she would have to rely on the parish, unless one of her children were to take her in. Neither prospect pleased her. She and Eddie had always been independent. They hadn't asked anyone for anything, and she didn't want to start now. In reality of course, she would have little choice in the matter if she wanted to survive at all. So, it was with some trepidation that the hamlet viewed the oncoming winter. No one said anything to Walter or Eddie, but they all knew that a harsh winter could bring danger to them both.

By the end of September Joe was back on permanent nights at the new furnace. The daily trek across the valley and back was just as onerous and he was more determined than ever to build himself a house in Dale Coppice. He decided that he would do just that, after spending this one last winter living in Banghams Wood. It was obvious to Joe that there were plenty of orders coming into the business. They were casting pigs more or less constantly, but also bellied pots, many of which were shipped off down the Severn to Bristol. From there it was said that they were sent all around the country, mainly by sea to other ports around the coast, and even to countries over the oceans.

# Chapter 6

1717: As it happened the winter wasn't as harsh as the previous one. The snow, when it came, lasted only a week or two and then melted away. It was, however, a pretty dreary time. There was plenty of rain which made the trackways inches deep in mud. Delivering the charcoal with old Ned pulling the cart was difficult to say the least. The weather was generally wet and damp with plenty of fog. It was an altogether miserable season, only punctuated by Christmas, which everyone determined to make the most of, as usual.

As they had all feared, in late February, Walter went down once again with a bad cold which rapidly turned to bronchitis and this time progressed to pneumonia. Within a week he developed a high fever and they all knew what it meant. Margaret and Abigail were sent for, and as he struggled for breath, all his children gathered around him to say their goodbyes. He knew exactly what was happening to him, he had watched his father going the same way. He told them all not to be sad. He would be going to be with his beloved Jane.

On the 12th day of March 1717, Walter Bangham took his last breath.

Once more, on the following Sunday, a sad little procession made its way to the burial ground. Because of the condition of the trackway, the coffin had to be carried by the men, Joe, Will, Dick, Arthur, Tom and Alf, which was no easy task and more than once they had to pick their way through the mud. Somehow, they made it and after a short service in the chapel, Walter was laid to rest.

For some weeks, the family found it hard. Walter had always been at the centre of their world and without his influence they all seemed to lose direction for a while. As when any pivotal member of a family passes on, there was a certain amount of adjusting of roles. Will, although not the eldest, still tried to take on the leadership role. While this was accepted by Dick and Dorothy and of course, Martha, it certainly wasn't by Joe, Elizabeth, Margaret and Abigail, who had all, each in their own way, already 'left' the family. This brought tensions as you would expect, particularly between Joe and Will, further exacerbating the rift between them.

Will was very worried. Without Walter he could no longer produce charcoal, and as yet, he had not decided what else he would do to bring in some money. Tom and Alf, who worked full time at the quarry, offered to help him get a place there as they were busy at the moment supplying limestone to the Darbys, among others. Although this was something he wasn't keen to do long term, he decided that at the moment he had little choice and agreed to work there, if they would have him. So, after some fifty years, charcoal production ended in Banghams Wood. It was the end of an era, and change was indeed coming to the Gorge.

Elizabeth went into premature labour shortly after Walter's death. She had been working hard to support the Bangham household as well as her own and had probably done too much, precipitating the early onset of labour about four weeks before her due time. However, helped by the other women, the baby was safely delivered. It was a little girl weighing just six pounds, but she seemed healthy enough. They called her Jane, after Elizabeth's mother, of course. Arthur was overjoyed at having another little girl. She could never replace Eliza, but he would love her just as much.

The river of course was high all through that winter, making navigation more difficult, which in turn meant that on occasion raw materials from the south, bound for the furnaces, were late arriving, and the wharf filled up with goods waiting to be transported in the opposite direction. Everyone battled on as best they could and somehow the furnaces were kept going. The men saw little of Mr Darby. It was rumoured that he was unwell, although no one knew exactly what was wrong with him. A general air of apprehension grew. There was no natural heir to the business ready to take over from him. His son, also Abraham, was still a child. During breaks, the men often wondered among themselves, what would become of the works, and therefore their jobs, should anything happen to Mr Darby. Joe was optimistic as usual, assuring anyone who would listen that 'Somebody'll take it over, just thee wait an' see.'

Spring came in early after the reasonably mild if wet winter. Arthur and Elizabeth were happy with their little family. There was plenty of work at the quarry with the increasing activities over at the Darby works. It seemed they could never take enough limestone to keep the furnaces running. Elizabeth, having once accepted that she would never be a mother, was entranced by her little girl but was sad that Walter hadn't lived long enough to meet his grandchild. She and the rest of the women worked hard in the garden plots, hoeing and planting to ensure a good supply of vegetables for the year.

It was the Sunday before Easter that Abigail came home for a visit. Elizabeth thought it odd that she came to her house first, rather than going home, but when she came in, she could see immediately that something was wrong. Abigail was pale and looked worried and Elizabeth noticed a thickening around her waist, which immediately rang alarm bells. When Elizabeth quietly asked her what was wrong, she broke down in tears saying that she thought she was going to have a baby. Elizabeth asked her who the father was, but she steadfastly refused to say. Knowing what a temper he had, Abigail was terrified of how Will would react. She knew he wouldn't take kindly to having to keep her and a baby, as well as Martha and Dorothy.

Elizabeth was shocked but not entirely surprised. There were always men around ready to take advantage of an innocent young girl. Of course, they were never around to face up to the consequences. She wasn't looking forward to telling Will about this. She hoped he wouldn't take out his anger on Abigail. She decided that she would first talk to Joe to work out some plan as to what could be done. Abigail would now have to leave service at the Hall and come back to live in the hamlet, which would mean another two mouths to feed without any extra money coming in. She told Abigail to say nothing to Will until she'd had a chance to speak with Joe and she was obviously relieved to leave it in Elizabeth's hands for the moment. Abigail spent the afternoon with Elizabeth, not wanting to show herself to Will in case he suspected something. As she was leaving she decided to pop her head in the door, intending just to say hello before setting off back to the Hall.

However, Will had been disappointed that she had been home and not come across the clearing to see him earlier, and told her to come in for a minute to warm herself at the fire before setting off back to the Hall. As she entered the room, he could see she was moving awkwardly with her back to him. He'd seen women move like that before when they had something to hide, and he asked her,

'Have you got something to tell me, our Abigail?'

Never any good at telling lies, she looked down at the ground and said,

'I'm sorry our Will, I didn't mean for it to happen.' and started to cry.

'No! Abigail! Not you! You're nobbut a child still! Who did this? Tell me Abigail, who did this to ye?'

Abigail said nothing, still crying and shaking her head violently.

'It's no use Abigail, ye'll have to tell me. He must be made to pay for what he's done. Was it one o' them toffs up at the Hall?'

Will was shouting now. Elizabeth heard him across the clearing and came running over.

She burst into the cottage and scooped Abigail up in her arms.

'Leave her alone Will!' she shouted. 'She's not telling us and that's that. What's done is done and we'll all just have to make the best on it!'

'Well, I won't be leaving it there – I want to know who did this. She's still a child. I'm going to be asking around and one way or another I'll find out and when I do, he'll be sorry he'd been born.'

When Abigail had calmed down, Elizabeth walked her back to the Hall, telling her not to worry, and to leave Will to her. She would make him see sense.

Will had managed to get work at the quarry, although he didn't enjoy it one bit. He had been used to working for himself and wasn't used to being given orders. Unlike Joe, he found this particularly difficult and he never bothered to hide his displeasure, which did not endear him to his employers. However, they were busy and needed the labour, so they had put up with his surly attitude, for the time being at least. He was now more determined than ever to find work on one of the Severn Trows as soon as he could. He knew that with the increased activity over at the Darby works, there were more boats than ever coming and going along the river and he had heard they were always looking for deck hands. Before that though, he mused as he worked, he had something else to deal with. He wasn't going to let the matter of Abigail's ruin, as he saw it, drop, before he'd found out who was responsible.

Will was still at the quarry on the day following Abigail's visit as Elizabeth went across the clearing to speak to Joe as she had promised. He was shocked, of course, and angry, but not with Abigail. It was as he had feared all along. She was altogether too pretty and good natured to be overlooked by a predatory man, and there were plenty of them about. Elizabeth told him Will had taken it badly and was determined to find out who had put her in the family way. Joe told Elizabeth to give him time to think about what could be done. He told her he had some ideas about his own future and maybe in some way he would be able to help Abigail as well, and that was how it was left for the time being. As for Will, Joe knew he could be hot-headed and wasn't one to let this drop. He feared what he would do if he ever did find out who the father was.

Of course, Joe had long intended to build himself a house in Dale Coppice and as he walked across to the works that evening, he was beginning to see how he might also help Abigail out. Once the baby was born, she could come and live with him. She could keep house for him and he would provide a home for her and her child. However, he was a bit concerned that when he left Banghams Wood, he wouldn't be there to keep an eye on Martha. She was such an innocent and had always looked to Joe for support. Will didn't have much patience with her unfortunately. He also had an idea that Will had an intention of seeking work on one of the trows and may be away from the house for days on end. Still, he determined to discuss his idea with Elizabeth the next day.

After much deliberation over the next few days, the two of them, along with Arthur, came up with a plan. All they needed now was to convince Will that it would be the best solution all round. The idea was that once Joe and Abigail left the hamlet, Elizabeth, Arthur and the children could move across to the Bangham house with Martha. Will, Dick and Dorothy would then move into Arthur's house which was the smaller of the two. That way, Martha would be looked after, and Dorothy was now old enough to keep house for her two brothers.

The following Sunday, Liz and Joe sat down with Will and told him about Joe's plan to build a house in Dale Coppice. At first he didn't listen to the rest of their idea, about Abigail and the baby going to live with Joe, because all he could think about was that with Joe gone, he would be trapped again, unable to escape the family responsibilities once more. Of course, he knew that Martha couldn't be left on her own while he went off down the river. So when they finally managed to explain that he and Dick could go and live with Dorothy in Arthur's place, it came as a relief. If he was away, Dick and Dorothy would be fine on their own.

So it was agreed that Abigail would stay with Will until after the baby was born, at which time, Joe would move into his own house, and Abigail and the baby would join him. The rest of the plan could then be implemented. It seemed like a good solution all round, and when Abigail next came to visit, she was delighted. Joe had always been her favourite. By the end of April, her condition became more obvious and she had to leave her position at the Hall and return to the hamlet.

In the meantime, Will had been making enquiries among the farmhands and quarry men and now had a good idea who had made Abigail pregnant. There was an under-butler called James Furlong, who it was well known couldn't keep his hands to himself whenever there was a young lass around. When Margaret came down one Sunday, Will asked her outright whether it was him. Although she denied it, she looked very uncomfortable and wouldn't meet his gaze.

She realised that he hadn't believed her.

'Leave it Will,' she pleaded. 'Nothing good can come of you getting involved now.'

'Leave it?!! Nay, I canna leave it! I won't let him get away with it.'

No-one said anything else for fear of making matters worse but they all exchanged worried glances, fearing what Will would do next.

They didn't have long to wait. Will came in late from the quarry on the Tuesday evening in an agitated state and Dorothy, who never missed a thing asked him what was wrong. He snapped at her that nothing was wrong and she should mind her own business. At that, she made some excuse to go over to Elizabeth and Arthur's house and told her that something was wrong with Will.

When Elizabeth confronted him, she could see the fear in his eyes and he admitted that he'd sorted that bastard out once and for all. She immediately knew what he meant.

'Oh my God Will, what have you done!?' she exclaimed.

'I just give 'im what 'e deserved our Liz. I guarantee 'e won't be touching no more lasses.'

Elizabeth sent Dorothy and Martha across to her own house while she tried to get out of Will exactly what had happened.

Eventually he admitted that he'd been up to the Hall and seen James making his way back to the kitchen from the privvy. He'd confronted him, saying he knew it was he that had put Abigail in the family way and what was he going to do about it. James had replied that if he hadn't done it someone else would have, as Abigail was rather too free with her favours.

'I couldn't let him say such things about our Abigail, could I?' he said. 'I just had to hit him. I struck him hard on the jaw and he fell backwards. He went down like a felled tree, and as he landed his head struck the edge of the paving stone. I swear I didn't mean to kill him Lizzie! Just to let him know he couldn't get away with it.'

'You mean you actually killed him, our Will?!' she said with a look of horror on her face.

'Aye,' he replied, 'well, I think so. He never moved after anyhow.'

'Oh God! Will, you'll have to get away from here or they'll string you up, for sure!'

Will looked full of fear and indecision.

'What must I do, our Liz? Where can I go?'

Elizabeth thought for a moment and then said,

'Did anyone see you do it?'

'I don't think so,' he said quietly.

'Then your best chance is the river! You must get down to the river and hope to God there's a trow ready to leave for Bristol. It's a big place and you'll be able to lose yourself there, or even work your passage to America. I've got a bit put by and you'll have to pay your passage on the trow. You must get away before anyone adds two and two together and comes looking for you.'

'Oh Sis, how can I leave you all like this?' he pleaded.

'Well, if you don't want to swing on the end of a rope, you don't have a choice. Get some things together while I go and find what money I can spare, and neither of us must tell any of the others what's gone on. The least they know the better.'

Will threw his clothes in a bag and after quickly eating some bread and dripping and taking a swig of ale he was ready to leave when Elizabeth came back with the few coins she'd managed to find.

'Now go, Will, quickly, before they come lookin' for ye. If they do I'll try to send them off on a wild goose chase to give you a bit more time, but hurry now and hope to God there's a ship ready to leave straight away.'

Will hesitated for a moment, completely horrified at what he'd done and how in a second his life had changed forever. Then he said,

'I'm so sorry Liz, to be going like this. Will you all be alright without me?'

'Too late to think about that now,' she said. 'The main thing is you need to get away and right now! Don't look back our Will. God protect you.' and with that, she gave him a fierce hug and pushed him out of the door, before the emotion of the moment caught up with her and she broke down in tears.

Will ran down the track to the Buildwas bridge then along the north side of the river to the wharf, where to his relief, there was a trow that looked as though it was just finishing loading pig iron, probably bound for Bristol. After a quick word with the captain and the exchange of a few coins he settled himself down in a corner of the deck, making himself as inconspicuous as possible. Within the hour, the trow pulled away from the wharf and Will Bangham was leaving the Severn Gorge, maybe forever.

Elizabeth calmed herself down and then went over to her cottage. They were all full of questions, of course, and she did her best to hide what had gone on but they all, with the exception of Martha, had a good idea. When she said that she wasn't able to tell them anything, in the end they accepted that. It didn't take long of course, for them all to realise that Will had gone, and once news got around about James the under-butler being attacked, they soon worked out for themselves that he'd had no choice but to leave Banghams Wood and would probably never be able to return.

Joe was angry with him for being so stupid and doing such an evil thing as to attempt to kill a man. No man had the right to take another's life. As it turned out, James wasn't in fact dead, although he didn't regain consciousness for two days and there had been some doubt as to whether he would survive. Well, now Will had made his bed he'd have to lie in it, thought Joe. This of course gave them all plenty to think about. With one of the main providers gone from the Bangham household, there would have to be changes sooner than they had anticipated.

As it happened, Dick was now working full time with the horses up at the Hall and Moses had said that it was time he retired. He had told Dick that he would speak to the master to see if he would take him on as the horse man. The master agreed as he'd seen the way Dick had handled the horses. It would mean a room above the stables for Dick, so as to be on hand should the horses need any attention. Since Abigail had left the Hall, there was a vacancy for a scullery maid and it was decided that Margaret should ask if they would take Dorothy on. She was horrified, until they told her that perhaps she might get a chance to learn to read, as there were plenty of books around at the Hall.

That was settled then, once Joe had built his house in Dale Coppice, Arthur and Elizabeth would move across the clearing into the Bangham place with their two and Martha. There were plenty of people looking for somewhere to live, with the growth of the Darby Works and the Quarry, so perhaps their own cottage could be let out for a few pence a week which would help with the family budget.

They did all miss Will of course, coming so soon after Walter's death as well. The Bangham family was now somewhat depleted, and soon there would be no Banghams as such, left in Banghams Wood

# Chapter 7

At the Works, what they had all feared, came to pass on May 5th. Mr Darby finally lost his two-year battle with illness and passed away. This was of course sad in itself, but more than that, the men now worried what would become of their jobs. The funeral was a simple affair as Quaker rituals tended to be, but the men and their families lined the road to Dale End with their caps removed and heads bowed as the coffin was carried on the horse drawn wagon. It was taken along the road to Madeley, across the river and up the steep slope to the Quaker Burial Ground at Broseley. Joe had remained at the works until mid-morning, in order to pay his respects. He was sad to watch the funeral of Mr Darby, the man who had given him his chance and always treated him fairly. It was heart-breaking to see Abraham, his young son, at just six years old, fighting back the tears and trying to be a man for his mother's sake, riding in the carriage behind the coffin with his mother and the other children.

Over the next few weeks there was much specu-lation about what was to happen to the works. By now there were scores of men, working either in the foundries or the furnaces; many families around the Gorge directly dependent on the Darby works, and also many more in the coal mines and quarries which supplied their raw materials. The whole district held its breath until it became known that a Bristol Merchant, Thomas Goldney and Mrs Darby's son-in-law Richard Ford were to take over the running of the business. Joe was pleased to hear that one of Mrs Darby's relations, a Mr Joshua Sergeant had taken it upon himself to look after the interests of the Darby children. Joe would not have been pleased to hear that they had been totally disinherited because of their father's early death.

For a while, little changed at the works but as the weeks went by Joe noticed that the place was taking on a more organised air. Richard Ford managed the day-to-day business of the works and he was obviously determined to make his mark on the place. Joe had to confess that things had been a bit lax for the last few months of Mr Darby's illness. Mr Ford called all the men together and explained that although he was a fair man, he did expect a full day's work for a full day's pay and that there were many men in the Gorge and beyond who would be only too willing to take the place of any man not prepared to work hard. Well, Joe thought, I suppose he has to start as he means to go on, if the business is to survive and prosper, which after all is in everyone's interest.

The range of goods was increased, and all manner

of cast iron domestic utensils were now being produced at the furnaces. Quantities of kettles, skillets, cooking pots and smoothing irons were being shipped down the Severn to Bristol or loaded on to carts to be taken by road to Shrewsbury or further afield, even, Joe had heard, as far as Manchester.

Abigail seemed happy enough now that she felt her future would be secure with Joe. He made enquiries among the men at the Works about finding a plot in Dale Coppice. A few of them, John Spencer, Ed Boden and Will Lloyd had already built their squatter cottages there and were pleased that Joe intended to join their settlement. As they said, there was strength in numbers and neighbour could help neighbour in time of trouble. They all offered to help Joe raise his house when the time came. Abigail's baby was due in the autumn, so Joe intended to use the summer to get his house built and ready for when the baby arrived.

Elizabeth spent any spare time she had, getting the Bangham house ship-shape for the time when her family would move into it. Little Jane was thriving. She was a bonny baby, who reminded her of Abigail when she was little, and reminded Arthur of Eliza. They both loved her dearly.

Things weren't going so well with Mary and Eddie. He seemed to be growing weaker and looking older with each passing week, although no one could really put a finger on what was wrong with him. He didn't seem to be in any pain, at least none that he admitted to. However, in the second week of June he took a turn for the worse, suffering a huge loss of blood. He took to his bed and there he stayed for several weeks with Mary catering for his every need, until one morning when she left him for a few minutes to bring him a drink of water, he quietly slipped away. After 40 years of marriage and four children raised safely to adulthood with Eddie, Mary was understandably distraught. Ella and Rose helped her to lay him out and Mr Johnson was sent for. Young Jimmy was inconsolable. He had been very close to Eddie, who had spent a lot of time with him, particularly since Eliza had gone, and Elizabeth did her best to comfort him. Poor child she thought, he must feel that everyone he loves is taken from him.

Two days later another sad procession made its way down the track to the Buildwas burial ground at Holy Trinity. Mary's children all came and her eldest daughter Susan insisted that she should go and live with her and her family in Madeley Wood. She didn't object. She had long since come to terms with the fact that she would never manage on her own without any income, and she and Eddie had never had the means to save anything. Susan stayed with her for a few days to pack up her belongings. With old Ned in harness on the cart, the men of the hamlet loaded them up and with Susan and Mary sitting at the front, with Joe, they set off down the track towards the Buildwas bridge. Everyone had gathered to watch them leave and there were quite a few tears to be seen. Mary had been a good neighbour to them all and she would be sadly missed.

It had been a fairly dry spring in 1717 in the Gorge and the reservoirs which fed the wheel that powered the bellows at the furnaces were so depleted by the beginning of June that, much to the annoyance of Mr Ford, both the furnaces had to be blown out. The furnace men, including Joe, were laid off. There was some maintenance work to do on the structure of the furnaces but by the end of June that was all finished.

Mr Newton told the men that unless he could find them the odd bit of work in the ironworks or the foundry, which had reasonable stocks of pig iron and plenty of orders, there would be no more work until the reservoirs filled up again. Joe decided it was time to put his plan into action and went with the other men to choose the plot upon which he would build his house. It took him the best part of a month to amass the lumps of stone, and the timber he would need. It was decided that the house raising would be undertaken on the first weekend in July.

The Banghams Wood men came across, and Elizabeth and the other women had made food for them to bring with them. They began the work early one day and with the help of the Dale Coppice men, John, Ed and Arthur, worked into the small hours building the simple structure that would qualify as a squatter's cottage. By the time dawn was breaking it was all but finished. Four walls and a turf roof stood where none had been before. Joe had his house. The Banghams Wood men set off wearily down the track to their homes, with the exception of Joe, who wouldn't leave his house that night. John's wife Susan brought him a hot drink and some bread, for which he was mightily grateful. Then after heartily thanking everyone who had helped him raise his house, he threw himself down to rest on a blanket on the ground.

He fell into an exhausted sleep and was woken up at about nine o'clock by the sound of children playing. He rose and washed at the pump, and John emerged from his cottage to invite him to come in for a bit of breakfast. He gratefully accepted although he knew they would have precious little for themselves at the moment, with John being laid off from work for the summer. There was porridge and a little honey and a swill of ale and Joe felt all the better for it and ready to begin his day's work. He intended to make and fit the door and window frame to his cottage, to keep out the wind and rain before the weather turned. Dick came over every few days with some food for him as he wouldn't risk leaving the cottage empty in case someone else should decide to take up residence. The other Dale Coppice residents also shared what they could with him.

It took him a further four weeks hard work to get his cottage into a truly habitable state. He did manage to do a few labouring jobs down at the Works which helped him to buy the few things he needed from Madeley Wood market. He made a couple of beds, one for himself and one for Abigail. In time, he would add another couple of rooms to the cottage, but it would suffice for the time being. In fact, it was looking quite cosy by the time he brought Abigail across the Gorge to take a look at what would soon be her new home. She was delighted with it. In a couple of months' time, she would be moving in with Joe and her baby and she was happy.

Joe settled into his new home and found his neighbours to be pleasant enough. John and Susan Spencer lived in the cottage next to his with their children Elizabeth who was about eighteen and Tom, sixteen. They had lived in Dale Coppice for ten years or so, John working for the Darby company as well as doing some farm labouring whenever he needed to. Ed Boden and his wife Mary with their three were in the next cottage along, and in the far cottage were Will and Margaret Lloyd, a young couple who hadn't been married very long and as yet had no children.

August turned out to be wet and the reservoirs started to fill up again. By the beginning of September 1717, Mr Ford judged it to be safe to blow in the furnaces. When Joe turned up for work, Mr Newton took him to one side and said that one of the furnacemen had finally been forced to stop working due to ill health. This meant they were a man short, and he wanted Joe to take his place. He would be working permanently in the hearth of the furnace, which Joe knew would be hard and dangerous work, but Mr Newton said it would mean working days now and he would still be paid twelve shillings a week. Given that he would soon have Abigail and the baby to feed and clothe, he readily agreed to the move. It would make life easier for Abigail if he was working days and all in all, he felt it was a good move.

The furnaces were soon in full production again, and busier than ever. Orders had poured in over the summer months and they were working flat out to fulfil them. Joe felt satisfied he had achieved his aim of moving across to Dale Coppice and life was easier without the daily trek to and fro across the Gorge at each end of his shift. He did miss his sisters and Dick of course but couldn't really say the same about Will. Of course he did wonder what had become of him. Bristol was a gateway to the wider world, and it was quite possible that he was right now on his way to the New World. Perhaps they would never know. What Will didn't know though, was that James had recovered from the attack, and in fact, he couldn't remember a thing about what had happened and therefore was unable to point the finger at Will. Of course, people had their suspicions, as he had disappeared the very next day, but no proof, and had Will chosen to come back he would probably have got away with it. As it was, the family just had to accept that their brother was gone, most likely forever.

In Banghams Wood, life had taken up its new rhythm after Walter's death and Joe's departure. Abigail had continued to live there for the time being, until after the baby was born, when she would move across the valley to join Joe. Martha, with Dorothy's help, was coping surprisingly well at keeping house for Abigail and Dick. Elizabeth and Arthur were struggling a little financially, but Elizabeth was a good manager, and they were happy enough. Baby Jane was thriving and Jimmy seemed to be getting over the loss of Eliza and Eddie, and had started to play more with the other children of the hamlet.

Eddie and Mary's house stood empty for a good three months, then one evening at the beginning of October, a new family arrived, piled along with their belongings on the top of a cart, pulled up the track from Buildwas bridge by an old carthorse. They arrived without notice and initially, the current residents of the hamlet were rather resentful of the intrusion. This was a tight knit community where shared joys and tragedies over the years had bound them together. They had jointly endured hardships and deprivations, experienced each others bereavements and joyous occasions alike. They felt that the arrival of a family of strangers in their midst would be bound to cause disruption, maybe even some realignment of loyalties. They surveyed the family and the pile of belongings on the cart with curiosity of course, trying to judge what manner of people they were.

The man looked to be in his thirties, and his wife about the same. Their clothes suggested that this move was a downward step for them, as did some of the items piled on the cart. The furniture was definitely not home made and there seemed rather a lot of it. There were several bundles which looked to contain clothes or household linen and baskets full of kitchen utensils and earthenware pots. The children, one boy and one girl, were scrubbed clean with their hair topped with smart hats, and wearing clothes that would have been at home up at the Hall.

As it happened, this had been one of the rare dry days that autumn, but as they pulled up the cart, it began to rain and Arthur, Tom and Alf all offered to help unload their belongings. As they did so, they chatted to the newcomers, and it appeared that they had come from Madeley Wood. They were Benjamin and Dorothea Blake, and the children were David and Susan. Apparently, they were some relation of Mary's who had leased them the cottage. Apart from that, they discovered little about the reason for the apparent lowering of their station in life. No doubt, they thought, this would become clear over the days and weeks ahead.

Arthur took it upon himself to point out a few of the basic rules of living in the hamlet, explaining that the pump was for the use of all. They would be made welcome as long as they were considerate of the other residents, keeping their little plot tidy and their children under control and not bothering anyone else. Benjamin Blake assured Arthur that their only wish was to settle peaceably in the hamlet and be good neighbours to one and all. With that, everyone left them alone to settle in to their new home. Elizabeth dropped by later that evening with some bread in case they had not brought any with them. They were very grateful and thanked her for her kindness.

As the days went by their story began to unfold. One day Dorothea was chatting to Elizabeth as she tended her vegetable plot and she explained that Benjamin had owned a trow on the river and had been doing good trade for the past ten years. Then tragedy had struck. Down in Gloucester docks there had been a collision and the trow, along with all its cargo had sunk. Benjamin had lost his means of making a living and the loss of the cargo had also cost him much of his savings as he had to recompense his customer in order to at least preserve his reputation. He hoped to get a new barge to rebuild his business, but in the meantime the family had had to give up their rented home in Madeley Wood and Dorothea's aunt Mary had kindly suggested they take her cottage until they could get back on their feet.

Elizabeth felt sorry for their bad luck and she liked Dorothea. They immediately struck up a friendship which was to last many decades, even though their lives would grow apart once again before too long.

By the beginning of November, everything was ready for Abigail and the baby in Dale Coppice. Joe had added another bedroom for the two of them and furnished it with a bed and a cot for the baby. It was on the 4th of November that Abigail called out for Elizabeth in the night, saying that the baby was coming. She laboured for twelve hours, and Elizabeth could see that it was a big baby. Abigail was quite small and slim, and it was hard going for her. Finally, at 2 o'clock the following day, Michael was born. He was a fine healthy baby with a shock of ginger hair, and Abigail was delighted with him. She stayed with Elizabeth and Arthur for three weeks before Dick took her and the baby in the cart over to Joe's cottage. Elizabeth was upset to see them go. She had enjoyed having Abigail around. They had always been close, but they had grown even closer over the last few months. Still, she knew it was for the best. She and Joe would soon make a good home for young Michael.

# Chapter 8

1718: Abigail and Michael soon settled in with Joe. She was grateful to him for taking them in and worked hard to create a comfortable home for them all. Her experience as a scullery maid and helping Elizabeth with the vegetable plot and the cooking, had equipped her well for the running of a home, despite her youth. She did find it hard though, to get used to the noise from the works, which never stopped. Day and night there was the roar of the furnaces, the hammers of the foundry and the men shouting to one another in the distance, trying to make themselves heard over the din. She noticed the air was full of soot from the furnaces and any clothes left out on the line more than a day were covered in it.

More than once, in spite of what had eventually happened to her at the hands of Furlong, she remembered fondly, the quiet, ordered days of life up at the Hall, and even in the hamlet in Banghams Wood. Still, she thought, she wouldn't want to go back into a life in service, where as a scullery maid, she had been at the beck and call of everyone. At least, living with

Joe she was free to organise her day as she wished. She loved Michael, in spite of the way he'd been conceived. However, she was sad that what had happened to her had in the end resulted in Will having to leave Banghams Wood. Although she was touched that he had tried to avenge her, she did feel guilty that she had been the cause of his disappearance from the family.

She soon made friends with Elizabeth Spencer, who, although she was a little older than Abigail, seemed pleased to have another young woman in the hamlet to talk to. Abigail suspected that there was a little more to it than that though. She had seen the way Elizabeth looked at Joe and made any excuse she could think of to pop into Abigail and Joe's cottage whenever he was at home. For his part, she wasn't sure whether he'd noticed or not. It was infuriating. He seemed completely absorbed in what was going on at the works. His new job on the furnace floor was hard and he came home completely worn out. Abigail determined she would say something to him about Elizabeth soon. He needed to open his eyes, he wasn't getting any younger himself, she mused. He was going on twenty-two now, which to Abigail, seemed ancient.

By mid-December Joe decided it was time to visit Banghams Wood to see how Elizabeth and Arthur were faring. Since Will had left, Arthur had taken on the role of head of the family. Of course, Dick was now living over the stables at the Hall and Dorothy was in service, so there was only Martha and his own family to look after. He was a good man and Joe didn't doubt that he would fulfil the role, but he did want to put his mind at rest regarding Elizabeth. He knew she would be missing him and Will and the others and he wanted to see her before the winter weather made visiting Banghams Wood nigh on impossible.

He crossed the valley on the following Sunday. Although Abigail would have loved to see Elizabeth, she didn't go with him because she wouldn't risk young Michael's health by exposing him to the weather. It was cold, and a wet westerly was blowing up the Gorge as Joe crossed the Buildwas bridge. He hadn't seen the family since Abigail had moved across to his place several weeks earlier and he was eager to listen to all their news. When he entered the cottage door, Elizabeth shrieked with delight at the sight of her favourite brother.

'Eee Joe! Y'are a sight for sore eyes!' she exclaimed, declaring that she'd greatly missed him, then added, 'I never expected you today, but you'll eat with us? There's plenty to go round. It's a pity Margaret won't be coming, it was only last week she was here.'

'That's a shame,' Joe declared, 'I was hoping I might see her, or Dorothy, but never mind, it's good to see you and Arthur and the little ones. How've they been?'

'They're both fine reet now, thanks,' Elizabeth assured him, adding 'How's our Abigail and Michael?'

Joe reassured her that they were both in good health and settling down to life in Dale Coppice. He told her that Abigail had made friends with Elizabeth Spencer, who lived with her family in the cottage next door. Something about the way he spoke, gave her a clue that perhaps it wasn't only Abigail who had made friends with Elizabeth Spencer, but she said nothing, storing the information away for future reference.

It was good to see Elizabeth back in the Bangham family home. They had moved in shortly after Abigail left and the place was looking cosy and well ordered, just as Joe would have expected. The smell emanating from the cooking pot suspended over the fire was teasing his taste buds into life as he settled down on the settle, opposite Arthur at the hearth. They chatted amicably while Elizabeth busied herself with feeding little Jane. It turned out that a family had moved into Arthur's old place. Thomas Baker had been taken on at the quarry a month earlier and had been looking for a place for his wife, Laura and his two young children, to move into. Arthur said he had seemed to be a good worker and he offered him his house at a rent of a shilling a week, which he had gratefully accepted and the family had moved in almost immediately.

Joe asked how the Blake family were settling in since they had moved into Mary and Eddie's old place. Arthur said they kept themselves to themselves most of the time. Apparently, Benjamin was trying to finance another trow so that he could start up his haulage business on the Severn again, so Arthur didn't think they would be with them for very long. Elizabeth seemed to be friendly with Dorothea though, and they often helped one another out with chores around the hamlet. Arthur said he had wondered whether to talk to Benjamin about perhaps working for him on his trow if he finally restarted his business. Joe said it sounded like a good idea given there would certainly be plenty of river work in the future, the way the Darby works was growing, with raw materials and finished goods being sent up and down the Severn several times a day.

Elizabeth declared that dinner was ready, serving up a ladleful of the meat and vegetables onto each plate, and they all sat round the table to eat. As they ate, Joe enquired about the goings on at the Hall. Had Dick and Dorothy settled in up there? How was Margaret? Had there been any rumours about why Will had left Banghams Wood?

Elizabeth told him they were all fine. Dotty had taken well to life at the Hall. She was a bright girl and was already well thought of, or so Margaret had told them. In fact, one of the maids who had had a little education was teaching her to read, and she was loving every minute! Dick was thoroughly enjoying caring for the horses and it was obvious he wouldn't want to be doing anything else. As for Will, Margaret said she hadn't heard anything. After all, no one at the Hall knew anything about Will and she wasn't about to enlighten them. Elizabeth had said nothing to the others about his assault on James until she'd heard that he wasn't dead and was fully recovered. When she had told Margaret about it, she said it was what she had suspected all along.

Joe stayed for another hour after supper and then declared he must be on his way. He said his good-byes, gave his sister a hug and set off towards the river. It was dark now but there was a full moon and he was easily able to pick his way down the familiar track to the bridge, enjoying the night sounds he had known all his life. An owl hooted some way off, to be answered by one closer to hand. The cry of an infant fox looking for its mother sounded off to the left followed by rustling in the undergrowth as no doubt she answered its call. It had been good to catch up with Elizabeth and to see the old place again. After all, he had been born and grown up in the cottage in the wood that bore his name, and his new place didn't quite feel like home to him yet.

On the other side of the river, as he walked up the lane beside the brook, the noise of the foundry and the hammers in the forge grew louder and the air became thick with fumes from the furnaces. Normally he didn't notice it, but now, after visiting Banghams Wood, in contrast to the peace and fragrancy of that place, the noise and the smell of Dale Coppice assaulted his senses. Still, this was a small price to pay, he thought to himself, for the steady work and good pay he received from the Works.

As the days grew shorter and winter tightened its grip in Dale Coppice, its inhabitants prepared for the harsh conditions which would inevitably soon arrive. The woodpiles were replenished, and any gaps around windows and doors were sealed against the winter winds. The hog had been killed, butchered and shared out in the hamlet according to the number of mouths to be fed. This year, Joe had been allocated his share even though he and Abigail had just arrived. This was a measure of the respect in which he was held among the Coalbrookdale men. They knew that he would more than earn his share in the months and years ahead.

Christmas in Dale Coppice seemed strange to Joe and Abigail. It was the first time either of them had spent it away from Banghams Wood and the rest of the family. Not that there was much of the family left there Joe mused, as he was clearing out the hearth to set it again to cook their meal on Christmas Day. Abigail had prepared chicken, ham and vegetables to go into the pot, which was soon bubbling away over the fire. After they had finished supper there was a knock on the door and when Joe opened it Elizabeth Spencer was standing there, and shyly said that her mother had sent her round to see if he and Abigail would like to come over for a drink of ale as they were having a bit of a party, it being Christmas and all.

Abigail smiled as she watched Joe's face turn pink, which told her she had been right all along, he did have a soft spot for Elizabeth. Of course, he was happy to accept the invitation. Without hesitation he threw his coat on and donned his cap. He damped down the fire and Abigail picked Michael up, wrapping her shawl around the baby and herself, and they followed Elizabeth back to the cottage next door. The whole Spencer family made them welcome and their first Christmas in Dale Coppice turned out to be every bit as enjoyable as any they had had in Banghams Wood. This was particularly true for Joe and Elizabeth. It was obvious to everyone that there was an attraction between them and from that day they were seldom apart, except when Joe was at the furnace.

The winter turned out to be as harsh as anyone could remember. The snow scurried around the clearing in Dale Coppice, drifting into huge mounds against the cottage walls until it reached the eaves and could grow no higher. Each morning the residents of the cottages had to dig their way out of their doorways. It was the end of February before the last of the snows had melted away and the March winds began to blow along the Gorge. Birdsong once again competed for attention against the constant drumming of the hammers in the forge, and the trees began to burst into life once more.

As 1719 wore on, demand for the domestic goods being manufactured at the Darby Works continued to grow. Joe was now skilled at iron making, experienced in judging when any adjustment of ingredients was needed to ensure a good product. The Coalbrookdale Company was developing a reputation for the quality of its goods and shipments were being sent far afield. Joe was always proud to hear that Coalbrookdale products were finding their way into homes and businesses up and down the land and even to the Americas!

Whenever he got the chance, he would chat to the hauliers to find out where the shipments were heading. He was particularly interested to talk to the Bristol hauliers, conscious that they were a link to an outside world he would probably never himself see. One such merchant was Solomon White. He owned his own Severn Trow and plied his trade constantly between the Gorge and the port of Gloucester where goods would be trans-shipped to be taken on to Bristol. One day in early March, he sought Joe out to give him a letter which he said he had been given by a man who asked him to deliver it to Joe personally, even though it was addressed to Elizabeth Green. Joe guessed that it might be from Will. They hadn't heard from him since he had left Banghams Wood.

As the letter was addressed to Elizabeth, Joe decided he must go over to Banghams Wood on Sunday to deliver it to his sister. To be fair, it wasn't much use Joe opening it himself as he couldn't read. Nor could Will for that matter. He must have paid a letter writer to draft it for him. The following Sunday, Abigail and Michael crossed the Gorge with Joe, to visit Elizabeth and Arthur. Perhaps Margaret or Dorothy might be there and if they couldn't read it, maybe they would know someone up at the Hall who would be able to decipher it for the family.

As it happened, neither Margaret nor Dorothy were

at Elizabeth's that Sunday, much to Joe's disappointment. He immediately gave Elizabeth the letter which
he told her had probably come from Will. She opened
it carefully, almost reverently, as though it was a thing
of wonder.

'Well, there's a lot of writing here Joe,' she said,
'but it might as well just be a load of scribbles, as
I can't decipher it and I don't know anybody round
here as can.'

'Well I do!' declared Arthur, 'Benjamin Blake is your
man! He's sure to be able to read and write, nobody
can run a business the way he has without learning
their letters.'

'You're right Arthur! Benjamin will be able to read
it. Will you go across and ask him if he would mind
coming over to read it to us all, Arthur?'

Arthur gladly agreed and disappeared across the
clearing to speak to Benjamin Blake, who returned
with him after about ten minutes or so. He took the
letter and with all the family seated round, full of
anticipation, he began to read:

*Dear Liz and all,*

*I want to let you know that I am in good health
and trust this letter finds you all the same. I have been
working at the Bristol Docks since I arrived here. The
work is hard but no harder than I'm used to. I have met
people from all over the world, here in Bristol. I hear
stories of all kinds of wild places and the animals that
live there. I've heard that over the ocean, in the Americas, a man can make his fortune. There is land to be*

*had that a man can call his own. No greedy landowners there. They call it a land of opportunity Liz, and I am moved to go there myself. By the time you receive this letter, I will be aboard the Matilda, halfway across the ocean, bound for America. One day I will return with a fortune for all of us to share Liz. Please do not worry about me. I am happy now that I am bound for a new life in a new world.*

*God bless you all,*

*Your loving brother, Will*

After Benjamin had finished reading, all were silent, as they took in the news that their brother was at that very moment on a ship somewhere in the middle of the great ocean, sailing to the other side of the world. Elizabeth broke the silence as she spoke softly,

'Oh our Will, whatever will become of you?' then turned to Arthur and buried her face in his shoulder, weeping quietly for the loss of her brother. Joe thanked Benjamin for reading it to them and took the letter from him. Benjamin said he was glad he'd been able to help, saying he was sorry it had been such upsetting news for them all, then took his leave.

Joe wasn't sure what he was feeling. He was angry at Will for getting himself in the situation of having to leave home through his recklessness, but he was relieved that at least it sounded as though he was following his dream. He knew Will had always wanted to explore the world beyond the Gorge and now he had his chance. He turned his attention to Elizabeth, trying to console her, saying that at least Will seemed in good health and fine spirits as he set out on his adventure.

'It's what he always wanted our Liz, you know that,' he said quietly, 'to get away from this place and see something of the world. Well now he has his wish and we must try to be glad for him.'

'I know you're right Joe, we must try, but it's hard and we all know we may never see him again.'

The conversation about Will ended abruptly as young Michael decided he was hungry and exercised his lungs to let everyone know it.

'Lordy Abigail!' Elizabeth exclaimed, 'that's a hearty cry! You've got a strong lad there and no mistake!'

'I know Liz,' Abigail agreed, 'when he's hungry he certainly leaves me with no doubt about it,' as she sat down by the fire and put him to her breast.

'Well I'd best get the rest of us fed an' all,' Elizabeth declared, and set about preparing the vegetables to add to the rabbit Arthur had caught that morning, which was already cooking in the pot.

While they waited for the meal to cook, Joe asked Arthur what news he had of Benjamin Blake's plan to set himself up with a new business. Arthur said he had spoken to Benjamin only last week and he said he hoped to have his new boat within the next month or so. He also said he had asked Benjamin if there would be any jobs going. Benjamin had told him that he would certainly be taking men on and if Arthur was interested he would be happy to keep him in mind. He did stress that the work was hard but Arthur had insisted that it couldn't be any harder work than what he had endured for years on the land and then up at the stone quarry, and he had told Benjamin that he definitely wished to give it a try. Joe told Arthur that the Darby works was taking on new men all the time, and if he liked he would ask for him. Arthur thanked him but said that he would really rather try his luck on the river than work at the ironworks with all the fumes and dirt it threw out. When the wind blew from the north, it was now even finding its way across the river and into Banghams Wood!

The smell emanating from the cooking pot, told Elizabeth that supper was ready to serve and she told them all to sit at the table while she filled their bowls. As it was still early in the year, and the days short, as soon as they had finished, Joe announced that he and Abigail must be making their way home to Dale Coppice. Elizabeth said that the afternoon had gone all too quickly and that they must come back soon, hopefully when Margaret or Dorothy were visiting. Joe promised that they would. In fact, now that the worst of the winter was over, perhaps they could visit more often, he told her.

With that, Abigail wrapped her shawl tightly around herself and Michael, and she and Joe said their good-byes and set off down the track to the bridge. The light was fading fast but Joe knew every twist and turn of the track, he'd trudged it often enough after all. Fifteen minutes later they had reached the bridge, just in time to see a barge loaded up with coal passing underneath it, heading for the wharf downstream. The river was high, as it usually was at this time of year and a brisk breeze had blown up. Looking down at the black water swirling around in the wake of the barge, Abigail shivered and said,

'I do wish Arthur wasn't set on going on the river Joe. I heard only yesterday about a boat that got sunk down towards Bridgnorth way, and seven men died. It seems to me once the river takes them there's only one end.'

'I know,' Joe replied, 'but we live in a dangerous world Abigail and accidents can happen anywhere, whether it's in a quarry or on a river. Don't worry, Arthur will take good care, with Liz and the children waiting for him back home.'

This seemed to settle Abigail's mind and she declared that they had better hurry home now as Michael would soon need feeding again. As they walked back up the hill to Dale Coppice, Abigail was deep in thought. She had long since realised, before Joe himself did, that he and Elizabeth were meant for each other. She knew it wouldn't be long before they were betrothed. What she wondered, would happen to her and little Michael? Would Joe still want her to live in Dale Coppice with them after they were married? Still, this wasn't something she could talk to him about until he had got round to asking Elizabeth to marry him. Men were so infuriatingly slow sometimes she mused.

So, no one was surprised when Joe and Elizabeth

announced that they were to be married. They had hardly been out of each other's sight since Joe and Abigail had settled into the hamlet. Joe extended his house, adding another bedroom and a brewhouse, determined to make it fit for his new wife. So it was, that one beautiful June morning, two processions wended their way to Holy Trinity at Buildwas. Joe and Elizabeth strode hand in hand down the track by the brook, followed by John and Susan Spencer and Abigail and Michael. Joe glanced lovingly at his bride to be. He thought she had never looked lovelier, in a white dress with a blue shawl around her shoulders. She wore a wreath of wild flowers around her golden curls and carried a posy of daisies in her hand. As they neared the Buildwas Bridge, they met the Banghams cart as it crossed the river, pulled by Ned with Elizabeth and Arthur with the children, and the rest of the family all piled on top.

The service was short, the main event, and indeed the purpose, was the reciting of the marriage vows and the signing of the register in the presence of the witnesses. Afterwards, Joe lifted Elizabeth up onto the wagon and climbed up beside her. Richard took the reins and led the procession along the riverside and up the hill to Dale Coppice for the celebration. Elizabeth and Arthur had brought a roasted hog joint and a barrel of ale to contribute to the meal, and the Spencers provided the rest. It was a fine sunny day and tables were set up in the clearing for the wedding guests. A fine feast was laid out and afterwards one of the men brought out his fiddle and dancing soon commenced. Later, on the cart on the way back home to Banghams Wood, Elizabeth remarked to Arthur that it had been 'a reet fine do!' and she was glad that Joe and Elizabeth had been given a day to remember. She was sure they would 'mek a go on' it' she declared, and Arthur nodded in agreement. This was to be old Ned's last duty, as old age finally took its toll and a month after the wedding he died in his sleep. The family all grieved for him of course, he had served them well for over eighteen years.

Joe and Elizabeth settled down to married life and within a year she was pregnant with their first child. However, it was an ill-fated pregnancy which failed at the seven-month mark. When the child was delivered it was a poor little mite who could never have lived to see the world. Elizabeth and Joe were devastated, and it was a year or so before they were ready to try again. Eventually try they did, and before long Elizabeth was pregnant again. To their delight, on 26th May 1724 a beautiful little girl, who they named Elizabeth after her mother, was born. She had her mother's blue eyes and golden hair but was unmistakeably a Bangham.

# Chapter 9

1724: The last few years had been busy ones in and around Dale Coppice. Each month would bring more newcomers. Often they would be relatives of one or other of the families already settled in the hamlet, but occasionally complete strangers would turn up, determined to find work in the valley. Its reputation for being a hive of industry had now spread far and wide, and acted like a magnet for families with no other means of earning a living.

The men who had founded the settlement became leaders of the group, and as needed, they called a meeting so they could all agree the rules by which Dale Coppice would be run. Everyone knew that in some of the settlements around the Gorge there was much rowdiness, drunken behaviour and even debauchery, particularly among the newcomers, and they were determined to keep Dale Coppice a fit place to live and bring up their families. Of course, everyone who worked at the Darby Works also knew that the owners wouldn't tolerate any drunkenness among their work force. The work was far too dangerous for that, and in any case the Darbys were Quakers who were renowned for their sobriety.

So there were now ten households in Dale Coppice. Six of the families were dependent on the Darby Works for their livelihoods. The other men worked either at the quarries or the mines thereabouts. The women tended their vegetable patches and looked after the hogs, which were owned communally and when they were slaughtered the meat was shared out between the families according to their need. In the last couple of summers when water had been short and the furnaces were blown out, some of the men had found work repairing the furnaces ready for the next season, or in the foundry. When without work, Joe and some of the men kept busy coppicing and building a couple of clamps to produce some charcoal, which was still needed in other furnaces and for domestic use around the gorge. It wasn't as lucrative as working at the furnace, but it served to keep their families fed.

At the works there had also been much change. As well as bellied pots and other domestic items, the Darby's had occasionally produced steam engine cylinders. Joe was always excited to be involved in the casting of parts for steam engines. He was bright enough to understand that these machines were indeed going to bring great change to the world. So far, while the engines were fixed to the ground, they had been used to pump water out of the mine workings, or at the pitheads, to raise and lower the cages down to the coal seam. Now there was sometimes talk of engines that would be able to turn wheels set on tracks. Wooden rails were already used in the valley to carry coal and stone from the mines and quarries, using a wagon hauled by a team of horses. The idea of placing a steam engine on a wagon to drive wheels which ran along tracks didn't seem too far-fetched to anyone with a scintilla of imagination, and Joe had plenty. However, it was to be many decades until these developments came about, and Joe Bangham would never live to see them. In the meantime, the Coalbrookdale works continued to cast parts for the Newcomen engine, and the men took great pride in their work, becoming famous for the quality of their workmanship.

Abigail had asked Joe and Liz whether they minded having her share their home, but both of them told her that she could stay with them as long as she wanted to. Nevertheless, she did dream that one day, she might have a home of her own. Since Liz had moved in, it hadn't felt like her place anymore, and Abigail felt that she had to defer to her in matters to do with the household, as she was Joe's wife and it was, after all, his house. Nevertheless, she did her best to help Liz with the chores and generally felt she earned her keep.

Arthur had been working the barges for the past two years now. Benjamin Blake, now Owner Blake, had been as good as his word and had given Arthur a job on his trow. Arthur loved the work, hard as it was.

At least he could see something of the world outside the Gorge. They sailed the Blake vessel, the Oriel, an upstream trow, down river as far as the Gloucester Docks, when they had to tranship the cargo to larger vessels, or downstream trows, for the second part of its journey to Bristol and the wide world beyond. Then they would reload the Oriel with goods bound for the Gorge, or sometimes, Shrewsbury. The boat would then be hauled back up river against the flow, with the help of gangs of bow haulers based in pubs along the river bank.

Elizabeth still wasn't too keen on Arthur working the river. He was away for days on end and she constantly worried that one day, he wouldn't return. She had lived by the Severn all her life and she knew its moods. It could be calm, gently flowing along when the level was low in the summer months, but when the north westerly drove sheets of rain along the valley, or the snows of winter melted too quickly, it could rapidly turn into a raging torrent as it forced its way through the narrow gorge. She had heard enough tragic tales of men and boats lost on the river to know that however careful a man was, no matter how well he could swim, the river showed no mercy. Once the fast-flowing water of the river in flood took them, few men could resist the pull of its currents. Still, she had to admit that he was earning good money. Owner Blake valued his diligence and reliability and paid him accordingly. She just prayed that God would protect Arthur. It was all she could do.

The winter was harsh that year. Snow piled high along the tracks, thawing slightly, then freezing overnight, making moving around treacherous. Joe was thankful that he only had the relatively short distance from the hamlet to the works to cover, remembering the winter of 1715, when he'd had to battle his way through the snow and ice from Banghams Wood, across the Gorge to the works. Liz had turned out to be a wonderful mother and a capable homemaker, and they were ecstatically happy now that they had their beautiful baby girl. That winter there was always a good fire with a pot bubbling away when he arrived home, tired and hungry from his day's work at the furnace and the trudge back through the snow.

It was at the end of February 1725 that the snow which had turned to layer upon layer of ice over the long winter months, began to melt. The rate of melting brought alarm and dread around the Gorge. Everyone wanted to see the end of it of course, but not like this. They knew that if it melted too quickly the river wouldn't cope with the volume of water tumbling down the valley sides, not just in the Gorge, but all the way upriver to its source in the Welsh hills. Arthur was away on the Oriel taking a cargo of iron goods downriver to Gloucester. Elizabeth judged they should be on their way back upriver in the next few days and prayed to God that they would stay put in Gloucester until the worst of the floodwater had passed. As predicted, by the third day of the thaw, with rain now pouring down hastening the melting of the remaining snow, the river had turned into a raging torrent, almost reaching the top of the arch of Buildwas Bridge. The wharf was packed with boats waiting for the flood to subside before making the hazardous journey downriver. No boats had arrived upstream for two days and there was much concern among the owners and bargees families alike. Still, there was nothing to be done except to sit tight and wait for the water level to fall.

Elizabeth was beside herself with worry. As she glanced at Jimmy and Jane playing by the fire, she felt sick to her stomach with the thought that they may no longer have a father, or she a husband. By the end of the third day after she had hardly slept for two nights, she was desperate to find out if there was any news. She felt completely isolated in Banghams Wood. The Blakes had moved out over a year ago, now that they owned their new boat and their finances had improved. Their house had been occupied by another quarryman and his family, who would know nothing of what might be happening down on the river. The next day, the rain had stopped, and the snow and ice were all gone. She left the children with Martha while she trudged down the now muddy track to the bridge to see if she could find out what was happening. She was horrified at the sight of the river, which was still far too high, just managing to find its way under the Buildwas Bridge. Making her way along the north side of the river, towards the wharf, her heart was hammering in her chest at what she might be about to hear.

As she approached the wharf, she could see a crowd of people, mostly women on a similar mission to her own. There would be many men from the Gorge somewhere on the river down towards Gloucester. Until boats started to arrive, there was no way to know whether they were safe. Although the rain had stopped, there would be plenty of water still to flow down the Gorge and no-one knew how long it was likely to be before the appearance of the sails of the first trow to make it home safely.

Elizabeth found Benjamin Blake in the crowd and immediately approached him to ask for news of the Oriel. He had none, but said a messenger had been sent by horseback to Bridgnorth to see if they could gain news of any boats that had been in trouble in the flood. He assured her that he had a good and ex-perienced crew on board the Oriel, which was a strong well-built boat and he had every confidence that it would soon return safely. He persuaded Elizabeth to return home to the children and as soon as there was news, he would send a message to her.

Reluctantly, Elizabeth agreed, bade him farewell and started back along the riverbank towards the bridge. She had only gone about a hundred yards when a shout went up that a boat had been sighted and she turned and hurried back to the wharf. It was a long way off in the distance and there was much speculation as to what vessel it was. She found Owner Blake by the edge of the dock, peering in the direction of the oncoming sails. He knew the outline and colour of his own ship's sails and was disappointed to see that this wasn't his trow, and then the man standing next to him shouted out that it was in fact his boat, the Severn Lady.

Realising the crew may have news of other boats yet to appear, Elizabeth remained beside Benjamin on the wharf, awaiting the arrival of the Severn Lady. After about ten minutes the boat was tied up at the wharf and the crew, looking weary, began to disembark. The other owners crowded round them, asking what news they had of their boats.

'It's been bad,' one of the men told them, 'the level of the river rose faster than I've ever seen it. Boats that were tied up fared best, but the ones in the middle of the river had a hard time of it.'

The crowd were clamouring for answers. More than anything they wanted to know if any of the boats had been lost.

'Just one to my knowledge,' one of the men replied, 'but I'm sorry, I can't be sure which one. I didn't see it myself, just heard of it from another boat that tied up beside us at Bridgnorth.'

Elizabeth was now filled with dread. A boat had been lost! She knew only too well what that meant. The river in flood would have taken anyone unfortunate enough to fall into it. There would be little chance of rescue for the crew of the stricken vessel. Owner Blake was obviously a very troubled man. Apart from the possible loss of life, the loss of another boat would have finished him. He was now pinning his hopes on the messenger returning from Bridgnorth being able to identify which boat had been lost, and said as much to Elizabeth, who was now determined to wait at the wharf until the man returned with news.

It was an hour later when they saw him riding along the riverbank from Buildwas Bridge. As he approached, he was surrounded by the crowd all shouting at once, desperately needing to know what was the name of the lost boat. Eventually, he was heard to call out the name Miranda. So, it was the Miranda, owned by Owner Reynolds, Elizabeth heard with relief. Her Arthur would be safe, thank God! Then she thought about the other women whose husbands wouldn't be coming home and tears of relief, mingled with tears of sadness for them, trickled slowly down her cheeks.

Owner Blake came over to her and said,

'I've just asked the messenger for news of the Oriel and he tells me that she is tied up at Bridgnorth. Elizabeth, I'm so glad for you, well, for us all of course. Now, you go home to the children and I'm sure Arthur will be with you soon. If there is any other news before then, I will let you know.'

She thanked him, wrapped her shawl tightly around her and then set off once again for the bridge. Now that she was sure Arthur was safe, her thoughts turned to home and the children who she had left with Martha. Martha does her best, she thought to herself, but I wouldn't want to leave her alone with them for too long. She tends to lose concentration sometimes and doesn't spot dangers as well as she might.

She needn't have worried. When she arrived home the cottage was cosy and warm with a good fire in the hearth and Martha was giving the children their supper of bread and dripping. Elizabeth hugged them so fiercely that Jimmy asked what was wrong and where his father was. She reassured him that he would be home soon.

It was two hours later, just as night was falling, that the door opened, and Arthur stood in the doorway illuminated against the gathering gloom by the light from the fire. Elizabeth flew into his arms, almost knocking him off his feet.

'By, that's a welcome and a half!' he declared as he hugged her close.

'I've been that worried though!' she exclaimed. 'We heard a boat was lost but no one knew which one. I thought you might be gone Arthur.'

'Well, it was touch and go at one point. We were in the middle of the river when the flood struck but we weren't too far from the wharf at Bridgnorth and just managed to get her safely tied up before the worst of it.'

The children joined their parents and hugged their father, not completely understanding but sensing that some kind of disaster had been averted.

There was much sadness in the Gorge over the loss of the Miranda. Sadly, only one of the seven bodies were retrieved, and only because it had become snagged on an overhanging tree branch. The others had been carried in the flood downstream towards Gloucester, and maybe even on towards the ocean. Such was the price of working on the River Severn. Its power could be used, but it would never be tamed.

Up at the Hall everyone had heard the news about the flood and the loss of the Miranda. Margaret knew that Elizabeth would have been beside herself with worry about Arthur if he had been on the river when the flood struck. She was due a day off and decided to visit Banghams Wood the next Sunday to see how things were with them.

It was a cold but fine day as she made her way down the track to the Wood. She hadn't visited for quite a while because of the snows of winter and Elizabeth and Arthur gave her a warm welcome. With the pot of vegetables and bacon bubbling over the fire, they settled down to share their news.

They talked, of course, about the tragedy on the river. Elizabeth told her how she had been at the wharf that day as the first trow made it home, and how relieved she had been to hear that the Oriel had been tied up safely at Bridgnorth. It had left many widows in its wake, and Elizabeth said how grateful she was that she wasn't one of them.

Margaret had news of her own to tell them. Being the horseman at the Hall, Dick had the job of going regularly to Bridgnorth with the wagon to collect supplies for the stables, but for some months seemed to have been finding more and more excuses to make the ten-mile journey to the grain merchants. After his last trip he had sought Margaret out to tell her that he had proposed to Margaret Andrews of Bridgnorth.

When Margaret told them that Margaret Andrews was the daughter of the Grain Merchant, they both speculated that Dick had 'done alright for himself'. Elizabeth was of course, thrilled to hear that Dick was to be married, and by the sound of it, his status in the world was about to rise. Margaret said she thought he would probably be moving to Bridgnorth as Margaret Andrews had no brothers or sisters living and she expected that she and Dick would take over the business when her father could no longer manage it.

Although Elizabeth was sorry that she wouldn't be seeing much of Dick once he moved to Bridgnorth, she was pleased for him. In any case, since he'd moved into the stables at the Hall, he had seldom visited the Wood. Margaret told her the wedding was to be in June, but Elizabeth doubted whether they would be able to go if it was to be in Bridgnorth.

Dorothy was doing well at the Hall, Margaret told them as they ate their meal. She had learned her letters, and the mistress had quite taken to her. In fact, her duties were no longer those of a scullery maid, as more and more, the mistress entrusted her to look after the children, who were six and eight years old. Dorothy was very happy to do this, Margaret told her, not really considering it to be hard work at all. In fact, of late she had been allowed to sit in with the children's lessons, taught by John Smith, the young teacher who had been engaged to run the Charity School in Madeley Wood. As the Master was a patron of the school, Mr Smith gave two days each week to the education of the children at the Hall. Margaret suspected that Dorothy's interest extended beyond education, as John Smith was a handsome young man and it seemed that the attraction might be mutual. Margaret said she hoped their relationship might blossom. Dorothy could do worse than to marry a schoolteacher.

Margaret asked whether Elizabeth had seen anything of Joe over the winter, but she replied that sadly, she hadn't. Margaret told her she had met Liz and Abigail with their children a couple of weeks back in Madeley Wood on market day. She remarked that young Michael was growing fast now. She said that she hoped he would steer clear of the Hall, as he was the image of James Furlong, the under-butler and that would have left no one in any doubt that he was indeed his father. Quite apart from his features, his shock of bright red hair would definitely have given the game away. Little Elizabeth was a bonny child, Margaret told her, with golden curls like her mother, and looked the picture of health.

Talking of Furlong the under-butler, brought Will into their minds and they wondered where he was and what he was doing. It had been eight years since he had left the Wood on that fateful night, and nearly seven since they had received his note from Bristol, saying that he was about to cross the ocean to the

Americas. Of course, there was no way they could have let him know that James had survived his attack, had not even remembered who had struck him, and no longer posed a threat to him. They just hoped that one day he would return. The family didn't feel complete without him.

As they were talking, Jimmy came in. He had been gathering kindling in the woods. He was fourteen now and growing fast. He had been apprenticed for some time to the coracle builder Bert Rogers down on the river. Coracles had been used on the Severn for generations for net fishing and eel catching, but with the increasing population it seemed that demand was growing faster than ever. Coracle building was a skilled craft and the Rogers' family had been making them for decades.

'How do you find working with Rogers, Jimmy?' Margaret asked him.

'I like it fine Aunt Margaret,' he replied, 'I'm learning how to build coracles and one day Bert says he'll let me try building one of my own.'

'That's wonderful Jimmy, better than working at the quarry or going down into the depths of the earth in a coal mine.'

'Aye,' Arthur agreed, 'but I do tell him not to get over-confident like. The river takes no prisoners, as we know.'

All this time, Martha hadn't spoken and Margaret cast a worried look in her direction.

'You don't have much to say for yourself today Martha. Are you not feeling well?'

Martha said that she was feeling alright, but she just wasn't her usual self. She usually made a fuss of Margaret whenever she visited, but today she had just sat quietly staring at the fire. Margaret looked questioningly towards Elizabeth, who just shook her head sadly without speaking. After they had eaten Margaret got up to leave and Elizabeth handed some scraps to Martha asking her to take them out to the hog pen, and while she was gone, she said.

'I am right worried about our Martha, Margaret. I don't know what's wrong with her but she isn't eating like she used to and last week she lost some blood.'

'Is she in pain?' Margaret enquired.

'She doesn't complain of any, but I'm not so sure. She is very quiet like you've seen. All I can do is keep an eye on her.'

'Aye, that's about the size of it Liz,' Margaret replied, as Martha stepped back into the room.

Margaret said she needed to be getting back up to the Hall, before the light went. Throwing her shawl over her head, wrapping it tightly round her chest and knotting it behind her back, she bade them all good-bye, and giving Martha an extra hug stepped out into the darkening afternoon.

# Chapter 10

1727: Dick and Margaret Andrews had been married in the summer of 1725 as planned and he had thrown himself into learning the family business, which was doing well. He loved the work and although he missed his beloved horses at the Hall, he and Margaret were happy together. They had moved into Margaret's family home with her father and Dick's life was now financially secure with a good future ahead of him, as Mr Andrews had told him that one day he would inherit the business as he was confident that he would do a good job and he knew it would be in safe hands.

Joe Bangham was well established at the Dale Company, as it had been called since Abraham Darby's death and the take over by Thomas Goldney 11. Richard Ford, the manager of the company was greatly impressed with Joe. He had been made foreman of his shift the year before and had eagerly accepted the responsibility of dealing with the other men, planning the work and ensuring that the job was done correctly.

As Joe was striding along the track back to the settlement that night he pondered about the Bangham family and how things were changing. Liz and Abigail had seen Margaret at the market a couple of weeks previously and she had told them how well Dick was doing in the Andrew's business. Joe was pleased for him, but understood that he wouldn't be seeing much of him in the future. It seemed that the family was drifting apart, with Will gone and Dick living in Bridgnorth. He wasn't able to get over to Banghams Wood to see Elizabeth and her family very often these days either.

As he strode into the cottage, young Elizabeth squealed with delight and ran up to him. He picked her up and swung her round as he always did. She was the image of her mother Liz, with her golden curls and ready smile and he doted on her. Abigail and Liz were sorting out the supper and Michael was busy drawing on a piece of slate with a lump of chalk. He was a bright boy and seemed particularly fond of drawing birds and animals. Abigail hoped that one day she would be able to send him down to the charity school which had opened at Buildwas. She was sure that, given some education, he would be able to make something of himself. As it was, he was a good lad and always willing to help his mother. He was particularly fond of going with her on market day, helping her to carry the provisions back over the hill from Madeley.

So it was that the following Wednesday, he and Abigail set off up the track along the valley side to Madeley. Liz didn't go with them on this occasion as little Elizabeth didn't seem too well. It was a fine day and they were happy in each other's company, chatting about the things they needed to get from the market. Abigail smiled fondly at her son. At eight years old he was a handsome little boy with striking features, and deep blue eyes. Of course, she knew that he had inherited his red hair from 'that man'. She still couldn't bring herself to speak his name and it hurt her greatly that whenever she looked at her beloved son, she was reminded of that fateful day when 'he' had forced himself on her. However, she pushed these thoughts from her mind as they began the descent towards Madeley and the market.

It was busy as always and they threaded their way through the crowd to the stall selling cheese. Abigail was holding tightly to Michael's hand, afraid to lose him in the crowd. She glanced down fondly at him and as she raised her eyes once more she was shocked to the core, as standing in front of her, blocking her way, was James.

'Well, well,' he said, 'what have we here?'

'Get out of my way!' she declared angrily.

Ignoring her, he took hold of Michael's free hand and pulled him towards the edge of the crowd. Abigail had no choice but to follow, unless she wanted Michael to be hurt. He was distressed by the way this man was pulling at his arm and shouted at him to let go. James didn't let go, but continued to pull them clear, leading them round the corner of the Inn wall.

'Get off him!' Abigail shouted, 'we want nothing to do with you!'

'But he's my son!' James shouted, 'I want to talk to my son!'

'What does he mean mother!?' Michael shouted, fighting back the tears.

'He's not your son!' Abigail screamed at him. 'He's my son and you have no rights where he's concerned.'

'Who are you kidding?' James sneered, 'You only have to look at him to know he's mine! He didn't get that hair from you, that's for sure!'

Abigail had no idea where this conversation might lead and the last thing she wanted was for Michael to hear anything about how he was conceived. She was desperate now to get away from him but he was still holding on to Michael who was, by now in floods of tears. Just at that moment, Owner Blake and his wife appeared round the corner and recognised Abigail. They could see that a man was pulling at Michael's arm and Abigail's eyes were full of fear.

'Let the boy go,' Owner Blake said with conviction.

James weighed him up briefly and could see from his bearing and appearance that he wasn't a man to be trifled with. Basically a coward, he let go of Michael's arm, at the same time swearing to Abigail that this wouldn't be the end of the matter. With that, he strode off.

Abigail thanked Owner Blake for his help and Dorothea asked her if she was alright now. Looking at the boy and the man, it had been obvious to both of them that he was the father of the boy. They had known of course, that Abigail had had to leave the Hall because she was pregnant, and now they understood how that had come about. Just another example of a man in authority taking advantage of a vulnerable young girl. They offered to help her buy what she needed and to set her on her way back to Dale Coppice, in case Furlong decided to look for her again. Michael clung to his mother but had now calmed down somewhat, and Abigail gladly accepted their offer of help. Half an hour later Abigail and Michael were making their way back along the track to Dale Coppice.

'Who was that man, mother?' Michael asked her suddenly. 'Why did he say I was his?'

'He's nobody!' Abigail replied sharply, having no idea how she would ever be able to explain it to Michael. He was inclined to ask her more questions, but something in her tone made him realise that he would be wise to say no more on the subject. He stored the incident away in his mind, and young as he was, was determined that one day, he would find out about the strange man with hair like his – he'd never seen anyone with hair that colour before, and somehow he knew that meant something, but not exactly what.

Arthur had been away downriver for the best part of three weeks and Elizabeth knew he would be home any day now. It was always difficult to know precisely when he would return. It depended on how many other vessels would be lining up for trans-shipment of their cargoes in Gloucester. The river trade was growing by the day. Each time the Dale Works increased production, which seemed to be more or less constantly, more boats had to be commissioned to ship the goods out to the ports and to bring raw materials and other supplies back upriver.

Elizabeth was working on the vegetable plot, planting potatoes and sewing carrots and turnips. It was back-breaking work and after she'd been at it for an hour or so, she stood up, placed her hands on her hips and arched her aching back. As she glanced towards the track, as she always did, just in case Arthur should appear, she gasped aloud as she saw him in the distance, coming round the corner of the lane. He had another man with him and at first, Elizabeth didn't recognise him.

She could see there was something familiar about the way he walked, throwing out one foot slightly with each step. Then suddenly, a light of recognition flashed in her mind. It was Will! He looked older and broader, and walked with a slight stoop as he climbed the track, but it was definitely him.

Elizabeth exclaimed his name and started to run down the track towards the two men.

'Will!' she shouted, 'Where have you sprung from?'

She embraced Arthur, saying how good it was to see him home at last, then turned to Will.

'You're a sight for sore eyes and no mistake, our Will!'

'It's good to see you Liz,' Will said quietly. 'There was a time I didn't think I would see any of you ever again.'

With that, he threw his arms around her and

hugged her close. Elizabeth linked arms with both of them and the three of them trudged happily up the track towards the cottage. As they approached, Elizabeth called out to young Jane to come and meet her Uncle Will, and she skipped across the clearing.

As they entered the cottage, Martha was sitting by the fire and Will was shocked at her appearance. She had aged far more than the nine years that had passed since he'd left Banghams Wood. Her ready smile was gone and she just looked blankly at him as he entered the room, not seeming to recognise him. She seemed to have shrunk physically and her face was marked with the lines that told of pain she had endured.

Will looked round at Elizabeth, searching her face for answers, but she just shook her head sadly. He realised that once they were alone he would be able to get his answers, but this was not the time.

'Let me get some food together Will, and then you can tell us where in the world you've been all these years.'

As she busied herself, Arthur and Will washed at the pump, teasing young Jane by splashing her with water as, stripped to the waist, they threw it over themselves. Elizabeth, hearing Jane's laughter, glanced out of the window to see what was going on. She smiled as she watched them, thinking that this Will who had returned seemed rather different than the man who had left on that fateful night. He seemed happier somehow, and more confident. She wondered whether he already knew that James hadn't died that night and in fact, had no idea who had punched him to the ground.

Finally the food was ready and she called out to them to come inside. Arthur and Will put on their shirts and they all sat down at the table to eat, all except Martha, who said she wasn't hungry.

As they ate their meal, Will was keen to find out about the rest of the family. He was surprised to hear that Joe was married now, to a girl from Dale Coppice and that they had a daughter, another Elizabeth! He of course asked after Abigail and was pleased that Joe was taking care of her and that she had a son, Michael who was growing into a fine boy despite his unfortunate beginnings. It appeared that Will had been given the news about James by Arthur, as they travelled back from Gloucester. Although he was relieved that he was no longer in danger of being arrested, he said that he was actually sorry that he hadn't finished him off that night.

'He damn well deserved it for what he did to our Abigail!' he declared.

He welcomed the news that Dick was now married to Margaret Andrews, daughter of the Bridgnorth grain merchant and had therefore risen in status. They chatted for a while about all the rest of the family and then Elizabeth's patience finally ran out, anxious as she was to find out where he had been all these years.

'Come on then Will, what happened after you left here?'

'Well, it's a long story,' he said, 'it's difficult to know where to start. Did you get the letter I sent you?'

'Aye, we did, although it didn't tell us much did it? Except that you were bound for the Americas!'

'That's right, I set sail aboard the Matilda the day after I sent the letter off to you.

They all settled back to listen as Will began,

'When I left you, I managed to buy my passage to Gloucester on the Lucky Lady, then I travelled on a boat to Bristol and that's where I ended up for the next year or so. There was plenty of work on the docks, loading ships for the Africa trade and unloading the cotton and sugar from the Caribbean.

I heard many stories about the conditions on the ships travelling from Africa to the Caribbean loaded with human cargo, more dreadful than I care to share with you, Liz. I had thought that I might travel to America that way, but soon decided that I would have to find a different route as I couldn't stomach being a part of that nightmare world.

I still had a hankering for the New World as it appeared that, with a little luck, a man could make his fortune there. A better prospect seemed to be to join a ship bound for Williamsburg, Virginia, and make my way inland from there. Eventually, I had saved a little money, enough to pay my passage, steerage of course, and to have a bit left over to help me get settled in America. I took my chance when I heard the Matilda was preparing to set sail carrying goods for the colonies, along with people who were intent on making a new life in the New World.

'That's when I wrote you the letter Liz.'

They had all been listening intently, particularly Jimmy, who was eager to hear about the world outside the Gorge. Working down on the river, he had often wondered where the never ending flow of water ended up. Arthur had of course, often talked to him about Gloucester Docks, but the world beyond that, had remained a mystery to them all.

'That was quite a shock to us all Will, to know you were already aboard the Matilda and on your way to the other side of the world. We feared we would never see you again!'

Will smiled.

'Well, here I am. I wish I could say that the journey across the ocean was a pleasant one, but I cannot.'

'It must have been exciting though!' Jimmy piped up, eyes shining.

'Well, we all started off with high expectations. It did seem like the start of a great adventure. We were going to a new world full of opportunity, where a man could thrive and build a good life for himself and his family. As we cast off from the Bristol docks, the deck was full of people waving goodbye to loved ones standing on the quayside, who they may never see again. There were smiles and tears aplenty, I can tell you.

'It didn't take long to realise however, that this

was going to be no easy passage. Conditions below decks were dark and cramped, each person confined to a narrow bunk piled two high and with not enough length for a man to lay with his legs outstretched. What luggage we had, which wasn't much, had to share the space with us. Food was scarce, consisting largely of a kind of porridge made with oats and water, and a biscuit or two, or a lump of bread and a cup of gruel. Occasionally there was a piece of fruit to vary the diet a little. The privvy was a platform of open planks at the prow of the ship, to be used with little privacy.

We knew the passage would take around six or seven weeks, depending on the weather. The Captain told us the Atlantic storms could be terrifying, as we were soon to find out. Sailing largely into the prevailing winds, progress would sometimes be slow he told us, and our exact time of arrival in the New World was unpredictable.

We did our best to settle in to the routine of life aboard ship. Many were seasick to begin with. It was difficult to sleep because of the noise, the feeling of being shut in, and the uncomfortable thought of the ocean many fathoms deep below us.

By the end of the first week, we were beginning to realise just what an epic journey we were on. We had left the land far behind us and there was none ahead of us, just rolling seas as far as the eye could see in every direction. The nights were the worst. At least during the day we could go up on deck for a period and see the horizon, which helped us cope with the seasickness. At night, however, below decks it was dark, with the smell of unwashed bodies and vomit constantly increasing.'

'It sounds horrible, Will,' Elizabeth said softly.

'It truly was,' Will replied, 'however, we had made our decision to come and we knew we had no alternative other than to tolerate whatever the journey threw at us. It was about twenty one days out that dysentery struck. Liz, Arthur, I can't tell you how horrendous it was. People unable to get themselves up on deck had to shit where they lay. If they had relatives with them they had to clean them up and try to make them comfortable. Some had no relatives, like myself, and I dreaded becoming ill but I managed somehow to avoid the dysentery, thank God.

'The rats began to multiply and lice were everywhere by then. People began to die, particularly the old and frail, and many a body was consigned to the deep. Children too succumbed, and that was piteous to witness. Parents were distraught, carrying their little ones up to the deck to be slid off the board into the icy waters of the Atlantic Ocean. Just as many died, some were born. Three little ones had come into the world on that ship by the time we reached America.

'We were about four weeks out when we encountered our first Atlantic storm. We know the Severn can be wild, but this was something completely different. Huge waves, sometimes as high as a house crashed around the ship, tossing it about like so much driftwood. Some of the crew had to scramble in the rigging to furl up the sails or they would have been ripped clean off by the force of the wind and water. The passengers were all ordered below decks in case they might be washed overboard. One member of the crew had been up in the rigging when the ship took a dive into the trough of a huge wave and the force of it tore his hands from the ropes and he plunged into the ocean, never to be seen again. Conditions below decks had by now become almost unbearable and we lay, petrified in our bunks, clinging on for dear life as the ship was thrown around. Some people had fallen out onto the floor as the ship plunged down into a trough, and stayed there, unable to drag themselves up long enough to crawl back into their bunks. All day the storm raged, but thankfully, by nightfall, had begun to subside. There were other storms as our journey progressed but none as vicious as that first one.

'After five weeks, we were all desperate to see land again. Of the fifty people who began the journey, ten of the passengers and one crewman had perished and the rest of us were weak from lack of decent food. Day after day we searched the horizon for some clue that land was near. Then, one morning we saw birds circling some way off and knew that our ordeal would soon end. The next day, some of us were on deck when a cry of 'Land Ahoy!' went up from the Crow's Nest. We slept better that night, knowing that the next day we would be arriving in the New World to begin our new life.'

Will realised that the room had become dark apart from the light from the fire. Elizabeth got up and lit the candles.

'My story is only half told but it's late and perhaps the telling of the rest of it will have to wait,' he said, smiling.

Jimmy protested, desperate to hear about the New World, but Elizabeth agreed with Will.

'You're right Will, even though we're all eager to hear it. But it's right good to have you home, and no mistake!' she declared.

With Jane's help she cleared away the remnants from the meal, handing the scraps to Martha to take out to the hog pen. After she left the room, Will asked Elizabeth what was wrong with her.

'We don't know Will, but she has a lot of pain and sometimes loses blood. She's not been her usual cheerful self for a while now, but we will just have to see what happens.'

Arthur brought a pail of water from the pump and after visiting the privvy one by one, they splashed over their faces and prepared for bed. Elizabeth made up a bed for Will on the bench and then hugged him tightly, saying,

'It's so good to have you home safe and sound Will, I've missed you all these years.'

'I know Liz, I've missed you all too, more than you'll ever know.'

# Chapter 11

The next day Will was determined to visit Dale Coppice to see Joe and Liz. Joe had been in his thoughts often over the last years. He knew he hadn't been fair to him, resenting the fact that he had wanted to leave Banghams Wood. Once he himself had made the break, he understood exactly why Joe had needed to get away. He could see now that the Darby Works represented change to Joe, and that is what he craved. He had been unable to accept that coppicing and burning charcoal was to be his life. Once he himself was forced to leave and travel into the world outside the Gorge, Will came to realise that his resentment towards Joe had been fuelled by his own desire to escape, but he had felt trapped in the Wood by responsibilities after Walter died. He was eager to see Joe and to show him that he no longer felt any animosity towards him. In fact, he had decided that he also would like to settle in Dale Coppice and maybe find work at the Coalbrookdale Company. He had had enough of travelling the world. He was home and this is where he intended to stay.

Assuring Elizabeth and the family that he would be back in a day or two, to finish his story, he set off with Jimmy the next morning, towards the river, intending to ask Bert Rogers to ferry him across. Jimmy was full of questions, of course, and as they walked Will told him about some of the more pleasant experiences he'd had in America. He told him about the vastness of the plains, the mountains and the wagon trains setting out loaded with settlers, full of dreams of a better life. Jimmy was enthralled and determined that one day he would take that trip down the river to find his own fortune.

The Severn was running strongly as Bert skilfully steered the coracle towards the northern bank. The wharf was busy, with several boats unloading or waiting to be reloaded with goods bound for Gloucester. Will could see that it had been extended since the day he'd left on the Lucky Lady all those years ago. He clambered out of the coracle, and up the bank to the Madeley road, then took the lane towards Coalbrookdale. As he strode up the valley he began to realise the extent of the changes that had occurred since he had left the Gorge. The track itself was now a cobbled road. The further he went the louder was the sound of metal hammering on metal. The hiss of steam and the roar of the furnaces assaulted his ears. His lungs began to react to the acrid smoke from the piles of coal off to one side of the track, presumably being burned to produce the coke needed for the furnaces. The light of the sun was now dimmed by the smoke hanging in the air. There were horse-drawn wagons moving up the track from the wharf, carrying coal and ironstone, and every so often, one would be coming in the other direction carrying goods bound for the river. The overall impression was of a hive of industry, and Will had to admit that it was exciting.

It was mid-morning when he reached the settlement in Dale Coppice. As he strode into the hamlet, he saw a young woman with her back to him, filling a pail at the pump. A young boy was waiting to help her to carry it. As soon as Will saw the boy, with his bright red hair, he knew that this was Michael, and the young woman must be Abigail. He called out her name and she turned to face him.

'Will!' she declared, 'Is it really you?'

'Aye it is lass,' he answered, and running towards her now, he picked her up and spun her round, as he had used to do when she was a little girl. Michael was confused. Who was this man who picked up his mother and swung her round?

Abigail noticed the puzzled and rather frightened expression on his face and said,

'Michael, this is your uncle Will!'

'Hello Michael,' Will said.

'H.. Hello,' he answered hesitantly.

At that moment, Liz, who was now heavily pregnant, appeared at the cottage door and linking Will's arm, Abigail led him over to her, with Michael trailing behind, struggling with the half-filled pail of water.

'Liz, this is our brother Will, the one that went to the Americas years ago.'

Liz greeted Will, saying she was pleased to meet him at last as she had heard so much about him. She invited him in and asked if he would like some ale, which he readily accepted. Abigail asked him whether he'd seen Elizabeth yet and he explained that he had come upriver with Arthur and been over at Banghams Wood the previous night.

Liz explained that of course, Joe was at the works, but would be home for supper. She was sure he would be happy to see Will as he had often spoken about him over the years and wondered whether he would ever return. Will said he was glad to be back and hoped to stay now. In fact, he said, he wondered whether he might find work at the Company.

'Well,' Liz told him, 'they do seem to be taking more men on every week, so it shouldn't be too difficult to find something.'

Will and Abigail chatted about life in the Gorge and within the Bangham family since Will had left. She briefly considered telling him about her meeting with Furlong but decided against it in case he should take it upon himself to confront him again. Will said he was amazed at the way the Works had grown. Given the huge increase in river traffic, it had been obvious that great changes were afoot. Abigail asked him about his adventures since he had left the Wood, but Will said he would wait until Joe got home before

going into all that, rather than having to repeat everything. To Liz's delight, Will took great interest in little
Elizabeth, playing 'pick up stones' in front of the fire
with her while she herself got on with preparing the
evening's meal.

Finally, there was a rattle on the latch, the door
opened and the two brothers set eyes on each other
for the first time in nine years. Will had been a bit un-
easy, wondering how Joe would react, as they hadn't
parted on the best of terms. In the event, Joe shouted,

'Will! I had heard that you came upriver yesterday,
but I could hardly believe it! By, it's good to see thee
lad!' he exclaimed, striding over to Will and throwing his arms around him. The two brothers embraced
and slapped each other on the back in greeting, then
stepped back to observe what changes the years apart
had wrought.

Joe thought Will looked older and the lines on his
face spoke of hardships endured, but overcome. He
looked as though he could do with some good food inside him, as though he hadn't eaten too well for some
time. Later, as Will recounted his journey back across
the ocean, which had been no less unpleasant than
the one that had carried him to America, they understood why. In the meantime, Liz had served up the
hearty stew and they sat down to enjoy the meal, Will
tucking in with gusto as though he had indeed been
starving for weeks.

After they had finished and Elizabeth was tucked
up in bed, Joe wanted to know what had happened

to Will since leaving the Wood. He quickly told them about the outward journey, but out of sensitivity to Abigail who he still thought protectively of as his little sister, he missed out some of the less pleasant details. Then he went on to recount some of his exploits in America, how he had worked for a while on the docks in Williamsburg, and then, when he had saved up a sum of money, had heard of a wagon train of English settlers heading west through the Appalachian mountains into a country where a man could claim 300 acres of land and set up his own farm. While in Williamsburg he had met and fallen in love with a young woman, Sarah, and they were married before setting out on the journey West.

Will looked sad and pensive when he spoke of Sarah, and when Joe asked about her, his face darkened and he fell silent for a while. When he had recovered himself he explained that Sarah had been pregnant by the time they arrived in the Shenandoah Valley after an arduous journey through the mountains. He said it was hard to describe the conditions he found there. He was given land, but nothing else. They had to clear it of forest and build a log cabin to live in. The settlers had helped each other to build their cabins, much as people did in the Gorge, for which he was grateful. He said he could never have done it alone.

In the meantime they had to live in the covered wagons, which afforded little shelter against the weather. Finally, after four months they had their cabin. By then, Sarah was almost due to deliver their child. She went into labour in the middle of the night and fought bravely to deliver the baby. It turned out that the child was trying to come out feet first and Will didn't know what to do to help. Neither could he leave her to bring help. She battled for a full day before weakened by the long and difficult journey and the conditions they had been living in, she succumbed and she and the baby, a boy, were buried the next day.

Telling them about this had been desperately hard for Will. Although it had all happened four years ago, it was still raw. He had loved Sarah dearly and they had dreamt of building a life together. He knew he would never love anyone else the way he had loved her. After Sarah and the baby had died, he said he lost heart and couldn't face clearing the land to farm it alone. He managed to sell it and the cabin to a settler in another wagon train which had just arrived, bought a wagon and returned, defeated, to Williamsburg. There, he worked for a couple more years on the docks and then decided he'd had enough of the New World and would make his way back home. At that point he hadn't known what he would have to face regarding what he had done to Furlong, but his desire to come home had been greater than his fear, and he had boarded a ship loaded with tobacco three months ago, bound for Bristol.

By now the light had gone and they were all ready for bed. Michael had already fallen asleep on the straw mattress laid out for Will. They all expressed their sorrow at the loss of his wife and child, and Joe said he could stay with them as long as he wished. He would speak to Mr Ford the manager at the works in the morning, to see if he could get him work either at the furnaces or in the foundry.

Will thanked him and said he was glad to be home at last, and of course, relieved that there would be no repercussions about the reason for his departure. Out of respect for Abigail no one actually said what that was, although Joe and Abigail knew exactly what he meant.

The next day, Joe found Mr Ford and asked about a job for Will, explaining that he had just returned from America but now wanted to settle in the Gorge. Unfortunately Mr Ford, after some thought, said he wouldn't be able to find him something at the moment as he'd just promised work to a group of men from further up the valley. Joe was disappointed but under-stood and thanked him anyway. Just as Joe turned to leave, Mr Ford said he did need more men to work in a new mine he was planning to lease, and if Will was interested, he would be happy to give him a try.

When Joe returned home that evening, Will was still there, waiting for news and was of course dis-appointed that there was no job for him at the works. Joe told him about the new coalmine that was being opened up and Mr Ford had said there would be work there for him if he wanted it. Although Will had always sworn that he would never go into the mines, he knew he couldn't be too choosy right now and reluctantly decided to take up the offer. The next day he went back to Banghams Wood to give Elizabeth the news and to finish the story of his time in America. The following Sunday Margaret visited Banghams Wood, having heard the news that Will was back. They had a joyous reunion and Will had to tell his story all over again, much to Jimmy's delight.

After they had eaten their dinner, Will returned to Dale Coppice but before heading down to the river, insisted on walking Margaret back to the gate at the Hall. When they were alone and walking along the track he asked her whether anything had ever been said about why he had disappeared after his attack on Furlong. Margaret assured him that as Furlong had eventually fully recovered, but apparently had no memory of who had attacked him, no one had ever connected him to the attack. As Abigail was living in Dale Coppice and rarely returned to the south of the river, she was sure no one would ever connect Abigail's child, and therefore the likely attacker to Will, so he needn't worry. Of course, Margaret was unaware that James Furlong had already met Abigail with her child who was so obviously his son, at Madeley Wood market. If she had been, perhaps she wouldn't have been so sure.

When Will arrived back at Dale Coppice he found an unfolding tragedy. It was a week before Liz's due date but she had become worried during the day because she couldn't feel the child moving inside her. She knew the signs because of her first pregnancy, which had resulted in a premature still birth. This time she had believed it would be different because she was almost full term and everything had seemed fine. She and Joe were now distraught, sure they had lost another child. When she finally went into labour at midnight two days later, it was with some terror that she told Joe to bring Mrs Spencer to help Abigail to attend to her. She was right to be worried, the baby, a boy, was already dead. Liz and Joe were heartbroken once again. Losing another child like this was devastating and they began to wonder whether they would ever have other children. The baby, born dead, couldn't be baptised and therefore couldn't be buried in consecrated ground and consequently they buried him in the woods. Will's grief at the loss of his own wife and child, never far from his mind, resurfaced and the Bangham cottage in Dale Coppice was consumed by grief for many weeks.

# Chapter 12

1728 had brought changes to the Darby Works. Abraham Darby's son, now seventeen years old, joined the firm, and managed the company along with Mr Ford. Joe was pleased to see another Darby involved in the Works. He had had a lot of respect for Abraham Darby, and Joe could see that the young man had many of his father's qualities. He was to see a lot of Abraham over the next few years, as he was often to be found working alongside the men, determined to learn all he could about the business of making and forging iron in preparation for one day taking over the running of the Works. Trade was good, the high-quality domestic goods they were producing were selling well, not only in England, but right across the oceans, as far as Africa and America.

Will had been taken on by Henry Cartwright, the gaffer at one of the mines leased by Mr Ford. He had of course been aware that mining was tough work, but he hadn't been prepared for the conditions under-ground. First of all, to get into the mine involved climbing into a cage suspended by a single hook attached to a gantry at the top of the shaft. Using a wheel and pulley arrangement, propelled by a horse, the cage was lowered the hundred or so feet to the bottom of the shaft. That was terrifying at first. Will had heard more than one story of cages breaking loose and plummeting down the shaft, taking men to certain death. After a while he got used to it, but the journey to the coalface, dragging a wagon behind him through the tunnel with only a candle to light the way, was always an ordeal. Once at the coalface itself, he had to toil with a pick, hacking away at the coal then loading it onto the wagon, which when it was full, had to be hauled back to the bottom of the shaft, where he transferred coal to the cage to be raised to the surface. He worked a twelve-hour shift from six in the morning until six at night. The work was hard and the wages poor, but Will was glad to be able to pay his way and was determined to stick at it until he could find something better.

Joe decided that he needed to expand his cottage now that Will was living with them, and together they added two more rooms. One was for Will and Michael to sleep in and the other provided a much improved scullery and wash house to cater for the needs of their increased family. Joe was glad to have Will around, to share the responsibilities of financing the household. For a while, everyone was happy with the arrangement. Joe and Liz gradually recovered from the loss of their little boy and began to hope that they would soon have another child.

Christmas that year was particularly special. With two wages coming in, the family were able to buy a few extras, and invited Arthur and Elizabeth and the children over for the Christmas Day feast. The weather, though cold, was dry, as thankfully the snows didn't arrive until well into January. It was good to be able to gather together, a rare occurrence these days. Elizabeth brought with her some news about Dick and Margaret. Margaret had told her that the horseman, Fred, had been over to Bridgnorth a few weeks ago and was given the news that they had been delivered of a little girl on the 3$^{rd}$ of October. They had called her Elizabeth, which pleased the child's aunt, of course. There was also much joyful reminiscing of years gone by, and as is usually the case on such occasions, the memories evoked were largely the happier ones. As Elizabeth and Arthur said their goodbyes, they all agreed that this was something they should do every year. It was just as well that they didn't know what 1729 would bring.

It was during the third week of February that Liz realised she was pregnant again. She was of course nervous about it and whether this time her baby would be brought successfully into the world. She told Joe she expected to give birth some time during September. He was overjoyed, although also a little apprehensive.

The snows came and went without interfering too much with life in Dale Coppice. The Coalbrookdale Company was busier than ever, now casting parts for steam engines which were beginning to be installed in more and more pits in the area. They provided a more reliable method of pumping water from the mines, as well as lowering and raising the cages the miners used to get down to the coalface. This was a growing market and as usual the Company was at the forefront of the development of the technology. More workers were moving into the district every year and Dale Coppice was getting rather crowded. Some of the newcomers didn't fit in too well, many of them being heavy drinkers and best classified as rogues and vagabonds.

Liz and Abigail tried their best to keep their children away from them, but it wasn't easy. Michael in particular seemed drawn to the children of the more rowdy inhabitants. At twelve, he was developing a mind and a personality of his own and Abigail struggled to control him at times. He seemed particularly attracted to Tom Williams who was a year older and full of bravado. He swaggered about the place with an air of entitlement that annoyed most folks but captivated Michael, who was never far from his side. He had suffered years of mockery and teasing because of his bright red hair, which had made him self-conscious and rather withdrawn. Spotting his vulnerability, Tom knew that he could use it to his advantage and soon 'groomed' him into becoming his constant and often useful companion.

One day in May, Tom told Michael he needed help with something and that they would need to be away after supper, but not to tell anyone about it. Michael was in a quandary. He wanted to tell his mother. but knew if he did, she would stop him from going. Loyalty to Tom won out in the end and he slipped out of the cottage when the sun was sinking in the sky, to meet him on the track on Lincoln Hill as arranged. When Michael asked Tom where they were going, he just smiled and said they were off to make some money, but when Michael asked how, he told him to wait and see. They strode off towards the river, but at the crossroads they came upon a couple of older men. They had a dog with them and were carrying sacks containing something heavy. Michael knew enough to realise that these were men who would probably not be up to much good. He hesitated and told Tom he wanted to go home, but Tom and the men broke out laughing, saying he was just a baby wanting to go home to his mother. Michael flushed bright pink then squared his shoulders and declared that he was no baby and he had only been joking. Of course he was going with them, he said.

The group set off, not as Michael had expected, towards the river, but parallel to it. They moved quickly over fields and through woods for two hours, Michael struggling to keep up with them. The light was virtually gone as they arrived at what was apparently their intended destination and sat down in the shelter of some trees to plan their next move. Michael was already worried when one of the men took out a tin of blacking, and handed it round to the others, who began to black up their faces. Now he understood what this was all about. These men were poachers, intent on stealing rabbits or hares or some such. He was horrified. He had heard men talking about what happened to poachers if they were caught.

After the passing of an Act of Parliament some years back, a man could be transported across the ocean or even hanged for taking a single hare for the pot from private land! Michael wanted nothing to do with this. He desperately wanted to go home but knew that he could never find his own way back in the dark. He tried to refuse to black his face but the men insisted that he was one of them now and must get blacked up along with the rest of them. As he tried to resist, one of them grabbed hold of him and held his hands tight behind his back as the other ruffian smeared the blacking over his face.

Michael was terrified but knew there was no way out of it for him now. He was one of this gang of men intent on poaching and however much he wished he'd stayed at home and not listened to Tom, matters were now out of his hands. The men took heavy clubs out of the sacks. Michael and Tom were given the empty sacks and told to pick up the dead rabbits as they emerged from their burrows and were clubbed to death.

One of the men took the dog and went off in search of burrows. The dog was now straining at its leash, sensing blood. As it was let loose it yelped and scrabbled the ground at the entrance to a burrow on the far side of a small hillock, and after a few minutes rabbits began appearing at the exit, to be expertly clubbed by the other man. Of course, some got away but many were killed as they tried to escape. Tom and Michael collected the bodies, still warm, some of them not quite dead. They were told to finish them off by swinging them by their legs against the nearest tree. Michael was sickened. Of course he'd eaten rabbit many times, but never before had he been responsible for taking life.

A cry went up,

'Right men, that's enough, let's be off before the gamekeeper comes a lookin' what all the noise is about.'

At that moment there was a loud crack, and then another. This was unmistakeably gunshot. They all fell to the ground, peering into the darkness to find out where the shots had come from.

Then came a shout,

'Stay where you are! If anybody moves it'll be the end of 'im!'

One by one, men carrying guns appeared out of the blackness under the trees into the moonlight that was now flooding the clearing. Plainly this was not just one gamekeeper. It soon became apparent that the local militia had been summoned and now surrounded the gang, caught red-handed with sacks full of rabbits. The poacher holding the dog leash, let go, telling the dog to attack, but it hadn't got further than twenty yards before it was shot dead. Plainly, being unarmed, the gang was cornered and soon arrested.

Michael began to cry, completely unable to comprehend what was happening to him. How had he got into this dreadful situation? He was a good lad, never in trouble before, and now he would go to prison — or worse!

# Chapter 13

The Captain of the Militiamen waved his gun at the miscreants, telling them to sit on the ground with their backs to one another. One of the others stepped forward with ropes and bound their hands tightly. Michael was crying, his tears running down his cheeks in rivulets, streaking the blacking as they went. He was terrified, and then horrified as he felt the wetness seeping into his breeches as he lost control of his bladder.

They were held like that for what seemed like hours, until a wagon appeared through the gloom, and they were all loaded into it. Michael realised that they were being taken to a lock up somewhere, but not being exactly sure where he was, he had no idea where that would be. It could have been Shrewsbury, or Much Wenlock, or even Bridgnorth. One of the men asked the Bailiff where they were being taken but was told that they would know soon enough. Accompanied by four of the armed militiamen and the Bailiff, all on horseback, they set off along a path through the woods until they reached a rough trackway.

The moon was up now and it was clear by the downward trajectory the track was taking that they were heading towards the river. For several minutes Michael was hoping that perhaps they were being taken to the Madeley lock up, but when they met the river, the party turned to the right and his heart sank as he realised that they must be heading out of the Gorge and over to Much Wenlock. The chances of his mother knowing where he had been taken lessened with every mile. They were still sitting back-to-back, so he couldn't see Tom, or either of the men, but he could smell their fear. They all knew that, caught red-handed with their spoils, they would be shown little mercy. For sure it would be hard labour, transportation or even worse, the gallows for them.

His assumption as to where they were going was correct and before long, they crossed the Buildwas bridge and headed south along the track towards Much Wenlock. An hour later they halted outside a two-storey black and white half-timbered building next to a church. In the half light, the building looked huge to Michael, who was only used to seeing rough built single storey cottages. They clambered out of the wagon and with the guns prodding their backs were herded through a heavy iron door at the base of the building into a dank, dark cell and the door clanged shut behind them. Through the iron grille in the door, the Bailiff told them they would soon be brought before the Magistrate but failed to say when that would be. One of the men asked for water but the

Bailiff refused to bring any, saying that they would be given food and water in the morning.

It was cold as death in the cell, and there was only the flagstone floor to sit on, with a bucket in the corner where prisoners could relieve themselves. The stink of unwashed bodies and years of filth had soaked into the very stones, pervading the air. Each breath Michael took made him gag as he sat shivering in the corner, huddled up, trying to conserve what warmth his body still held. He was utterly without hope. How would his mother know where to find him? Who would help him now? He'd been caught red-handed and knew there would be no mercy shown. For once, Tom was quiet. Faced with the reality of what he'd done his habitual bravado seemed to have deserted him, and he sat, his legs drawn up and his bowed head resting on his arms clasped around his knees. The two men began quarrelling between themselves, each blaming the other for their predicament, until the gaoler shouted out to them to be quiet, or they would feel the force of his truncheon about their ears.

There was no sleep for any of them for what was left of the night. A few hours later the key turned in the lock and the gaoler opened the door. The light flooded in, and half blinded them after the semi darkness of the cell. He entered with some bread on a platter and a jug of water and placed them on the floor, another gaoler standing behind him to ensure the men didn't try to escape. Their hands were still tied together and with some difficulty they scrambled to get at the food, one of the ruffians pushing Michael out of the way to grab a handful of bread. The other man, who was older than the first and seemed to have a shred of humanity left, took some of the bread, tore a chunk off and gave it to Michael. They each took a swig of water which quenched their thirst for the moment but was not nearly enough to last the day.

Tom, who had regained some of his spirit, asked the gaoler when they would be going before the magistrate. He told them that it would be the following morning before he arrived, so they'd better make themselves comfortable, and with that, the door clanged shut once more, leaving them in semi darkness once again.

That day was the longest of Michael's life. Hour after hour passed with no respite from the fear that was eating away at his guts. They were given a little more bread and water later in the day, and a small piece of cheese each. The only light entering the cell was through the small grille in the door, no more than eight inches square. In the half light, a rat would occasionally make its leisurely way across the room, stopping only to collect the odd breadcrumb from the floor before strolling away and disappearing into the gloom again. Occasionally one of them would relieve themselves using the bucket but without any privacy. No one would tell them anything about what was to happen next. Michael slipped into a fitful sleep once or twice during the day and by the time night fell was so exhausted that mercifully he fell fast asleep and dreamed of home and his mother. When he awoke Michael realised once again that she would have no idea where he was. He was ashamed that his foolishness in following Tom Williams had led him to inflict this on his mother. How would she ever find him? He only hoped that she had heard news of the arrests. The disappearance of Tom as well as himself might prompt her to make the connection, and realise that perhaps it was they who had been arrested and taken to one of the Courts in the area. He could do nothing now but hope that this was the case and that she would somehow find a way to help him.

His thoughts were interrupted by the sound of the key being turned in the lock. The heavy door swung open, letting in the early morning light and mercifully, a breath of fresh air. The magistrate would be arriving in a few hours they were told and they would then be taken up to the courtroom above the cell. They were given a bowl of thin gruel each which they had to eat with their fingers, but they were all so hungry that it took them no time at all until they had cleared their bowls.

As the morning progressed, they could hear the sounds of people chatting and carriages rumbling along the street outside the door of the gaol and the occasional neighing of horses as men shouted instructions at them. There was a general bustle about the place and the sound of furniture being moved and footsteps treading the boards above the cell. They realised with some trepidation that the activity above their heads probably signified that the courtroom was being prepared for their appearance in front of the Magistrate. Eventually the door was opened once again, and a couple of gaolers armed with pistols instructed them to follow. They were led along to the other end of the building and up some stone steps to a door which was obviously leading into the courtroom.

At the door, Michael rocked on his heels, halting for a moment until he was prodded in the back with the pistol being held by one of the gaolers. He was conscious of his own appearance, his face still smeared with black, his breeches dirty and smelling of his own urine. What would everyone think of him? He surely didn't look out of place with these ruffians, but he knew he didn't belong here. If only he hadn't been so foolish!

The disgusted looks on the faces of the people in the public gallery as he walked down to the front of the courtroom, not to mention the way the Magistrate peered down at him with undisguised revulsion as he stood in the dock, convinced him that he was right. He could expect no mercy here. He was correct on that score, but matters deteriorated further when they were told that because of the seriousness of the charges they faced, and the fact that they had been caught red-handed, the Magistrate had decided that they would be sent to Bridgnorth to appear at the next Quarter Sessions on Midsummer Day to be tried before a jury for poaching. They all knew that this meant the death penalty was to be considered, should they be found guilty.

Michael's legs threatened to give way. Bridgnorth! He knew that was another ten miles further away from his home in Dale Coppice and he was now convinced that his mother would never find him, and that he could be hanged without her knowing a thing about it. At that point, darkness took him, and he slipped silently to the floor.

# Chapter 14

In Dale Coppice, two days earlier, Abigail was beside herself with worry. She hadn't seen Michael since supper. She hadn't even seen him leave the cottage as she'd been busy in the scullery, and so had no idea where he'd gone to. Night was falling fast and there was a full moon rising above the trees.

Joe and Will went around the clearing, knocking on cottage doors to ask if he was there. They knew he often hung around with Tom Williams and were not surprised to find, when they reached his home that he also was missing. As usual his father was drunk and completely unconcerned about the whereabouts of his son. His mother however, was obviously upset and worried. She told them Tom had disappeared some time ago without saying where he was going.

Joe and Will searched the coppice and surrounding area until the small hours of the morning, of course, without success. Abigail feared the worst, either something had happened to him or he'd got himself involved in something bad with Tom Williams, and, God forbid, had been caught. They all knew that there were poachers working the area, and each of them had the same thought. Where else would they have gone at dead of night without telling anyone? Still, though, the consequences were too awful to contemplate and each of them kept their thoughts to themselves.

After a sleepless night, Abigail watched the sun rise in the sky and wondered where on earth her son was. All that day she stood sentinel at the cottage door, waiting and praying for him to reappear. After another largely sleepless night she declared that she would go to find the Justice of the Peace in Much Wenlock, to see if he knew of any incidents in the area involving the boys. She knew it was at least an hour and a half's walk to Much Wenlock. Will and Joe were both working and wouldn't be able to go with her. They tried to delay her departure until the following Sunday when they would go themselves, but Abigail would have none of it. She had waited for news long enough and told them she would go by way of Banghams Wood, hoping that maybe young Jimmy or perhaps Arthur, if he wasn't away on the river, would go with her. She also knew she would have to pass by the Hall, which gave her some cause for concern. She had literally never set eyes on the place since the day she left it. She told herself she must take care not to be seen by anyone there. The last thing she wanted was for James Furlong to hear of her mission that day.

Fortunately, it was a fine day, and after she had eaten bread and dripping for breakfast and drunk a cup of water, Abigail threw her shawl around her shoulders and set off on her journey. Half an hour later she was knocking on Elizabeth's door in Banghams Wood. Pleased to see her, Elizabeth gave her a hug and asked her whatever was she doing here, and on her own too? Abigail recounted the events of the last few days and Elizabeth was obviously upset and worried at hearing that Michael was missing.

'I was wondering whether young Jimmy or Arthur, if he's here, might be able to come with me,' Abigail said, hopefully.

'I'm so sorry,' Elizabeth said, 'Arthur's away down-river and Jimmy's working on the coracles with Bert Rogers.'

Abigail was disappointed, but said she was determined to go anyway. Elizabeth said she would have gladly gone with her, but that she was currently nursing Martha, who was very ill, giving Abigail the distinct impression by sadly shaking her head, that it was only a matter of time. Abigail was obviously upset about Martha, but right now, her concern for her son over-rode all other emotions and she said,

'That's terrible Liz. Poor Martha. But then I must go alone. I need to find out what's happened to my son. I'll be alright. I'll go up past the Hall and take the track to Much Wenlock. I should be there before the sun's high in the sky.'

She went up to the bedroom to see Martha and was shocked by her appearance. She was very thin and pale and seemed to be struggling to breathe. Her face lightened when she saw Abigail, who bent down to kiss her forehead, saying,

'I hope you're soon feeling better, our Martha,' knowing full well that she never would.

Martha smiled wanly and nodded weakly. Abigail squeezed her hand and then quietly, sadly, turned and left the room. Elizabeth gave Abigail a drink of ale and some bread, and then waved her off as she disappeared along the track in the direction of the Hall.

As she passed by the gate into the Estate, she shivered, remembering the day Michael had been conceived. He had come to her room as she slept, and she had woken to feel his hands on her and his hot breath on her face. She'd tried to scream but he put his hand tight across her mouth until she could hardly breathe. Fear had made her give up the struggle. She had thought he would kill her if she resisted and so, she let him do what he had come to do. He had hurt her physically, of course, as she had never been with a man before, but the psychological harm he had inflicted on her would never go away. She could never quite rid herself of the feelings of guilt. She used to feel she must have brought it on herself by smiling at him one day as he entered the kitchen as she was cleaning the fireplace. Now that she was older, with more experience of the world, she knew that wasn't true. He had simply used her for his own gratification with no thought what effect that would have on her. Still, she felt that she should have resisted more strongly. And yet, she told herself, something good did come of it, and that was Michael, her pride and joy. And now, her mission was to find out what had happened to him.

She hurried along the track in the direction of Much Wenlock. After half an hour or so, she came to a farm, and asked the woman who was hanging washing outside the farmhouse, if she was on the right track to Much Wenlock. The woman told her that she was and should be there in half an hour. The terrain was rather rough, with many ups and downs in the stony road, and it was well over an hour before she found herself walking down the main street in Much Wenlock, towards the black and white timbered Guild Hall, where she assumed the Court and the Justice of the Peace would be.

She found the stone steps at the end of the building and climbed up to the door at the top. It was open and as she entered found herself in a long dark room with a long table at the far end behind which stood several large, ornate seats. She realised this must be the courtroom. To one side of the door, a clerk sat behind a raised desk. He glanced down at her with some disdain as he surveyed her appearance. She realised that he probably wouldn't be used to seeing someone of her station in life standing before him demanding his attention. He asked her what she wanted and she stated that she had come to see the Justice of the Peace. He told her that the Justice of the Peace was a busy man and before he found out whether he would see her or not, he needed to know what her business was.

Nervously, she explained that she had come to find out what had happened to her son, who had gone missing, and she feared that something had happened to him. The clerk enquired what name this boy went by. Abigail explained that his name was Michael Bangham and that he went missing three days ago from Dale Coppice, Coalbrookdale.

At the sound of the name and address of the missing boy, a light of realisation illuminated the clerk's face and he opened up the ledger before him. Running his finger down the page, he halted about halfway down and said,

'Yes, here we have it. I'm sorry to have to inform you that Michael Bangham is to be sent this very day to Bridgnorth Gaol to await trial at the Assize, for poaching and trespass, along with the rest of the miscreants he was taken with.'

Abigail's legs buckled and she grabbed the rail in front of the desk.

'I must see him,' she finally managed.

'Not possible I'm afraid,' replied the clerk in a dismissive fashion.

'But please, I must, I've walked from Dale Coppice today, but I won't be able to get to Bridgnorth. Please, just let me speak to him. He's my only child and I'm on my own. Please, I just need to see him before he's taken.'

Something in Abigail's tone touched the clerk and

he told her to wait there while he found out whether there was anything he could do. After ten minutes or so he returned, instructing her to follow him. He led her down the stone steps and through the room beneath the courtroom. At the end were two huge iron doors with small grilles in them. Abigail realised with horror that her beloved son must be locked up in one of them. Between the two doors a huge, rough looking man was standing and it was obvious that he was the gaoler. The clerk spoke to him, explaining that the woman he brought had been given permission to speak briefly with her son, Michael Bangham. He nodded then stepped to one of the doors and called out,

'Bangham! You have a visitor!'

After a moment Michael's distraught face, still smeared with blacking, appeared at the grille.

Seeing Abigail standing there he called out

'Mother! I'm so sorry Mother!'

At the sight of her son, Abigail burst into tears, then realising that this wouldn't be helping him, calmed herself and set about trying to understand how he came to be in this situation. Peering behind him through the gloom she could just make out Tom Williams, and immediately then, knew exactly how he'd got involved in all of this.

'I'm a 'feared Mother,' Michael said. 'They've told us what might become of us.'

'Try not to worry Michael,' Abigail forced herself to say. 'I'll find a way to come to Bridgnorth.'

A voice called out from behind Michael's back,

'Will you tell me ma missus? She'll be right worried.'

Abigail was too angry with Tom for getting Michael involved in all this, to make any reply.

'Right, that's it missus,' said the gaoler, who had been standing beside her, 'time to go.'

Abigail put her fingers to the grille to touch Michael's in a desperate attempt to comfort him. Then the gaoler took her arm and dragged her away as she called out to him that she loved him. His voice quivered with emotion as he called after her,

'Mother, I'm so sorry!'

As Abigail left the Guildhall, she knew in her heart that Michael was in mortal peril. She understood as well as anyone what happened to convicted poachers. It was either the noose or transportation. Either way she knew it may well be a long time before she saw her son again, if ever.

Even though she felt sick, she knew she should eat something. She'd had nothing since leaving Elizabeth, and she had the long walk back to Dale Coppice before her. She had a few pence with her and bought some bread at the bakehouse. After she'd eaten it and drunk from the town pump, she set off wearily on her return journey. With her mind spinning, she barely noticed anything as she trudged along the track towards home. All she could think about was her beloved son in that horrible place, soon to be taken to an even worse one, with no certainty that he would ever escape it alive.

Bone weary, she decided that she must go straight

back home rather than call in at Banghams Wood. The light was already fading as she made her way straight down to the river. There she found Jimmy by the coracle ferry and told him about Michael, asking him to tell Elizabeth. Then after she explained to Bert Rogers where she'd been, not being unsympathetic to poachers, he offered to take her over the river for free.

It was dusk as she walked up the track into the Coppice, almost stumbling with exhaustion. As soon as she entered the cottage she collapsed into the chair. Joe, who had just returned from the works, seeing what state she was in, asked,

'Abigail, whatever's the matter?'

The concern in his voice opened the floodgates and she began to rock back and forth, wailing and then crying, alerting them all to the fact that something dreadful must have happened. After five minutes or so, she had calmed down enough to tell them, through the sobs, that Michael was in Much Wenlock lockup and would soon be in gaol in Bridgnorth and on trial for poaching.

Everyone knew what that meant. and a shocked silence persisted for some seconds, until Joe finally stepped forward to put his arms round his sister, trying to reassure her that they would find a way to help her son. No one believed him.

When Abigail had calmed down, she remembered Tom Williams and asked Joe if he would go and tell his poor mother where her son was. As he stood outside their cottage door Joe could hear Williams shouting at his wife, obviously drunk as usual. Joe knocked on the door and after a minute or so, Tom's mother appeared. She had obviously suffered a blow to her face and Joe was tempted to go inside and sort the bully out once and for all. Of course, he knew better than to intervene between a man and his wife, and just quietly told her that Abigail had seen her son in the Much Wenlock Gaol. The poor woman reeled and grabbed the door jamb for support, thanked him for telling her and slowly closed the door, no doubt to suffer more abuse at the hands of her brute of a husband.

# Chapter 15

1729: Troubles seldom come singly, and the following day, Joe received a message from one of the wagoners bringing materials up from the wharf. He had been asked by Jimmy to tell Joe that his sister Martha was very poorly, and anyone who wanted to see her again in this life, must go to her bedside as soon as possible.

It was Saturday and Joe decided the family would be able to visit her the next day. Abigail was horrified that with all the worry about Michael, she hadn't even told them about Martha. Of course, she couldn't have known just how ill she was, but still she should have prepared them for the bad news. As she had already seen her, Abigail offered to stay at home and look after little Elizabeth. She asked Joe to speak to Dick, if he was there, to ask him to find out when the Assize Court was to be held in Bridgnorth.

Will, Joe and Liz set off early, and were in Banghams Wood by mid-morning. As soon as they arrived, Elizabeth asked after Abigail. Jimmy had told them about Michael, and she knew Abigail would be distraught. Joe asked whether Dick would be coming to see Martha, and Elizabeth said she'd sent a message with Margaret who was asking Fred, the horseman at the Hall to pass it on to Dick when he next visited Andrews Grain Merchants. She was expecting him to come in the next day or two.

'Well, when he does come, Abigail said to ask him if he could find out when the Assize Court would be.' Joe said, 'I intend to go with her if I'm able.'

'I will, of course, and that's good, Joe, she's going to need plenty of support. But I'm right glad you've come, it doesn't look like our Martha's long for this world, as you'll see for yourselves.'

With that, Will and Joe went up to the bedroom and Liz, who felt she didn't know Martha very well and didn't want to intrude, stayed downstairs with Elizabeth, who offered her some herb tea. Joe and Will were shocked at Martha's appearance. She looked all skin and bone with her eyes closed and sunk into her head. Her breathing was very shallow, and it was obvious to them both that she wouldn't last long now. Joe sat down beside the bed and took her hand, stroking it gently. She opened her eyes and her lips curved into the special smile she reserved for her favourite brother, whispering,

'Joe, you came.'

'Of course I did lass,' he replied quietly.

'I'm weary Joe,' Martha whispered, then cried out in pain as whatever was attacking her body made itself sharply felt.

Will came to the other side of the bed and stroked her hair to comfort her, his own face contorted as he felt her pain. Elizabeth came in with a herbal infusion to ease her pain. Joe lifted Martha's head and helped her to drink, then she flopped thankfully back onto the pillow. After some minutes it was obvious the drink had done its job, and she was much calmer. Her eyes closed and her breathing, although shallow, was even now. She had fallen into a deep sleep. Her brothers kissed her gently on the forehead and then, full of sadness, joined Liz, Arthur and Elizabeth downstairs in the living room.

'It's not good, is it?' Elizabeth asked, looking first at Will and then Joe, maybe hoping for some sign that she was wrong, but of course, she knew in her heart that their sister would not be with them much longer. After they had all eaten some bread and cheese and taken some ale, Joe, Will and Liz went up to Martha, who was still sleeping, one last time. Then sadly they said their goodbyes to Elizabeth and Arthur and left Banghams Wood to make their way back across the Gorge. No one spoke as they trudged wearily back home. They all knew they would never see Martha again in this life, and tragically, maybe the same could be said about young Michael.

In fact, it was three days later that the news was brought by Jimmy. Martha had passed peacefully away in the night and the funeral was to be held the next day. Will and Joe spoke to Mr Ford to ask if they might take an hour or two off work to attend their sister's funeral.

The next day dawned clear and bright and promised to be a warm one. As the Dale Coppice contingent strode along towards the Buildwas bridge, they were pleased to see Dick and Margaret just arriving in a horse-drawn trap from the direction of Bridgnorth. It was obvious to them all that Dick had definitely done well for himself. He and his wife were smartly dressed, and the trap was new and pulled by a handsome black and white pony.

Elizabeth, Arthur and Jane, along with Margaret and Dorothy, walked down the lane to the church behind the coffin, which was carried by Mr Johnson on his cart. Thus the family gathered once more at the burial ground in Buildwas, this time to lay poor Martha to rest. It was indeed a solemn occasion. It seemed to them that Martha hadn't had much of a life, never having the pleasure of sharing her life with a loving partner, and never having the joy of children of her own. Still, they all felt that they had done their best for her and given her as happy a life as possible in the circumstances.

After the burial, Dick told Abigail he was sorry to hear about Michael, and that he had discovered that the Summer Assize would be held in Bridgnorth on Midsummer's Day. Joe, Arthur and Will joined them to discuss the situation and to see how they might help their sister. Dick told Abigail that he and Margaret would be happy for her to stay with them until matters had been resolved, one way or another. Margaret agreed that she would be most welcome. Arthur suggested that he could ask Owner Blake if he would mind if Abigail travelled down to Bridgnorth when the Oriel next set sail downriver, which should be in two weeks' time. Joe said he expected the furnaces to be blown out in the next couple of weeks, and he would be happy to accompany Abigail and see her safely to Dick's house. The kindness of her family overwhelmed Abigail, given the emotional state she was in, and she broke down in tears. Dick put his arms around her and she buried her head in his shoulder, tears coursing down her cheeks. Eventually, she gathered herself and then asked if he might possibly visit Michael now that he had been taken to Bridgnorth, to make sure he was getting enough to eat and to tell him she would soon be there to visit him. Dick promised that he would of course do what he could for the lad.

Before the family parted, Dorothy had news of her own to give them. She and John Smith were to be married. He had finally proposed to her the week before and she had gladly accepted. This news brought some cheer to the family, and they all congratulated her warmly. She said the wedding was to be at the end of June, and the mistress had given them permission to be married in the private chapel at the Hall and she hoped that they would all be able to be there to share her wedding day. However, in view of what had just occurred and what was happening to Michael, no one could really say whether they would be able to attend or not, and Dorothy said that she understood, of course, that this wasn't the time to make firm arrangements.

Joe and Will were unable to return to Banghams Wood after the funeral as they had only been given a couple of hours off work. Consequently, after matters regarding Michael had been decided, the family parted company. Will walked ahead with Joe, Liz and Abigail following on behind. As they walked back along the north side of the river towards the wharf, Joe glanced at Will. He could tell by the expression on Will's face that he was angry about something. Knowing his brother as well as he did, he knew that his anger was better expressed than allowed to fester. To explore what might be troubling him, he said,

'Will, I can see you're angry. It's a bad do isn't it?'

'If you mean Martha, yes it is,' Will replied, 'she didn't have much of a life, did she?' Then after some moments, he looked back, making sure that Abigail was out of earshot, then went on, 'But what's really making me angry Joe, is the way people are treated in this country these days simply for taking food from the woods and fields. How can it be right for folks to be threatened with being strung up just for doing what they've been doing for centuries, catching rabbits for the cooking pot?'

'I know Will, it doesn't seem right. It doesn't seem enough for the rich to own the land, they think they have the right to own every living thing on it, including us, if we're honest! But the law is the law and I guess we have to abide by it, or change it, and as we don't have a say in who makes the laws, I don't see how we can.'

'I know you're right Joe, but we don't have to like it, do we? Maybe one day, we will get a say, and things might change. My God, I hope so. It's just not right that a youngster like Michael can be thrown into gaol and threatened with the noose just for getting mixed up with that bad lot. He's only a lad after all.'

They had reached the wharf and turned to say goodbye to Liz and Abigail, who turned up the pathway towards Lincoln Hill and home, the men along Dale Road, Joe towards the furnace, Will making for the mine.

The next two weeks were agony for Abigail. Michael was never out of her mind. He was still a boy, now forced into an adult world with all manner of ruffians. She feared for him, imagining all kinds of horrors which might befall him, being completely without protection in such company. She knew food would be scarce, certainly not adequate for a growing boy, and there would be no creature comforts such as a decent mattress to sleep on.

She did well to worry. Michael was given no special treatment in consideration of his tender years. He was thrown into the cells with the rest of the prisoners and when food did appear, he was lucky if he could manage to get his hands on a few scraps. If it hadn't been for the one individual who was kinder than the rest, who noticed that he hardly ever got anything to eat, felt sorry for him and shared a little of his food with the lad, he would have starved to death. As it was, he was rapidly becoming thin and weak.

Dick finally managed to visit him a few days after the funeral, and he was shocked to the core by his appearance. He immediately began to bring food for him, having bribed the gaoler to let his nephew out of the main cell to give him a chance to speak with him, and to make sure he could eat the food without the rest of the prisoners stealing it from him. After a couple of weeks, he began to look a little better. He was of course, in a state of permanent fear about what was going to happen to him. He told Dick that he'd had no idea what Tom Williams had planned when he'd gone with him that night, and if he had known, he would never have gone. He knew poaching was against the law and promised he would never do it again. Dick said he believed him and that he should try not to worry, saying that he would plead for him when the time came.

The Oriel was due to sail on the 6$^{th}$ June and as luck would have it, the furnaces had been blown out the day before. Owner Blake had agreed to allow Joe and Abigail to travel down to Bridgnorth, saying he wouldn't think of charging them for the journey. At six o'clock in the morning of the 6$^{th}$, Joe and Abigail set out for the wharf. Will had given Abigail a few shillings to take with her as she had no money of her own, in case she needed to buy anything for Michael, and Liz had packed some bread and cheese for their journey.

Arthur greeted them at the wharf, handing Abigail a bundle that Elizabeth had sent. Margaret had given her some old clothes, rejects from the Hall, and she had altered the coat, shirt, and breeches to fit Michael, so that he would be able to face the trial with a degree of self-respect. She had also washed and pressed a couple of dresses for Abigail herself, realising that as she was going to stay with Dick and Margaret, she would need something decent to wear. Abigail couldn't believe how kind everyone was being, and it gave her strength to know that both she and Michael were so loved.

They boarded the Oriel and settled down in a corner of the deck. Both Abigail and Joe were excited to be leaving the Gorge, in spite of the circumstances. Neither of them had ever been as far as Bridgnorth, even though, as Arthur told them, it was less than ten miles away. Abigail was pleased that at last she would be able to see Michael, as was Joe, but he had to confess he was also looking forward to visiting Dick and Margaret's home for the first time.

By mid-day they were tied up at the Bridgnorth wharfage. They thanked the master of the Oriel and said their farewells to Arthur, then disembarked. They were grateful to see that Dick was waiting for them. Having found out when the Oriel was due, he had brought the pony and trap to pick them up.

Ten minutes later they halted outside a house that neither Joe nor Abigail could believe was Dick's. After the squatter cottages they had lived in all their lives, this house looked huge. It had an impressive looking door in the middle with large windows either side, and above was a row of three more windows. It looked new, as though it had only just been built, which Dick confirmed was the case. His father-in-law, Mr Andrews, had insisted that he and Margaret needed a place of their own and had commissioned the building of this house for them. It wasn't as big as the Hall but was certainly comparable to the Rectory in Buildwas. They were very impressed, although it did make them feel rather like the poor relations, which of course, they were.

However, Margaret couldn't have been kinder and soon made them feel at home. She showed Abigail up to a small bedroom which she said was hers for as long as she needed it. There was a basin and jug of water on a stand, and she suggested that Abigail might like to wash after her journey, then told her to come downstairs when she was ready. Abigail was full of wonder at these surroundings. The windows had velvet drapes and there was a beautiful patchwork quilt thrown over the single bed. She briefly bounced up and down on it, truly amazed that such comfortable beds existed. She undid the bundle of clothes Elizabeth had sent and quickly washed her hands and face before putting on one of the dresses. On the dressing table was a brush and comb and she brushed her hair and looked at herself in the mirror. She couldn't believe the transformation!

She went downstairs and into the room on the left of the hallway which was apparently the dining room. The others were all there, and although obviously impressed with her changed appearance, no one embarrassed her by making comment. Margaret asked them all to sit down at the table and a meal of beef and vegetables was served by a young woman who apparently doubled as parlour maid and cook. Joe and Abigail were in awe. Neither of them had ever been served with anything by a servant. Of course Abigail had seen luxury from the other side, but never experienced it herself. It occurred to Joe, observing the easy way his brother dealt with the servant, that he had settled very well into this lifestyle.

When they had finished eating, Margaret suggested they go through into the sitting room. Once again Joe and Abigail surveyed the room with a degree of amazement, unable to believe that their brother owned all this. Joe in particular felt rather out of place in his old leather breeches and woollen frock coat, the only one he possessed. At least Abigail looked rather more suited to the surroundings in her new dress. However, Dick and Margaret soon put him at his ease, and he was glad he had come, not least because he could get to know his sister-in-law better. He'd had little chance to do so since her marriage to Dick. He liked what he saw. She had a pleasant face and thick brown hair piled high on her head and fastened with a comb. She was small in stature but carried herself well, obviously not having been subjected to hard labour. He could see why Dick had been attracted to her, and he was glad that they were well settled and apparently happy in each other's company.

They exchanged pleasantries for a little while until Abigail could contain herself no longer and asked Dick if he had seen Michael recently. He replied that of course, he had visited him several times since he had been brought to Bridgnorth. He did not, however, go into any detail about the state he had initially found him in. He explained that he had been taking him food and ensuring that he was given the chance to eat it. He told her he had explained to the gaoler that the lad's mother was arriving, and he had agreed to allow her to visit him tomorrow. Dick asked Joe if he would stay the night so that he might also see his nephew in the morning. Joe readily accepted the invitation. He told Dick that once he had seen the boy, he intended to hitch a ride on one of the trows returning upriver to the Gorge.

Dick asked Joe if he would like to take a look at the Andrews Grain Merchant business premises and perhaps to meet Mr Andrews. Joe readily agreed, eager to know all he could about his brother's life. Everyone back in the Gorge would want a full report. The men disappeared and Margaret and Abigail were left alone to get to know one another. Margaret said she was so pleased to spend some time with Abigail at last. She told her that Dick had always spoken fondly of her. Abigail felt she wanted to hide nothing about her past and Michael's origins, as she suspected that this woman was going to be important in their lives in future and she wanted to start their relationship as honestly as possible. She began to explain, but hadn't said more than a sentence or two before Margaret said,

'Please, Abigail, you don't need to explain. Dick has told me all about Michael and who his father was. You have had a difficult time and Dick and I want to be here for you, and for Michael. He is determined to speak for him at the trial and, if you are in agreement, to ask the Judges to release him into his care, as his apprentice, and assure them that he will nurture the boy and keep him on the right path, if they will give him another chance. Of course, there may be a fine to pay, but Dick is determined that he will pay it for you. He feels the lad is truly remorseful and was dragged into the affair by Tom Williams, who seems to be a thoroughly bad lot. Dick feels that if Michael is here in Bridgnorth, he will be away from his influence and free to grow into a fine young man. What do you say Abigail?'

Abigail sat in shocked silence for a moment or two, unable to comprehend that they would be prepared to be so generous to herself and to Michael. Obviously, it would mean Michael leaving home, and that would be hard for them both, but at least here, with Dick and Margaret he would be safe, and given the affluence of their lifestyle, he would definitely be increasing his life-chances by living here. Eventually she spoke, saying,

'Margaret, I don't know what to say. That is so generous of you. Although it would be hard to see him leave home so young, it would be a great relief to me to know that he would be in good hands, and with a better future ahead of him than I could ever give him.'

'That's settled then,' Margaret replied, 'When the time comes, Dick will plead for him, and he can be very persuasive you know,' she added with a warm smile.

Abigail was greatly comforted by this conversation, being able at last to see a better future for her boy.

When the men returned Joe was full of how impressed he had been with the Andrews' business, telling Abigail that it was a far bigger enterprise than he had ever imagined. Margaret told Dick that she had discussed their idea for helping Michael and was pleased to report that Abigail was in agreement. Dick said he was pleased and went on to explain it all to Joe, who was equally happy with the proposed arrangement for the boy.

'That's grand Dick, it'll be the making of him. He's not a bad lad, just needs to get away from Tom Williams and be given the discipline of decent employment.'

'Well, Joe, he'll get that alright. As you have seen, there's plenty of opportunity in the business for a hard-working lad.'

After a light supper they spent the rest of the evening talking about this and that, just catching up on family news. Eventually they all retired for the night. Joe was given a comfortable bed in one of the spare bedrooms and Abigail settled down to the best night's sleep she'd had in a while, feeling there was at last some hope that Michael might soon be free and setting out on a better life than she could ever have hoped he would have.

# Chapter 16

Abigail woke early, washed, and dressed and went downstairs to find Dick and Joe in the dining room eating breakfast. Dick told Abigail he had arranged with the gaoler for her and Joe to visit Michael at around ten o'clock that morning. Abigail said again how grateful she was to everyone for being so kind. She couldn't eat much. She was too nervous about what she would find in Bridgnorth Gaol. Michael had been in custody for nearly two months. Goodness knows what state he'll be in, she thought to herself. Margaret had asked the servant to put some food and drink in a bag which she handed to Abigail who also put in the clothes that Elizabeth had given her for Michael, and they set off for the gaol.

The cells were situated beneath the building where the Assize Court was to be held, and when Joe had explained their business, the clerk on duty at the desk disappeared, and returned a few minutes later with a huge, rough looking man, whom they assumed was one of the gaolers. He looked as though he would be able to deal easily with any trouble the prisoners might possibly cause him, and Abigail's heart went out to Michael, thinking of him being in the care of such a person.

However, when Joe explained that they were here to see Michael Bangham, his attitude softened a little and he asked them to follow him down the stairs to the cells. It was a dingy, dark place that smelled of unwashed bodies and worse. Abigail heaved involuntarily. On each side of the passage were what could only be described as iron cages and in each one there were six or seven men, and in some of them, women also. They reached the cage at the end of the passage and in one corner was a boy. Abigail hardly recognised her son. He was dirty and unkempt and thinner than the day he had left home. Both she and Joe were shocked, not only by his appearance, but also at the conditions in which he was being held.

As they stood at the door of the cage, the gaoler called out,

'Bangham! You have visitors. Come forward now!'

Michael looked bewildered for a moment, then cried out,

'Mother, Uncle Joe! You came!'

The gaoler unlocked the door and Michael fell into his mother's arms.

The gaoler secured the cage and led them back along the passage to a small cell near the bottom of the stairs.

'You've got ten minutes,' he said gruffly.

After checking the bag Abigail was holding to

ensure it didn't contain anything untoward, he left, slamming the door then turning the key in the lock, which sent a chill down Joe's back, giving him a hint of what it might be like to be locked up in this place. Joe's heart went out to his nephew who was crying now and saying over and over again that he was sorry, and that he was so scared. Abigail comforted her boy, trying to reassure him that she and his uncle Dick would do everything they could for him.

Even though Dick had been able to bring him some food, he was still thin, his face still bore the remnants of the blacking and his hair was matted. She had brought a damp cloth with her and gently cleaned his face and hands as best she could, then she brushed his hair and helped him to change into the clean clothes she had brought. Michael tucked into the food and drink as though he hadn't eaten for days. It was heart-breaking to watch.

'Time's up!' came the cry, and Michael clung to his mother as the gaoler opened the door and said, 'Come on Bangham, time to go.'

Abigail assured Michael she would be back to see him as often as she could before the trial, and told him to try not to worry, she was sure Uncle Dick, who had some standing in the community, would be able to help him.

Michael continued to hang on to Abigail, until fi-nally the gaoler lost patience and dragged him away, and back to the cage at the end of the passage. To see him so roughly handled, his face full of fear, broke

Abigail's heart. Once he was out of sight, Joe put his arm round Abigail's shoulders and led her back up the corridor and out of the gaol.

Once Joe had escorted Abigail back to Dick's house, assuring her he would try to get back for the trial on Midsummer's Day, he took his leave of them all to make his way down to the wharfage where he found Owner Onion's boat unloading some of its cargo and preparing to take the remainder upriver to the Gorge.

Abigail felt a little lost once Joe had gone. Although of course, as she was growing up, Dick had always been there in Banghams Wood, she had seen nothing of him in recent years, particularly since he had married Margaret and moved to Bridgnorth. She felt quite out of place for a while, particularly in these, what to her, were affluent surroundings. However, as the days passed, she began to feel more at home. Thanks to Dick's ongoing arrangement with the gaoler, she was able to visit Michael every few days, taking him food and drink. Margaret had kindly provided another change of clothes for him for the trial and on the 23rd of June, Abigail took them into the gaol for him to wear the next day. Time and again Michael had promised his mother that if he was freed, he would never get involved with poaching again. He had learnt his lesson, she was sure of it, and now it was up to Dick to convince their Lordships that he meant it, and that he would make sure that the lad was as good as his word.

By the time Abigail returned to Dick's house, Joe

had arrived, having once again travelled down on one of the trows heading for Gloucester. Abigail was pleased to see him, and with the support of her two brothers, she felt more able to face the coming ordeal of her son's trial. The day of the trial, 24th June, Midsummer's Day 1729, finally dawned. It was threatening rain from a black sky. Abigail, Joe and Dick made their way to the Assize Court. It was with some trepidation that they entered the gallery of the courtroom, where people not connected with the trials themselves were allowed to stand to watch the proceedings. This trial of four prisoners who had been caught red-handed by the militia poaching on the estate of one of the county's notables, had attracted quite a crowd and the gallery was packed. Everyone knew that, following legislation enacted some six years previously, poaching could be punishable by transportation to America, or even by execution on the gallows. Speculation was rife. How could these felons escape severe punishment when they had actually been caught in the act with their ill-gotten gains still in their possession?

The courtroom was a dark and noisy place. Crowded as it was, it was hot and sticky and the smell of unwashed bodies pervaded the place. The room fell silent however, as the seven judges entered the room from the left and took their places in their appointed seats on the raised platform at one end of the room. One of the judges, who all wore black robes and long white wigs, called out,

'Summon the jury!' and immediately a line of men,

twelve in number, filed in to take up their places in the twelve seats ranged against the wall opposite the public gallery. Each one of them was solemnly sworn in, promising to exercise judgement without fear or favour. They then settled into their seats to await the beginning of the trial.

At the back of the courtroom, opposite the judges' platform was another raised area surrounded by a balustrade about four and a half foot high. Abigail perceived that this must be the dock, the place where she would soon see her own beloved son standing, to receive his fate. Her legs were shaking as the judge once again called out,

'Bring forth the prisoners!'

It appeared that all four of the poachers were to be tried together, presumably as what evidence was to be presented, applied equally to the role of each in the crime of which they stood accused. They emerged one by one from the top of a staircase behind the dock, presumably leading up from the cells below. They were a motley crew, dirty and malnourished after their months of confinement. Michael appeared at the end of the line and took up his place to the right-hand end of the dock. He stood out from the others, wearing the good, clean clothes Margaret had provided and with his hair tidy and his face clean. Abigail prayed that his appearance would convey to the judges that he was cut from different cloth than the ruffians whose company he had recently kept.

The Clerk of the Court asked each of them in turn,

to state his name and the Parish from which he came. He then read out the charge for which each of them must answer, and one by one they were asked how they pleaded. They all, of course pleaded 'not guilty', as to plead guilty might result in an automatic death penalty.

However, there was plenty of evidence on which the jury would decide their innocence or guilt. The witness evidence was presented by the Bailiff of the Estate and substantiated by the Captain of the Militia. The Bailiff recounted that on the night in question, in the early hours of the morning he had been alerted to shouting of men and the barking of a dog in a wooded part of the estate.

Suspecting the noises were being made by poachers, he had sent for the local militia before approaching them. Within half an hour they had the poachers surrounded and declared their presence. One of the poachers, in an attempt to resist arrest, had set the dog upon the Bailiff but it had been shot dead by one of the Militia men before it reached him. Realising the game was up, the poachers had then given themselves up, been arrested and taken to Much Wenlock Guildhall, where they were officially charged with poaching and placed in the lock up before being sent to Bridgnorth to await trial. The Captain of the Militia was asked whether he agreed with the description of events which had been given by the Bailiff. He stated that he did, and had nothing to add.

This was the case for the Prosecution, and to everyone in the room, most particularly the members of the jury, it seemed there could be little doubt that they were all guilty as charged. In fact, it took no more than two minutes for the jury to emerge from their huddle and agree the verdicts. The Clerk of the Court demanded the verdict on each of the defendants in turn. One after the other, the foreman answered 'Guilty.' As the Clerk asked for the verdict on Michael Bangham, Abigail gripped Joe's arm tightly, afraid she was going to faint.

'Guilty,' came the reply. Abigail involuntarily cried out 'No!' and looked at Michael who now looked terrified.

The presiding Judge asked each of the men in turn whether they had anything to say in mitigation of their actions. For the two men, there was little to be said, but when it came to Tom Williams, just thirteen years old, he did his best to convince the Judges that he was full of remorse and swore he would never do such a thing again, if he was given a second chance. The Judge, looking at his appearance and his arrogant manner, seemed rather unimpressed. Then it was Michael's turn. Dick stood up and catching the presiding Judge's attention, asked if he could plead Michael's case for him, explaining that he was a merchant of some standing and reputation in Bridgnorth and that Michael was his nephew. Seeing that Michael did indeed seem out of place among the rest of the miscreants, and after conferring briefly with his colleagues on the bench, he agreed to allow Dick to speak for Michael.

Dick made his way down to the floor of the court and stood in front of the dock, facing the judges. The presiding judge asked him to state his name and business. He informed the court that he was Richard Bangham, a partner in Andrews Grain Merchants of Bridgnorth and uncle to the defendant Michael Bangham.

He explained that being the boy's uncle, he knew him very well, had indeed known him since birth. He told them the boy had been brought up well by his mother, but without the benefit of a father's guidance. Consequently, he had succumbed in recent months to the influence of malign forces, being cajoled into misdemeanours in the name of adventure, but on the night in question had had no idea where he was being led, nor to what purpose. The boy had no idea that the men were intent on poaching until it was too late. He had indeed tried to resist and run away back to his home in Dale Coppice, but was prevented from doing so by one of the men grabbing hold of him and while he held the boy down, the other had smeared his face with blacking as he declared,

'You're one of us now lad!'

Dick went on to say that Michael was full of remorse and understood that he had been led into doing wrong, but was determined, if he was given the chance to work hard and lead a good life, to make his poor mother proud. Finally, he said that if Michael was allowed to leave the court today, he would be taking him into his own home as his apprentice, and he truly believed that if he were to be kept away from Dale Coppice, taught to read and write and the meaning of hard work, he could grow into a fine young man.

The judge looked directly at Michael and asked him,

'Is all this true boy?'

Michael stood as tall as he could, and in his strongest voice declared,

'It is, my Lord. I have sworn to my mother that I will never get involved with such matters again and will gladly live with my Uncle, and do my best to make something of myself, if your Lordships will only give me the chance.'

There was a brief consultation among the judges before the presiding judge began to pass sentence on each of the felons in turn. To each of the men he declared that they would be transported to the Americas for a period of no less than seven years. The men rocked on their heels at this, but both knew it could have been worse. They could have been facing the death penalty. On Tom Williams he passed the sentence of three years hard labour.

Joe placed his arm around Abigail's shoulders in support, as the judge looked straight at Michael. He paused a moment before declaring that in view of his age and the fact that his uncle had pleaded for him so eloquently, the judges had decided to be merciful and then formally stated,

'Michael Bangham, you will pay a fine of £10 and be bound over to keep the peace for five years, providing that you remain in Bridgnorth and are apprenticed to Richard Bangham of Andrews Grain Merchants. On payment of the fine you will be free to go.'

Michael could hardly believe it. Abigail and Joe made their way down from the gallery and into the floor of the court, where Michael had now left the dock and was standing with Dick. He immediately flew into his mother's arms, who, with tears of relief tumbling down her cheeks, was thanking Dick for pleading so successfully for her son.

Michael turned to look at the other defendants who were now being led towards the stairs down to the cells. As he reached the top of the stairs Tom turned and looked at Michael with such a look of hatred in his eyes that Michael reeled under the force of it and couldn't help feeling that he had somehow betrayed his former friend.

Dick arranged with the Clerk of the Court that he would go immediately to get the money and the indenture papers and return forthwith to pay the fine to release his nephew. Consequently Joe, Abigail and Michael were obliged to wait in an anteroom until Dick returned. Within an hour he arrived back at court with the money and the indenture document which Abigail had already signed. The Clerk checked the document and recorded that it was all in order, then took the £10 from Dick and issued a receipt. He then declared that they were free to leave.

Within half an hour they arrived back at Dick's house, where Margaret had asked the servant to prepare a bath for Michael. Abigail spent the next hour tending to her son and when she brought him downstairs, he was barely recognisable. He looked quite the little gentleman, if a little under-nourished. Margaret, determined to begin the task of 'building him up' had asked Mary to prepare a meal for them all and it warmed all their hearts to watch the boy tucking into it.

Dick told Joe that if he would stay the night, he would get one of the men to take him and Abigail back to Dale Coppice in the trap in the morning. After the emotionally exhausting day they had all had and realising that Abigail would want to spend at least one night with her son before leaving, he readily agreed.

Dick explained the boy would be living with them. There was an attic room which they had prepared for him. He said he would let him rest for a week or so, to get used to his surroundings and to recover somewhat from his ordeal, but then he would be working at the business five days a week. On the sixth day he would be going to school in Bridgnorth where he must learn to read and write and do his numbers. If he was to progress in the business this would be essential, he declared, and asked Michael if he understood how important this was.

'I do Uncle,' he replied, and then went on, 'I won't let you down and thank you for all you did for me today.'

With that, Dick took Michael and Abigail up to the attic to see the room they had prepared for him. It was a low room with a small window in one side of the roof. Michael ran over to the window and standing on tiptoe, looked down on the street, and beyond, a hundred feet below he could see the Severn flowing swiftly by. This gave him some comfort as he knew this was the same water that had flowed along the Gorge only hours before. It was a link with home. After months of confinement with no view of the world outside, he was delighted he would now have his own window through which to look at the sky. Abigail was thrilled to see how pleased Michael was and once again thanked Dick for his kindness.

Michael was so happy with his room  they struggled to get him to leave it and come down to join the others. In the event he was happy enough to spend the rest of the evening by Abigail's side. After the months of worry, the relief in the room was palpable and there was much merriment, sometimes bordering on the hysterical. Eventually it was time to retire for the night and Abigail went up to the attic with Michael, happy to be able to fuss over him and maybe for the last time, to kiss him goodnight and tuck him up in bed.

By ten o'clock the next day, Abigail and Joe were ready to leave Bridgnorth. Michael had spent a restless night, unused to the comfort of a bed, having slept on the floor of the gaol for months. Of course, he didn't want his mother to leave him and clung to her when the time came, but she gently withdrew her embrace, saying that she was sure he would be fine with his Uncle Dick and Aunt Margaret, and they would look after him. She said she would visit him as often as she could, and Dick said he would make sure the boy got to visit the Dale from time to time to see his mother. With that, Abigail and Joe climbed into the trap and set off on the journey back to the Gorge. Michael ran after the trap, waving wildly, until it had turned the corner at the end of the street and disappeared. Then he stopped, turned and walked dejectedly back to Dick and Margaret who were waiting for him at the gate. So began Michael Bangham's new life in Bridgnorth.

When Abigail and Joe arrived back at Dale Coppice a couple of hours later, there was a strange atmosphere. For a start, it wasn't often that a pony and trap turned up in these parts, and it caused quite a stir. In addition, word had already reached the Gorge about the outcome of the trial. The poachers were local men, from Madeley Wood and Buildwas, and Tom Williams was himself from the Coppice. It was apparent that people thought they had got off lightly, fully expecting they would be given the death penalty.

Nevertheless, seven years transportation was still devastating for their families who would be left destitute and probably sent back to their home parishes for support, where they would no doubt end up in the local poorhouse. It was also highly likely that the men would never return, as in order to do so they would have to pay their own passage home.

Tom Williams hadn't come off much better, as three years hard labour for a boy of fourteen would be difficult to bear and there was some doubt as to whether he would survive it. His mother, Martha, was distraught. At the very least she wouldn't see her son for three years. Fred, his father was predictably angry that such a fate should befall his son and had already started telling anyone who would listen that Michael Bangham had lied to save his own skin.

# Chapter 17

In spite of the general atmosphere around the Coppice, Joe and Abigail were certainly given a warm welcome in the Bangham cottage. Liz had prepared a meal for them, and little Elizabeth ran to her father for the special fuss he reserved for her. Abigail was glad to be home again after weeks away in Bridgnorth. She would have preferred to have brought her son home with her, but she knew he would have a good life with Dick and Margaret, and she would just have to bear the pain of separation. After worrying for months what fate would befall him, she decided it was a small price to pay for securing his future.

A week later, Dorothy and John Smith were married in the chapel at the Hall. Abigail said that for obvious reasons she would not set foot on the Estate and Will also declined, saying that he daren't risk coming face to face with Furlong, afraid he might try to finish the job he started all those years ago.

Joe and Liz left the children with them, and along with Arthur, Elizabeth and Margaret attended the wedding in the private chapel on the Estate. Dorothy looked beautiful, wearing a white dress given to her by the mistress and wearing a garland of wildflowers around her head. Joe was pleased to see that she and John were obviously very much in love. He seemed a decent sort and being the schoolmaster, had his own house in Madeley Wood. After the service, they were transported across the Gorge to their marital home in the pony and trap, loaned for the day by the Master. As her siblings waved them off, they were confident that Dorothy's future would be secure with her schoolteacher. Another Bangham was to go up in the world, and they were glad of it.

As Joe and Liz made their way up the lane towards the Coppice, Joe's joyful mood persisted. Six months pregnant, Liz was blooming and looked the picture of health. After the troubles he had recently witnessed in Bridgnorth, he was glad to be here having seen Dorothy now settled and, walking beside his wife, he felt secure in his own happiness. His little daughter was thriving, and she would soon have a brother or sister. Will had changed after his time in America, and he was altogether more pleasant to be around. As for Abigail, of course she was no doubt sad Michael was no longer to live with her, but he knew she was relieved he was safe from the malign influences he'd suffered in the Coppice, and now he'd been given the opportunity of having a good life ahead of him. Joe had been extremely impressed with Dick and Margaret, and the way they had been determined to rescue the boy. It had taken courage for Dick to stand up in

Court like that to speak for the lad, and he had been proud of his younger brother.

For the next couple of months, life went on much as usual in Dale Coppice. Joe undertook some maintenance work on the furnaces along with some of his workmates and Will took some extra labouring shifts at the mine, so the family's finances held up pretty well. The weather around harvest time was poor though, and as a result, the cost of food rose steeply and many of the families in the area, not so fortunate as the Banghams as far as supplementing their incomes was concerned, suffered greatly.

The Williams for instance, already devastated by Tom's imprisonment and the loss of his wages from his work in the coalmine, had a hard time of it. Fred Williams of course, continued to drink and to blame everyone else for the decline in the family's fortunes, and his wife and the remaining children began to show signs of malnutrition. Things came to a head one day in late August, when his wife Martha, confronted him as he staggered into the cottage, having spent what little wages he'd earned in the previous week, in the ale house. Her desperation finally overcame her fear, and she could be heard all across the clearing, shouting at him, calling him cruel and a useless father and husband, as he could watch them all starve, rather than stop drinking. Suddenly, there was a roar of rage, followed by several screams and shrieks, and children shouting out to their mother. Then, suddenly, there was silence, except for the quiet sobbing of the infants. After a moment or two, Johnny, the eldest child came running out of the cottage and into the arms of Joe, who, along with Will, had been on his way to investigate

'He's killed me ma!' he shouted, over and over.

Joe asked Will to take the lad and ask Liz to look after him, then went over to the Williams' cottage and cautiously entered. The scene that greeted him was one of utter carnage. Martha lay on the floor covered in blood which was oozing from several gaping wounds. One of the younger children, barely two years old, lay beside her mother, calling to her to wake up. Fred Williams was sitting on the floor, slumped against the wall, blood spatters across his face, still holding the filleting knife in his hand, and looking completely bewildered, obviously unable to comprehend what he had just done.

Joe told him to drop the knife, and when Fred looked at it, he seemed to see it for the first time, suddenly flinging it across the room as though it was on fire. Joe picked it up and took it outside to make sure it was well out of reach, placing it on top of the lintel over the doorway. Will was waiting beside the door and asked Joe what had happened.

'He's finally done it Will, he's killed Martha,' Joe said, with the conviction of someone who had just witnessed the carnage within.

'Go to Mr Ford's place Will and tell him what's happened. He'll be able to send a rider to fetch the Justice of the Peace from Much Wenlock, quicker than we could. I'll stay here and make sure he does no harm to anyone else.'

John Spencer and several of the other men had gathered outside the cottage and with their help, Joe was able to restrain Fred, binding his hands and feet where he sat, still slumped against the wall. He had made no move to stop the men as they took the four remaining little children, traumatised by what they had just witnessed, to Joe's cottage, where Abigail and Liz tried to comfort them as best they could. Martha's body had to be left where it was, until the Justice had been, so that he could record what he saw as evidence of what had occurred.

Everyone knew, of course, that Fred Williams was bound for the gallows, and the children, soon to be orphaned, would be sent to the poorhouse. All agreed that it was a complete tragedy, but one that wasn't entirely unexpected as they had all witnessed the family's decline and knew that Tom's imprisonment had hit Martha hard. He had been her main emotional support. The hunger of the past few weeks had proved the last straw and had given her the courage to stand up to her husband, which had unfortunately led to her losing her life.

The Justice appeared along with members of the militia within a couple of hours to survey the scene and to take Fred into custody. They placed him in an open cart and trundled him off to Much Wenlock gaol. As the family had no money, Martha was placed unceremoniously in a coarse white shroud and after a couple of days, taken away on a handcart to the burial ground. Only Joe and Will attended the funeral, which was brief and without ceremony. The five children had been placed in the care of Benthall Parish and were now in the poorhouse at Mine Spout, across the Gorge, destined for paupers' lives which would inevitably be short ones.

The whole incident had been distressing for everyone, and hit Liz, now seven months pregnant, particularly hard, and even Abigail, though it had been Martha's son who had led Michael astray, had had some sympathy for her, understanding how hard it must have been, to see Tom locked up for years. However, their own lives were hard enough, and instincts of self-preservation soon took over, the memories of those horrific events beginning to fade.

With Liz now in the later stages of pregnancy, by mid-September she could no longer make the journey to Madeley Wood market and so it fell to Abigail to bring the supplies they needed. She was always nervous about going to the market, forever fearful of running into Furlong, particularly when she had had Michael with her. Now that he was safely installed in Bridgnorth with Dick, she felt easier about taking the risk. So it was, that during the second week of September, Abigail set out for Madeley Wood market.

She was feeling quite settled about Michael now, glad that he was out of harm's way in Bridgnorth. She had already bought a few provisions, including some flour, but was astounded at the price of it. The poor harvest had resulted in the cost of flour and bread rocketing. She was just wondering how many more of the things they needed she would be able to afford to buy, when she heard someone call her name. Relieved it was a woman's voice, she spun round to see Dorothea Blake and her husband striding towards her.

First of all, they said how sorry they had been to hear about Michael, who had always seemed to them to be a good lad. Abigail thanked them and confirmed that he was now in Bridgnorth with Dick, and safe from the bad influences he had been subjected to. Dorothea said she was glad she had bumped into Abigail, as she had been hoping to see her. She was in need of a domestic servant to help with the general housework and also to help the cook with preparing and serving meals. She had wondered whether, now Abigail didn't have Michael to look after, she would like to come to Madeley Wood and take the position on offer. The pay would be four shillings a week and her keep.

Abigail didn't know what to say at first, thinking about Liz and wondering what help she may need until after the baby was born. Then it occurred to her that with her mother and sisters living next door in the Coppice, she would have as much support as she needed. Dorothea went on,

'Abigail, if you're not sure, perhaps you'd like to think about it?'

Now sure that Liz would be fine and although she had always thought she would never go back into service, she knew the Blakes were good people and she had been feeling for some time she couldn't stay indefinitely with Joe and Liz, now that their family was growing, and so she said,

'No. Thanks, I am sure. I would like to take up your offer. When would you like me to start?'

'Well, as soon as possible, shall we say Monday week?' Dorothea answered.

Abigail said that would be fine and asked where they lived. Owner Blake explained how she would find the place and they parted company, Abigail thanking them once again for their kind offer.

As she walked back to the Coppice, Abigail was excited that her life was about to change. Since Michael had gone, she had been feeling rather at a loss. She knew she ought to try to earn some money to help support the family if she was to stay with Joe but couldn't think what to do about it. She hadn't wanted to work at the mines or picking coal on the tips, but until now had been determined not to go back into service. This was different though, she told herself. Owner Blake was a decent man, and she would have nothing to fear from him, she was sure.

She was a little apprehensive about telling Liz and Joe, but in the end, they agreed that it was a good move. Joe had always liked Owner Blake and Elizabeth was still friendly with Dorothea, sometimes visiting her on market days, and would no doubt keep an eye on Abigail whenever she did. Furthermore, as they reminded her, it would be easier for Abigail to visit Michael in Bridgnorth as the Oriel usually called in there on its way to Gloucester, and they were sure Owner Blake would be only too happy for her to hitch a ride when convenient.  So it was, that on the last Monday in September, Abigail packed her few belongings, said goodbye to Joe, Liz and Will, and made her way to the Blake's house.

The rain that had ruined much of the harvest had filled the reservoir early and allowed the furnaces to be blown in by the second week of September, and Joe was now back at work. Their second child, a son, was born on the 26$^{th}$ October. He was a fine healthy lad who they named Nathaniel. They were ecstatic, Joe proud he now had a son who would carry on the family name. He loved his daughter Elizabeth dearly, of course, but she would marry eventually, and a son was different, it meant continuity, and also security for Liz when his own time came to leave this life.

Word got around that Fred Williams was to be tried at the Shrewsbury Assize for the murder of his wife. Everyone was interested, but he had never denied it and with the outcome certain, none could see the point in making the journey all the way to Shrewsbury to witness his demise. Joe had offered to be a witness, but the Justice said that as he hadn't actually witnessed the act and also that Fred Williams had confessed, that wouldn't be necessary. So it was, that Mr Ford gave them all the news one cold January morning as they arrived at the Works, that Fred Williams was to go to the gallows that very day. Not one person shed a tear for him.

# Chapter 18

The Works was busier than ever during the winter of 1730 with several orders for steam engine cylinders on the books. There was talk of possibly building a boring mill so that the finishing of the cylinders could be carried out within the Company. Production of domestic items continued apace, with plenty of orders for cooking pots and other cast items for shipping to many markets in cities across the country. Shipments were still being sent across the oceans, through the port of Bristol. Iron wheels were also now being cast for use on the railway used for transporting goods down to the wharf, and raw materials in the other direction. Joe was as proud as ever to be working for the Coalbrookdale Company, taking great pride in the reputation for the quality of the iron their furnaces produced. Of course, he knew that all this progress was coming at a price.

This was very evident as soon as the furnaces were blown out and the smoke and fumes in the air dissipated. During the summer months the sun shone brighter, and the air smelled sweeter, but when autumn came and the furnaces were blown in once more, fumes hung in the air and the sunlight faded, partly blocked out by the tiny particles of soot that floated through the air, landing on the vegetation all around the Dale.

The winter that year was thankfully mild with little snow and frost, although there was plenty of mist and damp hanging around the Gorge, bringing with it the usual bouts of bronchitis among the inhabitants. Christmas was rather strange, with Abigail now away at the Blake's household and rather than coming back to Dale Coppice she went off to visit Michael at Dick's in Bridgnorth. Elizabeth and Arthur didn't visit because they were both suffering from the effects of the damp weather with heavy colds and coughs.

It was at the end of January that Liz noticed young Elizabeth looking rather flushed and she had a slight fever which as always, caused considerable anxiety. All manner of ills began with fever, from smallpox to measles, none of them pleasant and most of them dangerous. After a couple of days her condition worsened, the fever now raging through her body. The family were all distraught, Liz spending every hour she could beside her, sponging her down to assuage the fever and giving her herbal concoctions which she hoped would help her to fight whatever was causing it. The source of the trouble was unclear. No spots or lesions appeared on her skin, but the fever lasted for two more days before the crisis was reached. On the evening of the fifth day, Elizabeth became agitated, tossing her head about and flailing around in the bed. They feared they would lose their little girl, but then, around midnight she suddenly became still, and exhausted, fell into a deep sleep. The fever had broken, the danger had passed. All this time, Liz had been terrified that Nathaniel might catch the fever too, but thankfully he did not. Elizabeth was weakened by her ordeal, but Liz made sure she had plenty of rest and good food, and over the next few months her strength returned.

Will had been paying rather a lot of attention to a young widow, another Elizabeth, a cousin of Liz's, who had moved in with the Spencers after her husband had died in tragic circumstances. He had been working in one of the coalmines when the roof caved in, trapping him and two other men underground. They dug for two days to get the men out, but when they finally reached them, they were all dead, either from their injuries or suffocation. Elizabeth was left with a little boy, George, but with no means of support and was taken in by her uncle and aunt, John and Susan Spencer.

Elizabeth was a pleasant looking young woman, not what you might call beautiful. She had a kindly nature but with a sadness and vulnerability about her that Will found attractive. Since his Sarah had died all those years ago, he had never looked at another woman, but now he began to feel that he could love this quiet, gentle woman. He knew he had much love to give, and Elizabeth certainly seemed as though she needed someone to care for her and her child.

It was early March when he told Joe how he felt, and that he intended to ask Elizabeth to marry him. She would of course, expect to move into the Bangham's cottage with Will, and both the brothers realised this wouldn't be ideal. Will said that perhaps it was time for him to build his own cottage in the coppice. Joe told him not to rush into anything as he had heard that the Darby's intended to build some new houses for the foremen and their families soon, and he was hoping to get one, in which case, Will and Elizabeth would be welcome to stay in his cottage. Now that had been settled, Will started courting Elizabeth, who was always referred to as Betty, in earnest, and was delighted to find that the attraction was mutual. They began to spend more and more time together to the delight of the Spencers and Liz of course, who was very fond of her cousin, and it was in early May that Will proposed and was accepted. The wedding was on the first Sunday in June at the Holy Trinity Church in Buildwas, followed by a wedding feast in the Spencer's cottage.

A couple of weeks later, Liz discovered that she was pregnant again. She and Joe were pleased but realised the cottage would become even more crowded with the arrival of another child. The baby would probably be born in March, Liz told him, and as the time approached, he decided to speak to Mr Ford about the possibility of having one of the new houses once they were built. Joe was a valued worker who had been with the Darby Company for seventeen years and Mr Ford had no hesitation in promising him one of the houses to be constructed on the other side of the valley. However, he said it would be several months yet before they were ready.

In the meantime, both families settled down well together. Liz and Betty, being first cousins and good friends, cheerfully shared the household chores and childminding. As her time approached, Liz was happy to have Betty around to help with the trips to market and the heavier duties around the home. She went into labour in the early hours of 19th March 1731 and by evening she and Joe had another son, whom they called Benjamin.

Elizabeth and Arthur visited the next weekend to see their new nephew, bringing Jane with them. She was thirteen now and growing up fast. Elizabeth told them that Margaret had secured her the position of scullery maid at the Hall, and she was to start the following week. Given Abigail's experience at the Hall, Elizabeth said she had some misgivings, but Margaret had assured her that she would look out for her. After all, Dorothy had worked there for many years, until her marriage to John, without any problems. As the families shared their meal, Joe glanced at Elizabeth and Arthur, noticing that they were both looking older. Of course, he reminded himself, Elizabeth was fifty years old now and Arthur well over fifty, so it wasn't surprising that the years were beginning to take their toll. He would have to keep an eye on them as time went on. They had their own cottage of course, which gave them some security, but if Arthur should become unable to work, they would need some help if they were to avoid Mine Spout poorhouse.

Matters came to a head sooner than Joe expected. It was about a month later that Jimmy turned up in the coppice to let them know that Arthur had suffered an accident while on a trip to Gloucester. It appeared that a heavy container of iron goods had broken loose from the ropes holding it in place as the Oriel had collided with another vessel in the docks and had caught Arthur a glancing blow on his right leg. Everyone agreed that it could have been worse, it could easily have killed him. As it was, his leg was twisted with a nasty broken bone. He was in great pain and the surgeon was sent for. As the other men held him fast, the surgeon had straightened his leg and as Arthur screamed out in agony, placed it in a splint. but at least his leg was saved. Jimmy told them that it looked as though his father would be unable to work for some weeks, and maybe longer, if his leg didn't heal properly.

Joe asked Jimmy to let Elizabeth know that he would come over to Banghams Wood on the following Sunday to see how things were, and to find out what he could do to help them. He fervently hoped that Margaret would be there too. He hadn't seen her for many months and was eager to catch up with her.

So it was, that the following Sunday Joe had gathered what provisions the family could spare and was crossing the Severn in Bert Rogers' coracle on his way to Banghams Wood. As he climbed the steps under Benthall Edge, he mused that it shouldn't really be called Banghams Wood any more as no Banghams now lived there. Elizabeth was a Green since marrying Arthur. Still, he supposed, perhaps it would always be known by the name, as often happened with place names which were frequently retained long after their origins were lost to living memory.

As Joe arrived in the clearing, he saw his sister was feeding the hog, a duty once performed by Martha, but the responsibility now falling to her. It struck him that Elizabeth must miss Martha very much. As she glanced up from tending to the hog, she noticed Joe striding towards her and let out a delighted shout,

'Eee! Our Joe, it's so good to see ye!'

'And you, Liz. I was so sorry to hear about Arthur's accident. How is he?'

'Come in and see for yerself,' she replied, emptying the rest of the hog's food into the trough, then leading Joe into the cottage.

Arthur was seated on the settle by the fire with his leg raised on a stool for comfort.

'Joe!' he declared, 'Thanks for coming over. This is a poor do and no mistake. Looks like it's going to be weeks before I'm fit for work again.'

'So I heard Arthur. Well, I've come over to see if there's anything I can do to help out.'

'Well, I won't deny that it will be a struggle Joe, but we still have Jimmy's wages and the rent from my cottage coming in.'

'And,' interjected Elizabeth, 'I do have a bit put by, so if it is only six weeks or so before Arthur can get back to work, we should be able to manage.'

'Well,' said Joe, 'Liz has sent a few things to help out right now, and I'll get over again in a couple of weeks with whatever we can spare.'

'Thanks Joe, we won't forget it,' Elizabeth said, then went on, 'Our Margaret should be here within the hour, and she may bring a few bits from the Hall, as she usually does.'

Joe said he was glad Margaret was coming, he hadn't seen her for months and was eager to hear her news. He was wondering whether she had heard anything about Michael. The horseman at the Hall may well have news of him as he would be regularly visiting Andrews Grain Merchants.

Elizabeth said she had seen Abigail when she last visited the Blake's and she seemed to have settled in well. She had been down to Bridgnorth for a couple of days after Christmas, and said she was pleased and proud that Michael, now fifteen, was growing into a fine young man. However, she had been rather worried that he seemed determined to find out about his father and had asked her again why the man with red hair had said he was his son.

'That's a tricky one,' said Joe, sitting down on a stool by the side of the fire.

'It is,' Elizabeth replied. 'Michael's no fool, and if she isn't honest with him about what happened, he won't rest until he finds out in some other way. God forbid, he may even approach Furlong directly. On the other hand, if she does tell him herself, goodness knows how he would take the news that his father had forced himself upon her. I'm glad it's not my decision to make.'

'Definitely! That's up to Abigail.'

'Anyway, here I am nattering away and I haven't even offered you a drink of ale Joe.'

'Thanks Liz I don't mind if I do.'

At that moment the doorlatch rattled and Margaret walked in, flushed and a little breathless from the walk down from the Estate. Joe was shocked that she also was looking older. That's inevitable, he thought to himself, she's probably thinking the same about me. He stood up quickly and went to embrace her. When he hugged her, she felt a little thinner than he remembered, which rather alarmed him.

'Margaret, it's so good to see you. I was hoping you'd be here today.'

'It's good to see you too Joe. No doubt like you, having heard about Arthur I've come to see if there's anything I can do to help.' she replied, handing Elizabeth the basket of food which Cook had sent, it being surplus to requirements at the Hall.

'You're all so kind,' said Elizabeth, a little overcome by their assurances of help. Since they had brought Arthur home on the stretcher three days ago, she had been at her wit's end, worrying how they would manage. Of course, she hadn't said anything to Arthur, who felt badly enough about it already. With her two siblings being here promising their support, she began to feel that they would, after all, be able to survive without going to the Parish, which she dreaded having to do.

'So, our Margaret,' Joe began, 'how are things up at the Hall.'

'Much the same as ever Joe. Young Jane seems to have settled in, although I think she is a little homesick and I do my best to keep an eye on her Elizabeth.'

'I know you do, Margaret,' Elizabeth replied, 'and I'm grateful. I do worry about her.'

'Dorothy and John seem happy enough,' Margaret went on, 'He still visits the Hall once a week to instruct the children as the mistress doesn't want them mixing with the Charity School youngsters. Apparently when he is up at the Hall, Dorothy teaches reading and writing to the schoolchildren and he says she has made an excellent teacher, which is no surprise to any of us, I'm sure.'

'I'm so glad Margaret.' Joe asserted. 'Yes, we all knew she would go far. And what about Dick? Have you visited Bridgnorth yet? He's certainly gone up in the world. Who would have thought a Bangham would have become such a well-respected merchant? Still, I don't begrudge him any of it and he certainly made the most of his new-found status when he rescued Michael from gaol. You should have heard him in Court

Margaret. It took some courage to stand up in front of the judges and successfully plead Michael's case.'

'I know, I wish I had been there Joe. I haven't been over to Bridgnorth yet, but I must make the effort. I could ride over there with Fred, the horseman, any time, I'm sure the mistress would give me a day off. You know, of course that they had a little boy, Richard, a year ago?'

'No, I didn't. To be honest Margaret, I don't get time to visit anyone these days, what with being so busy at the furnace. Still, it's good to know they're getting on with building their family. They'll be lucky children, that family will surely prosper and so will they.'

'Aye, that's true enough Joe,' Margaret agreed.

All this while Elizabeth had been busy preparing their meal and now served up the vegetable stew. It wasn't lost on Joe and Margaret that it contained no meat, reminding them that the Greens would certainly need some support over the next few weeks. The family continued to chat over their meal and then Joe asked if there were any jobs he could do, that Arthur would normally have dealt with.

Elizabeth assured him that Jimmy had been very good, stepping into his father's shoes when necessary. Just at that moment, right on cue, he walked in carrying an armful of kindling he had been gathering in the woods and placed them by the fire.

'Come on now lad,' Elizabeth said, ladling some stew onto a plate. 'Get this down you.'

'Thanks Ma,' he replied, 'I'm ready for it.'

Jimmy was now eighteen and a fine young man. He had served out his apprenticeship with Bert Rogers and was now building his own coracles, selling them from a hut he and Arthur had built by Bower's shipbuilding yard down by the Severn. He was beginning to make some money out of it, as with all the newcomers arriving in the Gorge over the last few years, there was plenty of demand. However, as yet he was quite slow at making them, wanting to gain a reputation for quality instilled in him by Bert, and wasn't making as much money as he might.

After an hour or so, Margaret noticed the light was fading and said she had better be getting back to the Hall. Joe offered to walk with her up to the Estate gate, and they bade farewell to Arthur, Elizabeth and Jimmy, promising to come back as often as they could. Joe said Will would probably be over the following week and he would send them some money and food to help out. Elizabeth and Arthur both said how grateful they were.

As Joe was walking arm in arm along the lane with his sister, he asked,

'And what about you, our Margaret? How are you?'

'Oh, you know me our Joe, I'm fine. It's not such a bad life, you know. I sometimes just wish I could have married and had children of my own, but that wasn't to be.'

Joe had never heard her speak like this before, with that note of regret in her voice. He didn't know what to say. She looked so sad at that moment that Joe's heart went out to her and when they had reached the gate, he gave her an extra special hug to let her know how loved she was, even if she didn't have a family of her own.

# Chapter 19

Over the next few weeks, Joe and the family were good as their word, making sure Elizabeth and Arthur were able to manage financially, one or other of them visiting regularly. It was in fact about eight weeks before Arthur was able to return to work. His leg was fully healed although still rather weak and painful, but he didn't allow himself the luxury of further convalescence, being determined to start bringing money into the home again as soon as possible, and he sent Jimmy over to the Blake's to say that he was fit for work. Owner Blake said he was glad, and that he could join the next trip downriver, which was due to leave the Gorge on the following Monday morning.

Whilst at the Blake's house, Jimmy saw Abigail, who told him that she also was going down to Bridgnorth on the Oriel. As she hadn't had any days off for several months, Dorothea had agreed for her to take a few days to visit her son, her intention being to then re-join the Oriel on its return trip from Gloucester. Abigail asked Jimmy to let Elizabeth know that she was going down to sort things out with Michael once and for all. When Jimmy gave her the message, Elizabeth knew exactly what it meant and she was pleased that Abigail was determined to explain things to Michael, but also rather fearful of what consequences might follow. He was apparently doing well in Bridgnorth, and she hoped the news wouldn't knock him off course.

When Monday morning came, Owner Blake told Abigail he was going down to the wharf in the pony and trap as he needed to speak to the crew of the Oriel before it set sail, and he would be happy to take her down with him. Abigail gladly accepted his kind offer. She had managed to amass a few things for Michael from the market and packed them along with a few clothes in the old leather bag that Dorothea had lent her. She now sat with it on her knee, beside Owner Blake as they made their way down the Gorge to the Wharf where the Oriel was tied up.

It was early autumn and the trees on the thickly wooded slopes of the Severn Gorge had turned to golden red. Abigail thought she had never seen them looking so beautiful. She was excited at taking the trip down the Severn, but even more excited, if a little apprehensive, at seeing her son again. She knew it was time to tell him about his father and how he had been conceived. He had to know. There was no way to deny the connection between him and Furlong, given their features and red hair and she knew that if she didn't tell him soon, Michael would take matters into his own hands and confront him directly. All these thoughts were running through her head as they arrived at the Wharf.

She saw Arthur standing beside the trow and raised her hand in greeting. She thanked Owner Blake for his kindness as he stepped down from the trap, handing the reins to one of his men from the Oriel. As Arthur stepped forward, he asked how he was feeling now. Arthur said he was fully recovered and thanked him for agreeing to his return to work. Owner Blake then turned away to speak to Tom Blythe, the captain of the Oriel, handing him some documents and giving him various instructions about the journey ahead regarding the cargo and how it was to be handled.

Arthur helped Abigail down from the trap, handing her a small bundle Elizabeth had sent, telling her it contained a jacket Margaret had passed on, from the Hall. It was too small for Jimmy but should fit Michael and it was, he said, a good one, far too good to go to waste. He took Abigail's bag and led her up the gangplank onto the Oriel, settling her down in one corner of the deck, for her journey down to Bridgnorth.

The loading of the Oriel was completed within the hour and they were sailing South by mid-morning. By mid-day they were tied up in Bridgnorth and Abigail said farewell to Arthur as he helped her down the gangplank onto the wharf. She stood for some moments, a little unsure which way to go. She had never walked from the wharf to Dick's house, having only been carried there in the pony and trap before. As

Dick didn't know she was coming, there was no one to meet her. She asked one of the men on the dock the way to Andrews Grain Merchants, as she expected that both Dick and Michael would in any case be at the business premises.

After about ten minutes, as she rounded the corner of the main street it came into view. Although Abigail couldn't read the sign, it was obviously a business selling sacks of feed and grain, and various farming and horse-related items were suspended from nails along the wall, above the window of the shop premises. Next to the shop there was a large open archway, wide enough to allow the passage of wagons, which led into an internal courtyard.

Abigail stepped inside the shop, causing the large bell above the door to spring into life. A smell of leather, mingled with the earthy smell of grain and animal feed, enveloped Abigail as she stood nervously by the counter, waiting for the arrival of someone answering the call of the shop bell. After a few moments a young woman appeared through the door behind the counter and, smiling, asked Abigail what she could do for her. Abigail enquired whether Mr Dick Bangham, or Michael Bangham were in the building. Looking Abigail up and down, the girl said in an offhand way, that they were both there, and if she would give her name, she would enquire whether they were able to see her. When Abigail told her that she was Abigail Bangham, sister to Mr Dick, the girl became rather more focussed and said if Abigail would care to take a seat on the bench under the window, she would find them at once.

The girl disappeared and after a few minutes, Abigail could hear the sound of footsteps quickly descending the stairs beyond the door, and Dick bounded into the shop. He was obviously delighted to see Abigail standing there and told her so as he embraced her. He said he was sorry she'd had to walk from the wharf, but obviously, he hadn't known she was coming.

Abigail said it was fine and she had found her way easily enough.

'Michael will be delighted to see you Abigail,' he said, 'come with me and we'll see where he's got to.'

Abigail followed him into the back of the shop and down a narrow corridor before eventually emerging into the courtyard, where they immediately saw Michael in the far corner, stacking sacks of grain. Dick called to him and as he looked up and spotted his mother, his face broke into a wide grin. He tossed the sack he was holding onto the pile in front of him. Each time she visited, Abigail was amazed at how much he had grown, and today was no exception. He was almost as tall as Dick and looked as strong as any of the men working in the yard. Abigail swelled with pride as she watched him striding towards her, his face beaming.

He embraced his mother, obviously delighted to see her, and Abigail held him close for a moment or two.

Eventually they parted, but Michael held on to her hand saying,

'Mother! I didn't know you were coming. Are you staying for long?'

'Well,' said Abigail, 'I can stay until the Oriel returns from Gloucester in four days' time if Uncle Dick and Aunt Margaret will allow me.'

'Of course you can Abigail,' Dick interjected, 'Margaret will be delighted to see you.'

Then Dick turned to Michael, smiled and said,

'Take your mother up to the house Michael, and you can take the rest of the day off and spend it with her.'

'Are you sure Uncle?' Michael replied, 'There's still a lot of work to do here.'

'Don't worry,' his uncle asserted, grinning, 'You can make up the time later in the week if you really want to!'

With that, Michael picked up his mother's bag and she took his arm as they made their way along the street to the steps leading up towards the main part of the town, which had been built on a rocky outcrop some hundred feet or so above the River Severn. About ten minutes later they had arrived at the Bangham's house, Abigail being no less impressed with it than she had been that first day she had arrived to visit Michael in the gaol. She shivered at the recollection of that dreadful time, but when she thought about her current mission, she felt almost as much horror. What would this day bring, she wondered. She was determined to speak to Michael as soon as possible, to give him plenty of time to talk to her about matters before she would have to leave him again.

Margaret made a great fuss as she opened the front door in answer to the ring of the large cast iron doorbell as it responded to the pull of the chain that hung beneath it.

'Abigail!' she exclaimed. 'How lovely to see you!' adding 'I wish I had known you were coming. I would have met you at the wharf with the trap. I'm assuming you came down on the Oriel?'

'I did,' Abigail replied. 'I was wondering if I could stay with you for a few days, until the Oriel returns from Gloucester?'

'Of course, we'd be delighted to have you! Come on in, please!' Margaret declared.

'Uncle Dick told me I could take the rest of the day off to spend with mother,' Michael told Margaret.

'Of course, that's a splendid idea,' she replied, then asked him to take Abigail's things up to the spare bedroom on the first floor. Abigail followed him and after she had unpacked her bag, gave him the jacket that Elizabeth had sent, which he seemed pleased with, and went off to take it up to his room. Abigail washed her hands and face and brushed her hair, then returned to the drawing room where Margaret was waiting for her with her son Richard, sitting on her lap. Abigail made a fuss of the child, who had his father's looks but his mother's thick brown hair.

Margaret rang the bell pull beside the fireplace and

a few moments later the parlour maid appeared. Margaret instructed her to bring the ginger wine and two glasses, and then to prepare some lunch for them all. Abigail was overwhelmed once more with the affluence of her brother's home, but at the same time, felt privileged to be there. It was a source of pride to her that her own brother should have risen so far in the world. She told Margaret that if she didn't mind, after lunch she would like to spend some time alone with Michael as she had something she needed to discuss with him. Margaret, having some idea what that may be about, suggested that perhaps they might go for a walk along the clifftop path which passed in front of the house.

When Michael returned Abigail was sipping the wine, conversing easily with Margaret and looking very much at home in the comfortable drawing room. Young Richard immediately jumped down from his mother's knee and ran up to Michael who immediately picked him up and started to tickle him. Abigail was pleased to see that the child obviously thought the world of his cousin Michael. The parlour maid had now set out a light lunch for them all in the dining room and entered the room to inform her mistress that it was ready. They enjoyed a meal of broth and bread and then, after thanking Margaret, Abigail got up, saying to Michael that she would like him to join her on a walk along the clifftop, as she would like to admire the view of the River Severn far below. He readily agreed. It was his favourite walk, he told her.

Half an hour later they were sitting on a rock beside the clifftop path, looking down on the River, a view that Michael never tired of. It always reminded him of home as he watched the river flowing on its endless journey. Abigail was nervous. She knew she had to do this, to tell Michael about his father and what had happened to her all those years ago. She had to do it for Michael. In fact, she couldn't have done it for anyone else. She had never spoken to anyone about what had actually happened that night, but now she must. Michael mustn't be kept in ignorance about what kind of a man his father was. He must never be allowed to think he was a good man who he might feel he wanted to emulate. She couldn't risk him wanting to get to know him. She knew that James Furlong could easily have convinced the lad that what had happened was her fault, and she couldn't let that happen.

After five minutes Michael himself broke the silence.

'Mother,' he said, in a tone suggesting that something important was to follow. 'Mother,' he repeated. 'I have asked you this before, but..'

Abigail's palms suddenly grew damp and her stomach churned as she realised what was coming.

'I need you to tell me the truth. Who was that man we saw at Madeley Wood market all those years ago? He said I was his son, and his hair was like mine. I have never seen anyone else with hair like mine, so you must tell me now, is he my father?'

Abigail sat for some moments, not speaking, but

with her mind racing. She had practised this so many times over the years. She had always known the moment would come when she could no longer avoid telling him the truth, and she knew that moment had now arrived.

Finally, she managed, 'Michael, you are right, it is time you knew the truth.'

Michael sat forward, eager to hear what she had to say to him. Finally, after seven years, he hoped he was going to find out who his father was.

Abigail looked into his eyes and said,

'I'm going to tell you exactly what happened Michael, and it may not be what you want to hear, but I believe you are now old enough to understand, and I hope you will not judge me harshly.

'I was just fifteen years old, working at the Hall as the scullery maid. The man you saw at the market is James Furlong and he is the under-butler at the Hall. I knew nothing of the world, never having left Banghams Wood before the day I was sent up to the Hall. I was determined to do my best and worked hard. I had noticed James Furlong observing me sometimes and smiling at me, but I just thought he was being friendly and smiled back. You will never know how often I regretted ever smiling at him.

'Anyway, it was about six months after I entered service that one night as I was sleeping in my room in the attic, I was woken up with someone's hand across my mouth. I was very afraid as I didn't know who it was. I hope I don't need to go into detail about what followed in the next five minutes. I was terrified and thought he might harm me if I resisted and so I did not.'

Michael looked horrified.

'What are you saying mother. Did he force himself upon you?'

'Yes, Michael, he did. Afterwards he ignored me completely and I began to think it must have been my fault. I had smiled at him, and in my innocence, concluded that must have been why he did that to me. It was some weeks later that I realised that I was carrying you. I never told him because I didn't want him to have anything to do with you. I had to leave service to return to Banghams Wood, then when Uncle Joe built his house in Dale Coppice, we went to live with him there. I had hoped that you would never see him, and therefore never need to know the truth about how you were conceived.'

Michael was silent, obviously struggling to process the information she'd just given him. After some minutes, he stood up, and without a word, ran along the clifftop path, back the way they had come, leaving Abigail distraught. She realised he would need time and space to process what she had just told him, but as he hadn't indicated how he was feeling, she was terrified that he would be blaming her, thinking that maybe she had been too easy with her favours. She couldn't bear the thought of him thinking badly of her or losing respect for her. She sat for a full hour, completely unable to decide whether she should follow him back to the house and try to talk to him or leave him alone to ponder over what she had just told him.

Michael was in a state of utter confusion. He had waited so long to find out who his father was. It had recently become something of an obsession. As he was becoming a man, he needed to know what kind of a man had given him life. He needed to understand where he had come from. There had always been a void in his life where a father should have stood. His uncles had been kind and tried to be a father to him, in their different ways, but it wasn't the same. He had never felt a father's love, never been able to walk in his shoes. There were things he couldn't talk to his mother about, things only a father could understand, and he wasn't close enough to any of his uncles to confide in them in the same way.

Now he knew that his father, the man who should have been part of his life from the beginning, had never wanted him and he had only been conceived as an unwanted by-product of a selfish, evil act perpetrated on his mother. This was challenging his own view of himself. Was he like this man who had taken his pleasure from his mother against her will. From his position of power, he had violated an innocent, vulnerable girl, which was unforgiveable. He was his son, even looked like him, perhaps he was like him in other ways? He thought about the poaching affair. He had tried to forget about it as he was deeply ashamed of letting his mother down. Now it occurred to him that maybe he had a weakness in his character inherited from his father, a selfishness that had led him to ignore the hurt he may cause his mother, just to gratify his own selfish wish for excitement.

Then he thought of Miranda and was even more confused. She was the girl who worked in the shop, and he was finding it hard not to think about her. She was a pretty girl with plenty of spirit and every time he saw her, he had the urge to kiss her and hold her close. Such thoughts now seemed dangerous, even disgusting. Was this how his father had felt, and is that what led him to do what he did?

He had run into the house by the back door and past cook without speaking to her, going immediately up to his attic room. He needed to think. And yet, he didn't want to think. He wished his mother had never told him. He wished he could still imagine that his father was a good man. He would rather he had been a kind, dead man, than an evil one who was still living. At least then he would not have had to make the decision whether or not to meet him. He knew deep down that even though he was, in this respect, evil, he would still need to find out more about him if he was to understand more about himself. He also knew that this would hurt his mother deeply. She would not un-derstand his need to know more about this man, and may see it as a betrayal, or worse, that he blamed her for what had happened, which of course, he did not.

His mother! As he lay on his bed, another, even more disturbing thought came into his head. When she looked at him, did she see his father? Each time she had looked at him, smiled at him, hugged him close, had she been reminded of that night? How could she love him, being the product of an act, which had brought her shame and ruin? A deep pain rose from the pit of his stomach, and a feeling of dread engulfed him. Could the love that had surrounded him all his life be an illusion? If each time she looked at him brought her pain, how could she also love him? Was this one reason why she had sent him to Bridgnorth, so that she need no longer be reminded of how he came into existence. Now the tears began to flow. He thumped his pillow in a mixture of fear and anger.

Meanwhile, Abigail was utterly distraught, but not altogether surprised, at Michael's reaction to her news. She was afraid she was about to lose her son. Would he understand? Would he blame her for what had happened? Could their close relationship survive this? She knew it would inevitably be changed. It could no longer be that of mother and child. To understand and accept her after this revelation, Michael would have to grow up somewhat and come to realise that his mother was, after all, just a human being with feelings of her own, and not some kind of superior being whose sole purpose in life was to love and cherish him. At the same time, he would have to deal with the knowledge that his father was a selfish, cruel man who took what he wanted without thought for his victims, and Abigail was sure she hadn't been the only one. All these thoughts were going through her mind as she made her way back along the clifftop path to the house.

As she arrived, Dick was also approaching the gate from the opposite direction, on his way home from the business. As soon as she saw him, the emotions she had kept in check throughout the afternoon, came tumbling out, and she fell into his arms, weeping and saying,

'Oh Dick, I know I had to tell him, but it was so hard and then he just ran off without a word. What shall I do if he wants nothing more to do with me?'

Dick knew immediately what she meant.

'You did the right thing Abigail. The lad needed to know the truth, however painful. Give him time. He's a bright lad and he'll work it out for himself. It's a lot for him to come to terms with. If you like, I'll have a word with him. He may need someone to help him to think it through. I won't force him to listen, just let him know I'm here if he needs to talk.'

'Thank you so much Dick,' Abigail managed through her tears, and began to calm down, reassured that Dick would be there for Michael as he wrestled with his feelings.

Michael didn't come down for supper that night. He couldn't face his mother yet. He couldn't bear to see the rejection in her eyes that he was now convinced would appear. She now knew that he was aware that she had been shamed and humiliated when he was conceived. There was, after all, no more possibility of sustaining the illusion. She must either love him for himself or hate him for being the object of her shame. He wasn't yet ready to find out which.

When the rest of the family had eaten, Margaret took some food and drink up to his room, knocking quietly on the door before entering. Her heart went out to him as she saw his tear-stained face and look of deep sadness in his eyes. She lit his candle and placed the tray of food beside the bed, before urging him to eat it, then quietly left without waiting for a reply. He couldn't face eating the food and eventually fell into a troubled sleep filled with disturbing images of a man with red hair but whose face was blank.

He woke early next morning and was out of the house before Abigail came down to breakfast, still not able to face her. He threw himself into his work, trying not to talk to anyone, his mind still full of doubts, about himself, his mother and yes, his father and how much of his own character he'd inherited from him. He avoided Miranda all day. Right now, he could do without those disturbing feelings.

For her part, Abigail had hardly slept, convinced her son must think less of her, even be ashamed of her, after what she had told him. She wouldn't blame him. She had been ashamed of herself for a long time after it happened, convinced that she must have led Furlong on. Of course, she had long realised that as the innocent child she had been, it wasn't her fault he had decided to satisfy his urges at her expense. Maybe Michael would come to realise that too, she thought.

Dick had observed Michael during the day, seeing that he was just getting on with his work and avoiding speaking to anyone. By mid-afternoon, he decided to try to speak to him about what he was going through, and called to him to come up to his office above the shop. As Michael entered the passage to go up to the office, Miranda was coming the other way. Normally he would have smiled at her and said hello, but now he passed her with his head down and never even looked up, nor did he speak, even though she greeted him with her usual cheery 'Hello Michael!'.

He knocked on the office door and heard Dick tell him to enter. His uncle was sitting behind his desk, smiling at him.

'You wanted to see me, Uncle?' he enquired.

'Sit down, please, Michael.' Dick said, gesturing to the chair in front of the desk, then went on, 'I know your mother has given you some news that has upset you,' he began.

Before he could say anything else, Michael looked him in the eye and then asked,

'You mean, you know? Does everyone? Does the whole world know I came about in this way?'

'Michael, look, I understand how you must feel, but ...'

'Do you? How can you Uncle? My whole life has been a lie, my existence a source of pain and shame to those I love. It would have been better if I'd never been born!'

'Michael,' Dick said with an air of authority now. 'You must never say that or even think it. Your mother loves you, has always loved you since the moment she first held you in her arms. We all have and will always love you. How you came into existence will never change that.'

'How can she though Uncle? How can she look at me and not think about him and what he did to her?'

'Because, Michael,' Dick answered with his voice full of conviction, 'love is stronger than hate.'

At this, a glimmer of hope entered Michael's mind. Could this be true? Could a mother's love overcome hatred? He thought about that love. She had struggled to be father and mother to him, had sacrificed her own ambitions to the responsibilities of raising him, clothing and feeding him, sometimes at the expense of satisfying her own needs. Even when he had let her down by getting involved in the poaching business, she had stood by him.

The few words his uncle had uttered – 'love is stronger than hate' had resonated with something within him and he knew he was right. By her every action throughout his life, his mother had shown him that she did love him, and suddenly he was ashamed he had ever doubted it.

Dick said nothing, just sitting quietly, wisely letting the lad work it out for himself. Eventually, Michael spoke,

'Do you think I could take the rest of the afternoon off uncle, I really need to speak with mother. I think I owe her an apology.'

Dick smiled and said, 'Of course lad, you get yourself away to your mother.'

With that, Michael quickly left and ran all the way up the steps and along the lane to the house, seeing Abigail sitting quietly by the window in the drawing room. She looked up as he approached, and he smiled at her. She smiled back with some relief. As he entered the drawing room she stood up and faced him. He went to her and embraced her, saying,

'Mother, I'm so sorry!'

'What on earth do you have to be sorry for?' she asked.

'For ever doubting that you love me. I couldn't believe that you could, after what happened.'

'My dear boy, that was never in doubt. You are my son, my son alone, no-one else's, and I love you more than life itself.'

With that, mother and son embraced, clinging to each other for some moments, each afraid to let the other go in case anything else should come between. Abigail spent another couple of days with Michael in Bridgnorth and as she was boarding the Oriel to leave, he assured her he wouldn't be seeking James Furlong out. He now had no desire to get to know the man. He couldn't help being a little curious about him, but his disgust at what he'd done had negated any residual desire he may have had to get to know him.

Abigail felt closer to her son than ever before. She knew now she had been right to tell him, ensuring the one threat to their relationship had been removed. Michael, for his part, felt more 'whole' than he had ever felt. The void that had been the place where a father should have been, wasn't exactly filled, but at least he knew he need no longer go on searching for answers, and that brought him some peace. He also understood his mother better and felt an overwhelming desire to care for her and to make sure that her life from now on would be easier. He waved to her as the Oriel drew away from the dock, swearing to himself that once he was earning enough to have a home of his own, he would insist that she give up her life in service and come to live with him. He would make sure she never wanted for anything, ever again.

# Chapter 20

The next couple of years in Dale Coppice passed by without major incident. Will and Betty had remained lodging with Joe and Liz, an arrangement that suited them all well enough. However, with Will and Betty now expecting their first child together, and Liz pregnant again, the baby due in December 1733, the cottage certainly began to feel rather too small for them all, soon to be ten in number.

Abigail was still in service with the Blakes although she had told Joe and Will of Michael's plan to have her move over to Bridgnorth to live with him as soon as he could get his own place. In any case, Dick and Margaret were expecting their third child, and they would be needing the space for their own family, Michael told his mother. He was eighteen now and had completed his apprenticeship. Apparently, Dick wanted him to stay on at the firm as stock manager, when he would be earning a decent wage. Consequently, she was hoping to be moving to Bridgnorth within the year. Joe and the others were pleased for her, they felt she deserved to be looked after for a change. Of course, with this news, Joe felt that his duty to look after Abigail was at an end and he was free to move his family out of Dale Coppice.

So, it was decided that Joe would enquire again about a company house. The building of a row that had been talked about a couple of years earlier hadn't materialised, but now he had heard that Mr Ford was about to lease a row of cottages near the new furnace at Dale End, known as Nailer's Row. Joe had now worked for the company for twenty years and he knew he was a valuable employee, with much skill and experience. Consequently, he believed he would stand a good chance of being given the tenancy of one of the two bedroomed houses. He spoke to Mr Ford as soon as the opportunity arose, who didn't hesitate in telling Joe that he would be pleased to let him lease one of the houses, for as long as he worked for the company. Joe thanked him and hurried home to give the others the good news.

June 1733 found the family preparing to move. Liz was happy to be getting one of the houses. A brick-built house with two sizeable bedrooms upstairs and a living room and a scullery on the ground floor, seemed like a 'step up' for the family. In addition, she was pleased to be moving her children away from the Coppice. Far too many rough sorts had continued to move in over the last few years. She was sorry to be moving away from her parents, as they weren't getting any younger. However, her sister was still living at home and Betty and Will would still be next door.

It was decided they would make the move as soon as the furnace was blown out, probably at the end of June. It was actually during the first week in July that the family's belongings were piled on a cart, borrowed from one of the wagoners who transported goods to and from the wharf. The Spencers were genuinely sorry to see them leave. Joe and John had become firm friends over the years, and of course, the Spencers would rather their daughter remained in the coppice. Liz reassured them that she would be only ten minutes' walk away down the hill and would still see them often.

Will and Betty, now heavily pregnant, were looking forward to having the place to themselves. They had agreed to rent the cottage from Joe at a nominal rent of a shilling a week. They thanked him for all his help, and Will offered to go with the family to help unload the wagon when they arrived at the cottage in Nailer's Row.

The wagon was piled high with their possessions, with Liz and the children perched on top. Will and Joe walked behind as they slowly made their way down the cobbled Dale Road towards the river. Nailer's Row was about two thirds of the way towards the Severn, standing to the right-hand side of the road. As always, there were other wagons coming and going to and from the river and the works. As they pulled up at the house, Liz reminded herself they would have to keep an eye on the children, as the houses had no front gardens and the doors opened straight onto the roadway.

Furthermore, they were closer to one source of fumes and smoke as the new furnace was only a hundred yards or so further up the valley. With Joe's help, she clambered down off the wagon with Benjamin in her arms. Young Elizabeth climbed down behind her, helping Nathaniel to do the same.

When they entered the house, it seemed spacious. The living room was about twelve feet square with a cast iron fireplace with an oven beside the grate. Beyond the door at the back of the room was a narrow passage leading through to the scullery and washhouse. Beside the door to the washhouse, stairs ran up to the bedrooms. The front bedroom, being over the living room, had similar proportions and a small fireplace. The back bedroom was smaller, but Liz felt it was of ample size for the children.  Looking out of the back bedroom window, onto the communal area she was disappointed to see only one privvy to one end of the space. She had thought they would have their own private privvy but it was obvious that it was to be used by the residents of all five houses. Still, over-all, she was pleased enough with the house, which seemed well built with higher ceilings and larger windows than she had been used to. She felt she would be able to make a good home here for the family, one they could be proud of.

Joe and Will soon had their possessions unloaded. They were pretty basic after all. They had left quite a few pieces for Will and Betty, Joe saying that he would soon be buying or making new furniture for their new home. They had brought their beds of course, and the old trunk, along with the settle and a couple of stools.

Over the next few weeks Joe and Liz worked hard to make their new home comfortable. They managed to pick up a few pieces of second-hand furniture and Liz made curtains for the windows. Life was rather different than it had been in Dale Coppice. As the vegetable plot Liz had been cultivating for years was left behind in the coppice, she had to start all over again with a new patch, which would take some time to establish. In the meantime, Joe brought some provisions from the plot in Dale Coppice whenever he could. There was no communal pump as there had been in the Coppice, and twice a day she had to carry water from the spring several minutes' walk away up the road towards the works. Also, as she had suspected, Liz had to pay rather more attention to the children now that they were living on the main road. No longer could she allow them to go outside alone, to explore the woods around the cottage or collect kindling for the fire. There was more or less constant noise as the wagons trundled up and down the cobbles and the hammering of the forges and noises from the foundry further up the valley resounded day and night. Still, Liz and Joe were pleased with the house itself and particularly with the privacy it gave them.

Betty went into labour on 20th August 1733. Her labour was quick and reasonably easy and by eleven o'clock that night she had given birth to a healthy little boy, who they named Walter. A week later Joe and his family visited the coppice to greet the new baby and Susan Spencer had prepared a meal for them all in their cottage. Liz was happy to visit her parents and to catch up with everyone's news. Will said he'd been over to Banghams Wood to see Elizabeth the week before. Arthur had been away downriver but as it happened, Margaret had also been visiting. He said Margaret had looked rather thin and drawn and he was worried about her, but apparently young Jane was doing well, and was now a kitchen maid.

Later, as the family were returning to Nailer's Row, Elizabeth and Nathaniel walked in front holding hands, Liz and Joe, who was carrying Benjamin followed them down to Dale End. It was a lovely evening and the Dale looked particularly beautiful, with the late summer sun sinking in the West, throwing its golden light along the Gorge. He could see Banghams Wood in the distance and wondered how his sister and her family were faring.

Joe himself though, was content. He was proud of his little family, and the home he had now provided for them. Elizabeth, now nine years old was a bonny, bright girl with golden curls just like her mother, and she doted on four-year-old Nathaniel who was dark like his father. They were rarely apart, and he adored his big sister. Benjamin was two and a half and beginning to chatter in that delightful way two-year-olds do. Joe looked at Liz as they strolled down the lane and smiled. She glanced across and smiled back, saying

'What? What's so funny?'

'Nothing,' Joe replied. 'Just that I love you, Liz.'

'I know.' she said. 'I love you too,' and right then, life was good for this Bangham family. Of course, life was not always predictable, and the following months were to bring even more change to the lives of Joe and his family.

The summer had been dry, and it wasn't until mid-September that the pools were full enough for the furnaces to be blown in, but Joe and a few of the men had been busy for a week or so beforehand, preparing to restart production. Mr Ford had told him they were going to try a new formula in the furnace, using coal from a new source. This coal he told Joe, should produce a better grade of iron, which might be more suitable for making wrought iron. Heaps of the new coal had been slow burning over the summer break and were now cooling, ready for the coke to be transported to the top of the furnace to be added to the limestone and iron ore. It took a couple of days to load up the platform with the raw materials that would be needed.

The furnace was lit and the sluice from the pool high above was opened, allowing the water to flow and turn the wheel to drive the bellows, and the furnace was charged using the proportions of material specified by Mr Ford. Within a few hours the furnace was roaring, and within a few more it was time to draw off the first of the iron by knocking out the clay plug at the base of the furnace. Joe was always a little nervous as the first iron of the season began to pour out of the orange mouth, sparks flying everywhere. He was particularly apprehensive because the proportions of ingredients had been changed. The intensity of the heat was always shocking and however many times he witnessed it, a certain level of fear gripped Joe. Ever since he had witnessed the accident when one of the men lost his arm, he had known what damage the molten metal could do to a human body.

On this particular day, Billy Owens, a young man who had been working for the company for several years, and was one of the most experienced workers, was on shift. Knowing that Billy was competent, Joe gave him the job of knocking out the clay plug at the base of the furnace to allow the molten metal to flow.

'Right oh, Joe,' Billy said, and picked up the sledge-hammer, preparing to strike the plug. He swung the hammer and struck the plug, expecting that it would release a steady flow of molten iron into the trench below. However, whether it was because of the new formulation, or just a horrendous combination of circumstance, as the plug fell away, the metal didn't flow downwards, but shot outwards, hitting Billy full in the chest. As it bit into his flesh he screamed in agony. Joe quickly grabbed Billy, pulling him away from the metal, now pooling on the floor.

As soon as Joe was able to take a good look at Billy, he could see it was hopeless. The metal had cut across the middle of Billy's body, biting into his flesh, almost cutting him in two. The young man died almost instantly, and Joe realised it was a blessed relief that he did. The other men rushed over to where Billy lay. To their horror they could see that the lad was already dead. Mr Ford had arrived and told them to bring the handcart and in shocked silence the men loaded Billy's body onto it and took him home to his widowed mother, who was living in a cottage in Dale Coppice.

Joe was distraught. He blamed himself, as he had given Billy the job of unplugging the furnace. Maybe changing the formula had caused gas pressures to build up within the iron? He told himself he should have been aware that it might behave differently and maybe as foreman, he should have done the job himself. Logically, this was just an unforeseeable accident and Joe knew that, but it did nothing to assuage his feelings of guilt. He had gone with the men as they wheeled the body to Mrs Owens, and the sound of her wailing as she saw her son, continued to ring in his ears long after that terrible day. She was a widow, her husband having died in a mining accident some years before and Billy had been her only means of support. Joe knew she might now be destitute and could well end up in Mine Spout poorhouse. As it was, Mr Ford, being a good and honourable man and because Billy had died at work, paid for the funeral, and made provision for Mrs Owens so that she was able to live out her days in her home in the coppice.

The whole episode hit Joe hard. Although he continued to work at the furnace, the enjoyment had gone. The place now filled him with horror, and it took extraordinary effort for him to control his fear. He had a responsible job and he realised in a way that he hadn't previously, that the lives of his men were in his hands. Liz noticed the difference in him with sadness. He looked older and as though he was carrying a great burden. However often she told him he wasn't to blame for the lad's death, he couldn't forgive himself. Every day at the works he was reminded of Billy Owens, and how he would never know the joy of being a husband and father. In fact, over the years that followed, he took it upon himself to call on Billy's mother from time to time, to make sure that she was managing. It helped to lessen his feelings of guilt, but they never quite went away. After Billy's death, Joe was never quite the same. The memory of that dreadful day stayed with him, and not even the birth of their fourth and last child, Ann, in December of that year, could lift his mood.

The family continued to settle into Nailer's Row and to get to know their neighbours. There were a further four families living in the row. They seemed a decent enough lot to Liz and with a total of more than twenty children of various ages between them, the place was always full of the sounds of children playing in the backs. Initially, with thirty or more people all sharing one privvy it wasn't ideal to say the least, but at Liz's instigation, Joe soon organised the building of two more initially, and they all determined to build a further two so that in the end each house would have its own. Water was more of an issue. With no pump serving the row, it all had to be carried from the brook up the valley. Joe and the rest of the men, who were all renting their homes from Mr Ford, determined to ask him to install a water pump. Within the year they had their pump and life became a little easier.

At the Works, the demand for steam engine cylinders was growing steadily. No less than ten had been produced in 1732 and Mr Ford, anticipating increasing demand in the years to come, had constructed a boring mill, which had recently begun work. Tipped off by Joe that there were jobs going, Will approached Mr Ford to ask him if he could move from the mine to the boring mill. As he had been a good worker, and out of respect for Joe, Mr Ford agreed to give him a trial. Will was delighted. Although the money wasn't much better than what he'd been earning in the mine, it was more regular and he felt the conditions, although still harsh, would be much preferable to crawling on his belly for what seemed like miles in the pitch black, to reach the coalface.

The young Abraham Darby 11 had now joined Mr Ford in managing the company, and the following year, rainfall had been particularly low in the Gorge, prompting them to install a horse driven pump so that the water flowing over the bellows wheel could be returned to the pools and re-used. Production could now continue the whole year round, which was a mixed blessing for the furnacemen. Although they now had continuous work and therefore wages, there was now no respite from the drudgery of twelve-hour days. In addition, a system of double shifts on Sundays was instigated in order to keep the furnaces working at maximum capacity, which meant working two full weeks before taking every other Sunday off.

Predictably, Will voiced his opinion that it just wasn't right to expect men to work nonstop for thirteen days or nights, urging Joe to object. Although he was unhappy about it, there was no way he could object without losing his job. There were plenty of men around the district who would have been only too glad to take his place, however long the hours might be.

The years continued to roll along, and Joe's work seemed to grow harder each year. With no break during the summer, and working two weeks at a stretch, the strain on Joe, who in 1737 was now forty years old grew steadily. The long hours and hard physical labour were beginning to take their toll. He could see that the progress being made in the business was coming at a price, particularly to the workforce, but also to the quality of life in Coalbrookdale. Billy Owens hadn't been the last workman to lose his life working for the Company. As activity increased and the size and quantity of their products grew, inevitably so did the dangers. At least half a dozen men had been maimed or killed in the years since Billy's demise, mostly it had to be said, in the mines, the forges and the foundry. As for the air quality, as the furnaces were now working all year round, there was no opportunity for the fumes to disperse, and a constant bluish haze hung over the narrow Coalbrookdale valley.

The children were growing fast. Nathaniel was now seven years old, the image of his father with his dark hair, and a bright lad with endless curiosity. Benjamin, five, was more like his mother and his older sister Elizabeth, with his curly blond hair and ready smile. Ann, being just two, already had a mind of her own and reminded Joe of his sister Dorothy when she was small. Liz remarked to Joe that the time was coming to think about finding a place for Elizabeth. She was thirteen next birthday and old enough to go into service. Joe wouldn't hear of it. He had no intention of allowing his eldest daughter to be a scullery maid, remembering what had happened to Abigail, and how her life had been ruined by 'that man'. He hadn't seen Abigail for a couple of years as she was living in Bridgnorth with Michael, and he wondered how life was treating her. He hadn't seen Dick and Margaret either for that matter. There never seemed time to visit people these days. Work dominated everything and he hadn't even had the chance to see Elizabeth and Arthur during the past year. He decided that on his next Sunday off, he would definitely make his way across the river to find out how they were faring.

He arrived at the clearing a couple of weeks later having been ferried across the river by Jimmy, who had given him some disturbing news. He said that Arthur hadn't been too well of late. He'd a bad cough that never seemed to get any better and he knew Elizabeth was very worried about him. Joe had climbed the path from the river towards Banghams Wood, emerging from the trees behind the cottage, and found Elizabeth tending her vegetable patch. She hadn't seen him approach and he stood for a moment, just watching her. He could see immediately that she was looking older. She seemed bent over, and was moving more slowly than he remembered, pulling turnips.

He called her name and she spun round to see him striding towards her. Her face lit up and she shouted his name, saying how pleased she was to see him there. Wiping her hands on her apron she held out her arms to embrace Joe warmly. She hadn't seen him for over a year and it would be true to say that they both noticed that time was taking its toll on their sibling. Elizabeth had obviously lost some weight and looked rather tired. As for Joe, Elizabeth thought he looked older and a little more world weary, no longer the bright, eager young man who had strode off to seek his fortune across the valley, all those years ago.

Arm in arm they entered the cottage. Joe was pleased to see that, as usual there was a pot bubbling over the fire. Some things never change, he thought to himself. Elizabeth explained that Arthur was in bed as he hadn't been too well of late. She didn't say what was wrong with him but the look of fear in her eyes told its own story. A few minutes later, Arthur, having heard Joe arrive, came slowly down the stairs. Joe was shocked. His eyes were red-rimmed, and his skin was deathly white.

'Sorry to hear you haven't been well Arthur,' he said.

'Just a bit of a chest,' Arthur replied, before being struck by a coughing fit, the sound of which was obviously terrifying Elizabeth, and told Joe that this was no bout of bronchitis. They had all heard the sound of that cough before and knew exactly what it was. Arthur had a fight on his hands. Consumption took no prisoners and Joe had never known anyone who had beaten it.

When the coughing subsided, Arthur slumped in the chair before the fire, his head in his hands. He looked utterly weary. Elizabeth gave him a drink of honey and warm water from the jug she had previously prepared and stood in the hearth to keep warm. He was calmer now and they were soon sitting in front of the fire, catching up on all the news. Elizabeth asked after Liz and the children of course, and Joe confided to her that he didn't know what to do about Elizabeth. The family was growing, and his wages weren't keeping pace with their demands. Elizabeth would soon be thirteen and must soon be contributing in some way to the family finances. However, he told his sister, the last thing he wanted was for her to go into service. Even though Jane, her own daughter had found work up at the Hall, she understood Joe's reluctance. What had happened to Abigail had hit him particularly hard.

A thought occurred to Elizabeth. Last time Margaret had visited the cottage, she had mentioned that Dorothy had visited the Hall with John the week before, when he came to teach the children. She had told Margaret how well the Charity School was doing now and that soon they would have to get some help to deal with the smaller children, who really just needed someone to supervise them and to play some simple games with them, to get them ready for more serious learning that would follow. Elizabeth wondered whether Dorothy and John might be prepared to take Elizabeth in, to teach her to read and write and do sums, while at the same time she could help out with the little ones. That way, she would be getting some education and her keep, but not of course, be paid enough to send money home. Joe said that would be a small price to pay for her to learn to read and write.

Elizabeth suggested she could mention it to Margaret when she next visited. Perhaps she could ask her friend, the lady's maid, to write a note to Dorothy asking her if she could possibly call on Joe when it was convenient. Joe wondered whether that might not be asking too much of his sister, without telling her what he wanted to speak to her about. Elizabeth, however, thought it would be better to speak with Dottie face to face and if he wasn't able to get the time to go to Madeley Wood, she was sure that Dottie would be glad to spare the time to visit him if she was able. So it was decided, and Elizabeth said she would speak to Margaret on her next visit.

Joe spent another couple of hours with Elizabeth and Arthur and by the time he left he knew that poor Arthur would not be long for this world. As he walked down the steps to the river he was wondering how Elizabeth would possibly manage when Arthur's time came. She would still have Jimmy of course, and the rent from Arthur's cottage, but it would be difficult for her. He would of course do what he could, but that wouldn't be much. They were hardly managing themselves and there just wasn't enough money coming in to take on responsibility for Elizabeth as well. As he arrived at the river he put the matter to one side and gave his attention to clambering into Jimmy's coracle to be ferried across to the far bank.

'What did you think of father?' Jimmy asked, his voice full of concern.

'Well, to be honest Jimmy lad, I don't think it looks too good for him,' Joe replied.

'I know you're right Uncle Joe.' Jimmy went on, 'I'm right worried as to how Ma and me will manage, but I guess this isn't the time to be thinking about that, although I have been wondering whether I ought to ask Owner Blake if I could take father's place on the trow. The money would be better than what I'm making with the coracles.'

'Well, don't do anything rash Jimmy,' Joe told him, 'Let's just see how things work out first.'

'You're probably right Uncle,' Jimmy said, and with that, they parted company and Jimmy cast off the coracle to return to the other side of the Severn.

# Chapter 21

When Joe arrived at Nailer's Row he was eager to tell Liz about his plan for Elizabeth. She wasn't entirely supportive of his idea. She didn't really want to see her eldest daughter, who was now very helpful with the little ones, leave home just yet. At the same time, she knew the family finances were struggling to keep them all, and one less mouth to feed would certainly help the situation, and she would certainly be happy to see her daughter learning to read and write. Living with the schoolmaster and mistress would inevitably offer her opportunities of meeting people of higher social standing, greatly increasing the chances of her eventually marrying well and rising in society. Therefore she put aside her own misgivings at losing her daughter and told Joe she would certainly support his plan if Dottie could find herself able to take Elizabeth on at the school.

One Sunday afternoon, a month later, a pony and trap pulled up outside Nailer's Row. This was a rare event. In fact, no-one could remember such an occurrence. As Joe looked out of the window, he was delighted to see his sister sitting on the trap beside her husband who was holding the reins of a brown and white pony. Joe rushed outside to greet them. He assumed that Margaret must have succeeded in sending the note as planned, but he was utterly astonished that Dottie and John had made the effort to visit them.

He suggested that John tie up the pony at the post at the end of the row, and then helped his sister to climb down. He was unsure whether to embrace her. She looked so fine, clean and tidy in a neat jacket and skirt, and he was conscious of his own grubby appearance. He needn't have worried. This was Dottie, and she hadn't changed a bit. She threw herself at him and gave him a huge hug.

'Joe!' she cried, 'It's so good to see you!'

Liz, who had also been hanging back, a little unsure of herself, not really having had much to do with Dottie over the years, finally stepped forward. Dottie extricated herself from Joe's embrace and stepped towards Liz, arms outstretched.

'Liz, it's lovely to see you, it's been too long!' Then, seeing the children standing behind her, exclaimed, 'Gracious! I can't believe how they've grown!'

'Please, come inside,' Liz offered, with as much grace as she could muster, although she was a little daunted at meeting this young woman who, though family, seemed so confident and far above them in status.

By then John had tied up the pony and joined them.

'This is nice Joe,' Dottie declared as she surveyed the cosy room with its roaring fire with a colourful rag rug in front of the hearth. Liz had just completed the rug and was particularly proud of it. Everywhere there were signs that every attempt had been made to make it comfortable, presumably Liz's doing, Dottie thought. From the heavy curtains to the white lace cover on the trunk, and the little ornaments here and there, the whole gave an appearance of being a well-cared for home, albeit not an affluent one.

'Please,' said Liz, 'do sit down. Joe, pull up the settle nearer to the fire, and can you fetch the stool from the scullery?' The children sat on the trunk under the window, except young Anne, who climbed on her mother's knee.

Eventually they all settled down in front of the fire and the conversation turned to the reason for their visit. Liz was glad she had already mentioned to Elizabeth the possibility that she might be going to live with her Aunt Dorothy and her Uncle John at the schoolhouse. She hadn't been too keen on the idea, but when it was explained to her that she would be able to learn to read and write and would avoid going into service, which would have been the other alternative, she had begun to accept the idea.

'Dottie, John,' Joe began, 'I'm so glad you could see your way to visiting us. Can I assume that you received a note from Margaret?'

'We did Joe,' John replied, 'and we have been wondering why you asked us to call.'

'Well,' Joe went on, pausing rather awkwardly, then continued, all in a rush, 'as you know, our Elizabeth is going on thirteen now and we have been wondering, frankly, what is to be done with her. We don't want her to work at the pit heaps, or to go into service with strangers,' then, after another brief pause he said, 'Look, I'll come straight to the point if you don't mind, we were wondering whether you might be in need of some help around the house Dorothy, or even with the younger children at the school. She is wonderful with the little ones, and I'm sure she could be of real help to you.'

There was a short silence, when Joe and Liz were beginning to think they had been too presumptuous in even asking. Then Dorothy said,

'Well, as it happens, this may be the answer we are ourselves looking for, isn't that right John?' she said, smiling at her husband.

'It is,' he replied, smiling back at her. 'You see, Dorothy is with child, and will certainly be needing more help around the house and with caring for the child when it is a little older, as when I am away she would like to go on teaching at the school.'

Joe and Liz declared how happy they were to hear their news.

Dorothy went on,

'Thank you so much, both of you. Actually, you are the first to know. As for Elizabeth,' at this, she turned towards her, asking, 'Elizabeth, would you like to come and stay with Uncle John and I? I would be happy to teach you to read and write, and you would be able to help me around the house and with the children?'

Dutifully, Elizabeth replied

'Yes, thank you Aunt Dorothy.'

'Are you sure Dottie? I wouldn't be able to give you anything for her keep,' Joe said, rather shamefacedly.

'Don't worry about that Joe,' John interjected, 'Elizabeth will earn her keep, I'm sure.'

'When is your baby due Dorothy?' Liz asked.

'Dottie, please Liz, everyone calls me Dottie! The baby should be born in about six months, round about Christmas time.

'In that case Dottie,' Liz asked, 'when would you like her to join you?'

'Well, the sooner the better Liz,' Dottie answered quickly, leaving no one in any doubt that she welcomed the idea of having some assistance.

'Dottie, John, that's wonderful,' Joe declared, 'That's a great weight off my mind, I can tell you.'

'That's settled then,' Dottie said, 'you can bring Elizabeth over as soon as you like. Do you know where our house is, Joe?'

'I'm sorry, I don't Dottie,' he replied.

John proceeded to explain exactly where the school and the schoolhouse were, and it was agreed that Elizabeth would be brought over to them in two weeks time when Joe next had his day off.

The main business of the day settled, Liz insisted on offering them oatcakes and ale, and they spent the rest of the afternoon chatting about family news.

John was happy to talk about the school and how the numbers of children were growing, as the employers in the district began to see the benefit of educating their workforce, at least in the basics of reading and writing. The number of the benefactors to the school was growing by the year, John informed them, which could only be a good thing for the children of the district. As the light began to fade, Dorothy and John took their leave, saying they were looking forward to seeing Joe and Elizabeth in two week's time.

So it was, that two weeks later, Joe and his daughter made their way along the road to Madeley Wood, then climbed up the hill to find the school and, next door to that, the schoolmaster's house. It was a two-storey house and it looked rather grand, and a little daunting to Elizabeth. Most of her life had been spent in a squatter's cottage, and this house was definitely a step up even from Nailer's Row, never mind from a cottage in the woods. Elizabeth had been reluctant to leave her mother when the time came, and Liz was sad to see them go, but she knew it would be for the best. Her daughter was being given a chance to change the direction of her life. If she stayed with them she may never learn to read and write, and most certainly would never meet anyone of a higher social status who could offer her a good life.

Now, as they stood on the doorstep of the school-master's house, they both felt a little nervous. Joe had never seen where Dotty lived before and from the out-side it looked pretty grand. Not as grand as Dick's but certainly a step up from Nailer's Row. Understandably Elizabeth was full of trepidation at the prospect of living here, away from her family, and until the door opened, couldn't imagine what it would be like, never having stepped inside such a grand house before. Joe pulled the chain hanging beside the door. The brass bell rang loudly and within a minute or so John opened the door. He smiled warmly, saying,

'Joe, Elizabeth, how good to see you! Please, do come in, Dottie's in the parlour.'

Parlour! thought Joe. My, my sister has definitely gone up in the world!  He followed John into the room on the left of the hallway which was indeed, it would seem, the parlour. There was a cheerful fire in the hearth and Dottie, who had been busy with a crochet needle, stood up as they entered.

'Oh do come in you two and warm yourselves at the fire. I'll make us some warm milk and then I'll show you your room Elizabeth.'

Dottie disappeared into the room at the back which Joe assumed must be the kitchen. John asked them to sit down, and picking up the small bag of Elizabeth's belongings they had brought with them, placed it on a chair by the parlour door.

Joe surveyed the room with a mixture of pride and envy. He was proud that his little sister had done so well for herself, but then he had always known she would. The envy came from realising that he could never aspire to such a home for his family. Although wages at the works were higher than agricultural workers' pay, it would never be enough to be able to afford a place like this, with the accompanying lifestyle. However, he reflected, at least his daughter would be able to enjoy it.

Finally, Dottie returned with a tray carrying cups of warm milk, and oatcakes. When they had finished, Dottie offered to show Elizabeth her room. Elizabeth was thrilled to hear that she was to have a room of her own and happily followed her aunt into the hall and up the stairs to a room off the landing at the back of the house. It was a small room with a narrow bed and dressing table with a mirror and a brush and comb placed neatly upon it. A chair stood under the window with a cheerful cushion placed on the seat. Elizabeth was entranced. She had never imagined she would ever have a room like this, and it was to be hers alone! She had been sad to leave her family but having this room to herself certainly began to make up for that. She smiled broadly at her aunt, saying

'Thank you so much aunt, it's lovely!'

'Well, I'm glad you like it, and I hope you'll be very happy here with us.'

'Can father come to see it?' Elizabeth asked eagerly.

'Of course, come on, let's go down and get him.'

Elizabeth followed Dottie back down to the parlour, where she eagerly asked Joe to come up and see her room.

Joe could see why Elizabeth was so pleased with it. It was a neat little space that she would be able to call her own. She'd never had that luxury, always having to share her space with her brothers and sister. In fact, she was so happy with it that she didn't want to go back down to the parlour and insisted on testing the bed, then climbing on the chair to look out of the window at the yard outside. There were no factories here, just the woodland as far as she could see, and in the yard below, the brown and white pony that had brought her aunt and uncle to Nailer's Row, was peering out of his stable. Oh yes, she thought, she would be happy here!

Finally Joe persuaded her to come down to the parlour, while he took his leave. He could see that his daughter would be well cared for here, and he was glad she would certainly now have more opportunities in life than he could give her. He thanked Dottie and John profusely and said that either Liz or himself would visit their daughter as often as they were able, although with the long hours he was having to work, and Liz having the little ones to care for, he couldn't say how often that would be. John said he understood of course, but told him not to worry about Elizabeth, he was sure she would settle in well with them and she would certainly be kept too busy to fret too much about being away from home. Once she had settled in, Dottie would start by teaching her to read and write, in preparation for her to help out with the little ones as soon as possible.

With that, Joe embraced his daughter, telling her to work hard learning her letters, and to obey her aunt and uncle at all times.

'Of course I will father,' she declared, then clung fiercely on to him, not wanting him to leave.

He gently extricated himself, then, shaking hands with John and kissing his sister on the cheek, left quickly so as to avoid his daughter becoming upset at his departure. He knew it was to be several weeks before he saw her again, and as he strode away, he felt the emotion well up in his throat. She had always been the apple of his eye, and he would miss her greatly. Mentally shaking himself he took a grip on his emotions, telling himself once again that she would have a better life here, now and in the future, than he could provide for her. Squaring his shoulders, he quickened his pace and strode quickly down the track towards the river and home.

# Chapter 22

Michael had been Stock Manager at Andrews Grain Merchants for a couple of years now. in 1738 he had managed to rent a small house near the business and finally realised his long-cherished ambition of bringing his mother to live with him. No longer would she have to be in service to someone else. She could run her own home, which she took to with much enthusiasm.

It stood at the end of a small terrace of houses which had been built a century before. However, it had been well maintained and was of ample size for the two of them, having two bedrooms, a sitting room and a scullery at the back. Abigail had lost no time turning it into a comfortable home for herself and her son. She was thrilled to be living with him again after being apart for so long, and she was proud of the young man he had become. She knew she had been right to agree to him staying with Dick and Margaret. It had been the making of him. She was happy to be living in Bridgnorth, which was a bustling market town, quite unlike Coalbrookdale, or even Madeley Wood for that matter. Their house was in the lower town, near the river and although it was quite a climb up to the high town to visit Dick and Margaret, she did see them quite often. Dick sometimes called in when he was down at the business, which was literally only a few strides away.

For their part, Dick and Margaret were busy not only growing the business, but also their own family. Margaret was kept busy with their four children, Elizabeth who was nine years old, Richard was seven, Walter four, and the youngest was Joseph who was now two. They were well known in society in Bridgnorth with many influential friends in the district. Of course Margaret's family had been well established in the town for over fifty years, since her grandfather had set up the business in the 1680's. Dick, a quick learner, had taken well to the running of it and was proving to be a good businessman. They were prospering, and as the business grew, so did Michael's prospects.

He was now working in the office full time, and after some instruction from Dick, was keeping the company accounts as well as dealing with the stocks. Through his hard work and diligence, he had made himself indispensable to his Uncle Dick. It was an arrangement that suited them both. Mr Andrews, Dick's father-in-law had now retired and was in poor health, leaving Dick to run the company single handed. This meant that Dick needed to get out to visit potential clients more often and had less time to spend in the office, and he was glad to have someone he could trust dealing with the day to day running of the business.

Michael was happy to have his mother under his protection, and she in turn was more content than she had ever been. She had no need to worry over money and it felt good to be cared for. Michael loved to treat her from time to time, and she would often visit the market in High Town, when she would buy a little something for herself or to decorate the house. Christmas was approaching and it occurred to Abigail that it would be nice to look for a little something for Michael. So it was, that the next Wednesday morning she set out to climb the hill to High Town.

She had just closed the door and turned to walk towards the steps when she stopped dead. Passing by the door was a wagon, with two men sitting at the front. As she looked at them, her heart stopped. She hadn't seen him for years, but there was no mistaking the bright red hair, undimmed by age. He was the one person on earth she never wanted to set eyes on again. James Furlong. Her legs almost buckled and she shrunk back into the doorway to avoid his gaze.

She was panicking now. It was obvious that this was the wagon from the Hall, making its monthly visit to the grain merchants. Perhaps Furlong needed to visit Bridgnorth and decided to make the journey on the wagon with the horseman. Or, she realised with horror, he had heard that Michael was working here and was determined to confront him. What should she do? Peering round the door jamb she saw the wagon turning to go under the archway into Andrews' yard. She must warn Michael. The last thing she wanted was for him to be confronted by Furlong without warning. She wasn't sure whether Furlong knew Michael was there or not, but either way she knew there would be trouble if they met. She hurried along to the shop, and without waiting went straight through to the stairs and up to Michael's office, where she knew he would be at this time of day.

'Michael, he's here! He's just gone into the yard right now!'

'Mother!' Michael declared, 'Whatever is the matter? Who's here? What are you talking about?'

'It's him Michael. Furlong.'

'You mean, from the Hall? Dear God, what does he want here?'

'I imagine he wants to see you!' Abigail exclaimed.

'Well then, I'd best go and see him, but I hope he isn't expecting this to be a joyous occasion!'

'Michael! No!' Abigail exclaimed, but Michael, retorted,

'Mother, this has gone on long enough. He can't hurt us anymore, and he needs to know that it's useless to try. I want nothing to do with the man.'

With that, he jumped up from behind his desk, a thunderous look on his face that terrified Abigail. She was afraid of what he might do when confronted by Furlong. He ran out of the room, down the stairs and out into the yard, followed by Abigail.

When Abigail emerged from the passageway the two men were already confronting one another. She had always known Michael bore a strong resemblance to Furlong, but until she saw them standing face to face she hadn't realised just how strong. There could be no doubt, if ever there was. They were father and son. The sight of this man who looked so much like him, had stopped Michael in his tracks and for a moment he was lost for words.

Furlong spoke first,

'Do you remember me?' he asked.

Dear God thought Michael, he even sounds like me!

'Why should I?' Michael asked.

'Because I saw you once at Madeley Market, and I wanted to see more of you, but your mother wouldn't allow it.'

'What makes you think I would want to see you?'

'Because I'm your father.'

'No!' Michael declared, 'You are no father of mine. I know exactly what you did to my mother, and I could never accept you as my father, so you'd better leave now, and don't ever come here again. I want nothing to do with you.'

Predictably, Furlong's mood changed instantly, and he spat out the words,

'What I did to your mother? Good grief, what did she tell you?'

Abigail knew exactly what was coming and stepped forward in desperation, intending to stand between the two men.

'It's alright mother,' Michael said gently, and with some authority, asked her to step aside.

Seeing Michael's obvious affection for his mother, which he had never experienced himself, from anyone, Furlong felt an uncontrollable urge to hurt them both.

The words Abigail was dreading to hear, spewed out of his mouth

'I suppose she told you that I forced myself on her! Not a bit of it!'

Abigail glanced in horror around the yard, to see the horseman from the hall and the workmen all standing there, listening intently and watching the scene unfold.

After pausing to let that sink in, Furlong went on,

'She wanted it, but then she was always very free with her favours!'

At this, a terrible anger welled up in Michael's chest and he lunged at Furlong. Being younger and stronger, one blow from Michael's fist sent Furlong sprawling on the ground. Abigail cried out to her son to stop, afraid of what he might do. This man had already caused her to lose her brother for nine years and she didn't want to lose her son as well. Michael, however, would have gone on punching him if two of the other men hadn't run over to restrain him. Furlong was bleeding from his nose and had apparently banged his head on the ground as he fell.

'Get out!' Michael shouted at him, 'Get out of my

sight and never come back. If I ever see you here again, I'll kill you!'

Being the coward he was, Furlong stumbled to his feet and staggered towards the archway, but not before glaring at Abigail with such evil intent that her blood ran cold. Then, as he stumbled away, he called out to Michael,

'Just you wait, you'll regret this, you'll see!'

Michael went over to his mother, who was crying now. He put his arms around her saying,

'Come on mother, don't worry about him, he can't hurt you anymore.'

But Abigail wasn't so sure, she looked around again at the men, who had heard everything, and felt she would never be able to hold her head up in Bridgnorth again. Furlong had once again blighted her life. Would she never be rid of him?

Fred, the horseman, was only too eager to share the story of the events in Bridgnorth with the rest of the servants at the Hall. Everyone had agreed that Furlong deserved to be taken down a peg or two. The following Sunday was Margaret's day off. It was a bright late Autumn morning as she made her way down the steep path on Benthall Edge towards Banghams Wood, enjoying the red and gold of the autumn leaves. They were just at the point when a strong wind would have blown them down, but right now, they reminded Margaret that autumn really was her favourite season. When she arrived at the cottage, she lost no time in giving Arthur and Elizabeth the news about Michael and Furlong.

'Poor Abigail!' Elizabeth declared, 'Will she never be free of that man?'

'Well, from the state of Furlong's face, Michael certainly did his best to make sure he wouldn't trouble them again. He's such an evil man though, I fear he'll not give up that easily, now he knows exactly where Michael is.'

'I fear you're right,' Elizabeth agreed.

'Anyhow, tell me, how's our Jane getting on? I was hoping she'd be visiting last week, but she didn't come. Is she alright?'

'Yes, she's fine Liz,' Margaret reassured her. 'It was just that the Hall was full of houseguests last weekend, come for the shoot, so none of the servants were given time off. She asked me to tell you she'll definitely be down next Sunday.'

'That's good, I was beginning to get worried, and in any case, I think she should come and visit her father. He's not getting any better Margaret. I'm right worried about him to be honest.'

At that moment, Arthur, having heard them talking, appeared at the bottom of the stairs.

'Now now Liz, don't you be worrying about me, I'll be right as rain when I get rid of this chest. Good to see you Margaret,' he said, before another coughing fit took hold.

Margaret cast a worried look at Elizabeth, and they

both knew that sadly Arthur would never be rid of 'this chest' as he called it. His eyes were red-rimmed, his face pale and drawn. They knew the signs all too well.

'I told you to stay in bed today Arthur, you need to rest,' Elizabeth told him as the coughing subsided.

'We'll all get more rest than we want one day,' he retorted, stepping up to the fire and sinking wearily down in the armchair.

Elizabeth served some broth from the pot over the fire. Arthur said he wasn't hungry, but the sisters enjoyed their dinner and then chatted for an hour or so, about this and that, just catching up on family news. As they did so, they both noticed that the years were taking their toll on their sister and after Margaret had left, Elizabeth wondered what would become of her when she was too old to go on working at the Hall. She would have no home of her own to go to when the time came.

For her part, as she trudged back up the steep winding path to the top of Benthall Edge, Margaret was wondering how Elizabeth would manage if she was left on her own. How different, she thought, for the gentry. They need never worry what would become of them when they grew old. As for herself, she couldn't help feeling rather bitter that after years of service, the day would eventually come when she could no longer fetch and carry for them, and would be discarded, asked to leave to make room for someone younger and fitter. Without a home and family of her own, she may well end up in Mine Spout poor-house.

Ten minutes later Margaret knocked on the back door at the Hall, and it was opened almost immediately by Jane. She was twenty-one now and had grown into a bonny young woman. She had Elizabeth's eyes but Arthur's light hair. She was now one of the kitchen maids, helping the cook, Mrs Bramble, to prepare the copious amounts of food to feed the family and the host of servants living in the Hall. Jane was a willing worker, and popular among the other servants. In spite of the hard work demanded of her, she always seemed to have a ready smile and brightened up any room she entered.

'Aunt Margaret!' she declared. 'How were Ma and Pa?'

'Well,' Margaret replied sadly, 'I'm afraid your father isn't well at all Jane, and your mother is hoping you'll be able to visit him soon.'

'Yes, of course I will. Cook has said I can definitely take next Sunday off to visit them.'

'That's good Jane, they will both be pleased to see you. But if you've finished your chores, why don't you come and sit by the fire, and we can have a chat before bed?'

'Well, that would be nice, and I have just finished my work. I'll just ask Cook if she needs me to do anything else.'

The door to the kitchen was open and Mrs Bramble, who had heard the exchange, called out,

'Go on girl, go and catch up on Margaret's family news!'

'Thanks Mrs Bramble!' Jane replied, grinning at her aunt.

Margaret took off her coat and hung it up in the passageway and as they walked along towards the servant's hall, who should step out of the open door at that very moment but James Furlong. His face was still bruised from the encounter with Michael's fist, and from the look of hatred on his face, that wasn't the only thing that was bruised. His ego had obviously also taken a battering.

'Two for the price of one! What a treat!' he sneered as he planted himself firmly in front of them.

Margaret would have loved to punch him in the face herself, or at the very least and in no uncertain terms, tell him to get out of their way. Of course, as Under Butler, he was her senior in the hierarchy of the household, and she knew it was more than her job was worth to challenge him. She simply said,

'Please let us pass.'

He pushed his leering face up close to Jane's as he sidled past them, making sure that his body brushed against hers, and Margaret's blood ran cold as she understood the message he was sending. In his twisted mind, Jane was now fair game. Jane was visibly shaken.

As he disappeared into the kitchen, and they had stepped inside the servants hall, closing the door behind them, Margaret asked,

'Are you alright Jane? Has he tried anything on with you before?'

'Not really,' she replied, 'only he never misses a chance to leer at me.'

'Well for God's sake be careful, and make sure you lock your door at night.'

'I will Aunt, of course.'

That night Jane made sure that her bedroom door was locked and to make doubly sure she placed the chair up against the doorknob.

# Chapter 23

Furlong continued to seethe with indignation at his humiliation by Michael in Bridgnorth, and a plot began to form in his mind as to how he might make the Banghams pay. As he had stood inside the door of the servant's hall he had heard Jane tell her aunt that she would visit her parents on the following Sunday. Well he thought, maybe it was time to show this family they couldn't get away with humiliating a Furlong.

Sunday morning saw Furlong quickly making his way along the path across the meadow, towards the kissing gate leading to Benthall Edge. He knew the girl would be leaving the Hall after she'd finished her morning duties in the kitchen, and he would wait for her on the path leading down to Banghams Wood. When he reached the gate, he looked around to make sure no one was watching, then went through and hid himself in the bushes a few yards along the path.

About half an hour later he could hear Jane singing to herself as she strode towards the gate. He peered through the branches and could see her manoeuvring her way through it, carrying a basket, no doubt full of things for her mother and father, given to her by the soft-hearted cook.  Amazing how generous she can be with other people's food, he thought to himself. Jane was deep in thought as she passed through the kissing gate, then after walking a few yards along the path she looked up and was startled to see James Furlong step out in front of her.

'Well, well, what have we here,' he said menacingly, 'and all alone!'

Jane was terrified, but as her mother had told her many times, the only way to deal with bullies was to stand up to them. She stood tall and declared,

'You don't frighten me Furlong! You're just a bully who likes to take advantage of women.'

Incensed that she should have the temerity to stand up to him, he took a step towards her. She realised she had a choice. Knowing what he'd done to her aunt all those years ago, she knew she could either accept her fate, or attack. Fatefully, she chose the latter.

'I know exactly what you did to my aunt all those years ago, so don't think you got away with it. Everyone knows what you are.'

'And I know what you Banghams are,' he sneered. 'You think you're so good, don't you? But you're no better than the rest of us. I know it was that no good Uncle of yours that attacked me and left me for dead, and then scurried off like the coward he was.'

Jane was taken aback at this. The family had always assumed he didn't know who had attacked him.

'And you talk of that Aunt of yours! She likes to

tell herself that what happened was my fault, but let me tell you, she enjoyed it, and I don't suppose I was the first!'

Anger rose in Jane's chest, and she let rip,

'You liar! You're just scum Furlong, no woman's safe where you are and never was! Now get out of my way and let me pass!'

Furlong stood firm, showing no sign of moving, then Jane strode forward and tried to push past him. Angered by her determination to resist him, as she reached him, he lifted his hand, bringing it crashing down on the side of her head, and she fell to the ground. She tried to get up, but he struck her again and this time she lost her footing and fell sideways, tumbling down the steep sided valley. She screamed as she fell, knowing that the land here fell away steeply. Benthall Edge was at least a couple of hundred feet high. Her scream stopped abruptly as she hit a tree trunk and her neck snapped.

Furlong, realising that she could never survive such a fall, looked round to make sure there had been no witnesses, then turned and walked back to the Hall as though nothing had happened. Unfortunately for Furlong, there was a witness, and a reliable one at that. The gamekeeper from the Hall, Mr Sykes, had been out in the woods, setting traps, and he had heard the kerfuffle on the path above him. Looking up, he could plainly see Furlong and Jane. He could hear raised voices but couldn't distinguish what was being said, although the tones were clearly angry. Then he saw Furlong raise his hand and strike Jane and when she tried to get up, he saw him hit her again and she tumbled off the path.

The girl had screamed and he had watched in horror as she came crashing down Benthall Edge, passing the spot where he was standing and then, with a sickening thud that silenced her scream, she crashed against a tree stump some hundred feet below. Sykes clambered across to the path and made his way quickly down to where it passed beneath the spot he judged the girl to be. He scrambled up through the brambles until he found her, lying akimbo against the tree. Her head was at an odd angle and her eyes were staring up at the canopy of leaves above her. It was obvious that she was dead. Poor lass, he said quietly to himself, gently closing her eyelids.

He knew he wouldn't be able to move her himself, and he also knew he now had pressing business at the Hall. He had a murderer to apprehend.

Sykes had no choice but to leave Jane where she lay until he could bring some men to carry her home to her mother and father. He respectfully covered her face with the kerchief from around his neck and arranged her skirts to give her some dignity. When he had finished, he made his way back down to the path and then up towards the kissing gate and across the meadow to the Hall.

When he arrived, he went straight to the Master's study and knocked on the door.

The Master called out 'Come!' and he entered, saying,

'Sir, I'm sorry to trouble you, but there is a matter of great urgency that we need to deal with.'

'What is this matter that demands my immediate attention Sykes?'

Sykes proceeded to explain he had just witnessed the death of one of the servants. Jane, the kitchen maid had just been murdered by James Furlong, and he had seen the whole thing from beginning to end, and he described exactly what had happened.

'Are you sure the girl is dead?' the Master asked.

'I am sir. I went down to where she lay and there is no doubt of it. Her neck is broken.'

'Well, this is a bad business Sykes. Is the girl still lying where she fell?'

'She is sir. I could not move her on my own. In any case I thought that maybe as Justice of the Peace you might like to view the body before it was moved.'

'Good thinking Sykes.' the Master replied. 'I will certainly need to record what I see. First, we must deal with Furlong. Is he in the Hall?'

'I don't know sir. I don't think he knew I had seen everything, so I imagine he returned here afterwards, thinking he'd got away with it.'

'Come then Sykes, we must apprehend him and see what he's got to say for himself. I see you still have your gun. We may yet need it.'

With that, they left the study and went down the

back stairs to the servant's hall. They found Furlong sitting in front of the fire enjoying a drink of ale and looking as though he hadn't a care in the world, until he looked up and saw the Master standing there with Sykes behind him. Still he didn't realise the significance of this most unusual occurrence. The Master never usually came down to the servant's hall. Yet, here he was. He knew this would not be a social visit but didn't yet connect it with the events that had occurred earlier. The Master stood for a moment looking at him and then announced,

'Furlong, I have to place you under arrest for the murder of Jane Green, the kitchen maid.'

'What? No! I know nothing of this!'

'Sadly for you Furlong, I have a reliable witness who saw the whole thing.'

Sykes now stepped forward, glaring at Furlong, saying,

'I was in the woods this morning and I saw what you did, and what happened to the girl. You didn't even have the decency to see if there was anything you could do for her.'

The colour had drained from Furlong's face now. He knew that the game was up, although he still tried to plead his innocence, now changing his story somewhat, trying to assert that it was just a terrible accident. Sykes however, said he was willing to swear under oath that he saw him deliberately strike the girl twice, the second time causing her to fall from the path down the sheer drop of Benthall Edge, and as a consequence to break her neck as she struck a tree trunk.

Furlong looked visibly shrunk. He knew his fate was sealed. They tied his hands and locked him in a room in the cellar until he could be taken to the gaol at Much Wenlock.

The Master then instructed Sykes to find four men to accompany them to where the girl lay, and to bring the handcart. Sykes first went to find Margaret, knowing that Jane was her niece, to let her know what had happened. She was distraught. Elizabeth and Arthur would be destroyed by the news that their daughter was gone. She must go to them and be with them as they were given the news. She followed the men across the meadow and through the gate. She saw them stop just a few yards along the path where the Master had noticed the basket Jane had been carrying snagged on a branch a few yards down the slope. He remarked to Sykes that he could see many broken branches where the girl must have fallen. Margaret's legs almost gave way as she thought of her dear niece tumbling down that sheer drop, no doubt fully aware there was nothing to stop her plunging to her death. She must have been terrified.

The Master led the way down the path as it curved round to a spot where Sykes told him that Jane was lying just above them beyond the brambles. They found her as Sykes had left her and the Master surveyed the scene. It was obvious from the angle of her neck that she must have died the instant she struck the tree. He looked up the steep slope of Benthall Edge and could see the trail of broken branches marking out the path she had taken as she fell, and it led directly to the top, where he could just discern her basket, snagged on the branch. There was no doubt in his mind that the description of events given by Sykes was correct. He even noted a bruise to the side of her head where Furlong must have landed the first blow. The evidence was clear, Furlong was a murderer and he, as the Justice of the Peace would not rest until he got his just desserts and this girl and her family had justice.

As the Master turned away and returned to the path, he instructed the men to lay the girl on the handcart and bring her up to the Hall, where she could be attended to with dignity. Margaret stepped forward and said,

'Begging your pardon Sir, but I think her mother, my sister, would dearly want her daughter to be taken home. It's just in the wood at the bottom of the path. Would it be possible for the men to take her their instead?'

'Well Margaret,' he replied, 'now that I have seen her body, I can see no reason why she shouldn't be taken to her mother and father.'

Then he turned to Judd, one of the men who had come with them, and told him to take her down to her mother's home. The Master then strode back up the path with Sykes, to go back to the Hall to deal with Furlong.

While the men were retrieving Jane's body, Margaret hurried ahead to break the news to Elizabeth and Arthur. When she arrived at the cottage she found Elizabeth alone, sitting by the fire. She had been worrying rather, wondering what had happened to her daughter whom she had been expecting to arrive. When she heard the latch, she was relieved, thinking that it was her daughter at last. When the door opened and she saw Margaret standing there, she immediately knew something was wrong.

'Margaret!' she exclaimed, 'What's to do? Where's Jane? I've been expecting her since noon.'

Unsure where to begin, Margaret hesitated for a moment.

'Margaret, tell me! What's happened to her?'

'Oh Liz,' Margaret began, the tears already beginning to trickle down her cheeks. 'She's gone Liz.'

'What do you mean, gone?' Elizabeth said, with rising panic welling up in her chest.

'Liz, something terrible has happened,' Margaret began, 'She was making her way down the path to see you, when Furlong confronted her.'

'Nooo!' Elizabeth now knew what was coming and the colour drained from her face. She gripped the arm of the chair beside her, waiting to hear the worst news she would ever hear, but at the same time, not wanting to listen to the words.

'I'm so sorry Liz, apparently Furlong struck her, and she overbalanced and fell down Benthall Edge.'

Elizabeth let out a heart-rending wail and collapsed to the floor. A second later, Arthur appeared at the doorway to the stairs. He had heard everything and stood for a moment in complete shock and disbelief.

'Margaret,' he managed, 'this can't be true! Not our precious daughter!' Of course, immediately the nightmare of losing his little Eliza all those years ago flooded back. His legs now gave way and he flopped down on the bottom step of the stairs.

'Arthur, I'm so sorry!' Margaret said through her tears.

She stepped forward and helped Elizabeth into the chair, then she had no choice but to tell them that their daughter was, right this minute, being brought home to them by men from the Hall.

Elizabeth looked at her in disbelief.

'But look,' she said, 'I've got a stew bubbling for her supper!'

'Oh Liz. Come on, we must prepare.'

At that moment, there was the knock on the door that Margaret dreaded, and when she opened it, the men were standing there with the handcart carrying Jane's body.

As they picked her up and carried her into the cottage, a coughing fit took hold of Arthur, and he put his kerchief to his mouth. As he took it away it was covered in blood. Everyone knew what that meant, but for the moment their attention had to remain with Elizabeth, who had collapsed again at the sight of her beloved daughter being carried home with her face covered. Margaret once again helped her back into the chair by the fire.

The men placed Jane gently on the table in the living room and Margaret thanked them as they left, then turned her attention to dealing with Elizabeth and Arthur. She found a sheet and placed it over Jane, then tried to get Arthur back up the stairs to his bed. He was weak and it took some time for her to manage it. He was in complete shock and his eyes were full of despair. She gave him a drink of the herb tea that was beside the bed, then went back downstairs to attend to Elizabeth.

She found her standing over her daughter, having pulled the sheet back and removed the kerchief. Her face was contorted with pain as she bent down to kiss Jane gently on her forehead before looking up at Margaret with a look of utter despair and anguish.

Meanwhile, the Master and Sykes had reached the Hall, and as Justice of the Peace, the Master formerly charged Furlong. He still tried to protest his innocence, swearing it was all just a dreadful mistake. He hadn't meant to hurt her, and it was just an accident.

Ignoring his pleas, with his hands and feet bound, Fred, the horseman and two other men loaded him onto the cart and with the Master and Sykes riding beside the wagon, he was taken to Much Wenlock gaol and was thrown into the same cell his son had occupied years ago, to await his fate. No one doubted what that would be.

# Chapter 24

Margaret was desperately trying to decide what to do next. She knew she would have to return to the Hall soon but she couldn't leave Elizabeth and Arthur with their daughter lying dead on the table. She would have to send for Jimmy who would be working down on the river, but how could she get a message to him without leaving the cottage?

She went upstairs to Arthur and found him in a dreadful state. The blood soaked rag he was holding to his mouth told the story. He was in the last stages of the disease and wouldn't last long. What a desperate situation, thought Margaret. His daughter lying dead downstairs and him not long for this world either! She helped him to take a sip of the herb tea on the table beside the bed, but he coughed and spluttered, bringing up more blood. His eyes were full of pain and despair, unable to comprehend what had just oc-curred. Settling him down as best she could, Margaret went back down the stairs to see what she could do to help Elizabeth. Poor Jane would have to be washed and laid out as soon as possible but she wasn't sure Elizabeth would be capable of doing it.

As she entered the room there was a knock on the door. When she opened it she was relieved to find Rose Bottoms and Ella Forester standing there. They had heard the news and had come to see if they could help.

'Well, we could really do with some, thanks,' Margaret told them, and opened the door wide for them to enter. They both gasped in horror as they saw young Jane lying on the table, the sheet pulled up to her chin, and Elizabeth standing over her, gazing at her with tears streaming down her face, just silently mourning her loss.

'What can we do?' Rose asked Margaret.

Margaret replied softly, hopefully out of earshot of Elizabeth.

'Well, we do need to wash her and lay her out properly, but I don't think Elizabeth is up to it.'

However, Margaret obviously hadn't spoken quietly enough, as Elizabeth immediately said, with some passion,

'No! Thank you all the same, but if anyone's going to wash my daughter, it will be me!'

'Of course,' ventured Ella, 'but we can help you Liz, it's the least we can do.'

They had just finished and covered her with the sheet when Jimmy burst in. He was breathless, as though he had been running, which of course he had.

Hearing the news from one of the grooms from the Hall who had been on an errand to Madeley Wood, he had hurried home immediately.

'Oh Ma!' he declared when he saw Jane's body laid out on the table, covered with a sheet. He went straight to Elizabeth and took her in his arms. With the tears flowing once again she stood with her head on his broad shoulder, as he tried to comfort her. Eventually she calmed down a little, then Margaret said,

'Jimmy, it was that monster Furlong, you know. That man has been a curse to this family, but this time he'll get what's coming to him. The gamekeeper, Mr Sykes saw everything.'

'Where's father?' Jimmy asked, knowing that all this would devastate him, and could well overwhelm him given the state of his health.

Margaret told him that he was upstairs, and the look on her face and slight shake of her head told Jimmy that he needed to go to him immediately. He gently extricated himself from Elizabeth, helping her into the chair, then ran up the stairs, taking them two by two, to see how his father was faring. When he saw him, his worst fears were realised. His face was deathly white and his eyes staring. The blood stained cloth he had been holding to his mouth had fallen from his hand which was lifelessly dangling over the side of the bed.

Jimmy stood for a second, unable to comprehend that his father too, was gone.

'No! Aunt Maggie, come quick!' he called out loudly and bounded across to where his father lay, finally at peace.

He lifted Arthur's arm and placed it under the sheet, which he drew up to his chin, then gently closed his eyes on the world as Margaret entered the room.

'Oh my God!' she exclaimed. 'This will be the end of Liz!'

'I know Aunt Margaret. How will she ever cope with losing both of them? How will any on us, for that matter?'

His face was grim as he fought to control his own emotions. Realising he was now the man of the family, he squared his shoulders and leaving Margaret to straighten Arthur's body and cover his face with the sheet, he slowly went downstairs to give his step-mother the news.

Ella and Rose were thankfully still there. As soon as they saw Jimmy's face they exchanged worried glances, sensing that things were bad, and both in-stinctively moved to stand behind Elizabeth, to sup-port her as she was given the news that was surely coming. Elizabeth, who had been standing beside her daughter's covered body, looked up and saw Jimmy standing there with such an expression of pain on his face, she mistakenly assumed that he had just realised that his father wasn't long for this world.

'I'm sorry lad,' she murmured, 'he's bad, isn't he?'

'Oh Ma!' Jimmy exclaimed, quickly stepping towards her and once again taking her in his arms. As he held her close, he knew he had to tell her.

'Ma, I'm so sorry, but Da's gone!'

He felt her go rigid in his arms and she quickly pushed him away.

'What do you mean, gone? He's upstairs in his bed. You've just seen him!'

'No, Ma, he's gone. This was too much for him!'

Saying nothing, but with a look of disbelief still on her face, Elizabeth hurried up the stairs and into the bedroom. At the sight of Arthur's body covered with the sheet, an unearthly wail issued from somewhere deep within her and she collapsed to her knees beside the bed with her head on her husband's lifeless chest. Margaret knelt beside her and threw her arm around her sister to give her some support as her body shuddered with the deep sobs that engulfed her.

Downstairs, Jimmy pushed his own emotions to one side. He must take charge of the situation. He thanked Rose and Ella for helping with Jane. He said he would help his aunt and mother to deal with his father, but he wondered whether Alf or Tom might take a message to Johnson, the undertaker in Buildwas, to ask him to call as soon as possible. Ella and Rose both reassured him that a message would be taken down to Buildwas without delay.

Margaret knew she would not be going back to the Hall that night. She would have to help Jimmy to lay Arthur out, because looking at the state of her sister, she wouldn't be able to do much. Her sobs had subsided but she still knelt beside her husband, as she raised her head to look at Margaret, and her eyes looked as though all the life had left them also. Her beloved daughter was gone and now the only man she had ever loved was gone too. At that moment, she didn't want to live either.

Margaret gently helped her up and led her to the chair in the corner of the room.

'You sit there Liz, Jimmy and I will do what's necessary,' Margaret assured her. My God, thought Margaret, I'm not sure she will be able to take this. It's more than anyone should have to bear.

Jimmy understood what had to be done and brought up a bowl of hot water, and he and Margaret washed Arthur and laid him out, covering him with a sheet. As Jimmy went to cover his face, Elizabeth, who had been watching them, let out another wail and getting up with some effort, made her way to the bedside, kissing her husband for the last time, before the sheet was drawn across his face.

They had just finished when there was a knock on the door. Jimmy hurried down to open it, finding Tom on the doorstep.

'Jimmy lad!' Tom declared, 'We're all that sorry to hear the news about Jane and Arthur.'

'Thanks,' Jimmy answered quietly, unable to say anything else as he struggled to contain his emotions.

'I've come to give you a hand if you need it, and

Alf's off down to Buildwas to take your message to Johnson.

'Thanks Tom, maybe you could help me get Jane upstairs. She can lie beside me Da until Johnson gets here.' As he said these words, the emotion finally broke through, his face contorted with pain. Tom quickly stepped forward, placing a hand on Jimmy's shuddering shoulders. Tom had no words that could make any of this better, so he just stood quietly, sharing the moment with Jimmy.

Eventually, Jimmy recovered some composure and they went upstairs to arrange Arthur's body so that Jane could be placed beside him. Elizabeth, once again seated on the chair, with Margaret comforting her as best she could, watched quietly now as Tom and Jimmy moved her husband's body to one side of the bed. Minutes later, they carried Jane into the room and laid her gently beside her father.

The full horror of Elizabeth's situation was now laid bare. She felt her life was over. The two people she loved most in the world were gone and she knew she would never be happy again. Margaret stayed with her that night, making sure that both she and Jimmy had something to eat and drink, although neither of them really wanted anything at all. Margaret slept with Elizabeth and Jimmy slept in the chair by the fire downstairs. At first light there was a knock on the door and Jimmy was roused from his fitful sleep, shocked once more as he remembered the events of the previous day. It was Johnson, the undertaker, come to measure up and make arrangements.

He expressed his sorrow at the tragic turn of events that had befallen the family. Jimmy thanked him then led him up to the bedroom where Arthur and Jane lay side by side. He did what he had to do, ensuring the bodies were properly laid out, then told Jimmy he could arrange the funerals for three days time at the Buildwas burial ground at noon, if that was convenient. Johnson said he would return with the woollen shrouds and coffins early on the day of the funerals.

Elizabeth had fallen into an exhausted if fitful sleep, but had woken to the sound of Johnson and Jimmy talking in the next room, and she and Margaret had thrown their shawls around their shoulders and had just now appeared, in time to see Johnson leaving the room. Jimmy was shocked at the sight of Elizabeth. She looked old and vulnerable in her grief. He vowed to himself that he would look after her, just as his father would have wished. He went across to her and put his arms around her shoulders, gently guiding her down the stairs into the living room. Margaret followed them and began to busy herself preparing some breakfast for them all. Elizabeth still seemed in complete shock, still unable to process what had happened.

Eventually, when they had eaten, Margaret declared she would have to return to the Hall, asking Jimmy if he would be alright. She said she would somehow get word across to Dale Coppice, Nailer's Row, to Dottie in Madeley Wood, and also up to Abigail and Dick in Bridgnorth.

Word of the tragedy in Banghams wood, spread quickly through the Gorge. Margaret had given the message to John, asking whether he or Dorothy would be able to let Joe and Will know about the double tragedy that had befallen the family. Indeed, news of Jane's death had reached them even before Dorothy arrived in the trap the next day. Joe was at the works, but Liz explained they had already been given the dreadful news about Jane. When Dorothy told her about Arthur, she was shocked to the core, declaring,

'Poor Elizabeth! How will she ever get over this?'

She said that Will of course had taken the news about Jane particularly badly, wishing more than ever he'd finished Furlong off all those years ago. Refusing refreshment, Dorothy said she was sorry but she had to get back up to the school as she was teaching the little ones that afternoon. Liz promised to tell Joe about Arthur as soon as he came home, and meantime, she would make her way up to Dale Coppice to let Betty know.

At about the same time as Dorothy was arriving at Dale End, the news had broken in Bridgnorth. Elizabeth had spoken to the Mistress about trying to get word to Abigail and Dick. The whole household at the Hall was in shock over what had happened, and she said she would do what she could to help. In fact, she had suggested that Margaret ask her lady's maid to write a note to Dick, and then instructed the Butler to tell the stable boy to ride over to Bridgnorth to take it to Andrew's Grain Merchant. Dick and Michael were both in the office when the boy arrived with the note. Dick quickly opened it but as he read the contents the colour drained from his face.

'Oh my God!' he declared.

'What is it Uncle?' Michael quickly asked him, 'What's happened?'

'I hardly know where to start.' Dick replied. 'Poor Elizabeth.'

Unable to find the words to tell Michael this terrible news, Dick collapsed into the chair behind his desk and handed him the note.

As Michael read it, he too turned white as a sheet. It was too much to take in. His cousin Jane was dead, and at the hands of that monster Furlong! And Arthur gone too! His Aunt Elizabeth would never cope with this double tragedy, and then his thoughts immediately turned to his mother. How would she take the news?

With mounting horror, Dick declared 'Your mother must be told! Would you like me to do it?'

Michael hesitated, and then said 'If you don't mind Uncle, I think I should be the one to ...'

'Yes, of course,' Dick replied. 'As for myself, I intend to ride over to your Aunt Elizabeth's this afternoon to see if there is anything I can do to help.'

With that, Dick went down into the yard and asked one of the men to saddle up his horse. Then he wrote a note to Margaret, explaining what had happened and that he would be home in the evening, telling Jed the young apprentice, to take it up to the house. Minutes later he was riding along the road towards the Gorge. Meanwhile, Michael had arrived home, finding his mother busy sewing in front of the fire. She looked up as he came into the room.

'By, you're home early lad!' she said, smiling, 'I haven't even christened our supper yet.'

The smile disappeared from her face when she saw Michael's expression.

'What is it? What's the matter?' she demanded.

'Oh mother, I don't know how to tell you.'

'Good grief lad, tell me, what on earth's happened.'

He still had the note in his hand, and he wished he could have just handed it to her, but of course, she had never learnt to read. He had to find the words.

'Mother, I'm so sorry, there is no other way to tell you this. Cousin Jane and Uncle Arthur are both dead.'

'Cousin Jane! How can that be, she's only a lass! I know Arthur's been ill for a while and not expected to get better, but Jane as well? Our Liz will be distraught! What on earth happened?'

Michael paused and took a deep breath before answering, knowing he would soon have to answer his mother's next question.

'Oh mother, the poor girl was murdered!'

'Oh Mother of God! Murdered! How? Do they know who did it?'

So now the moment had come. He had to tell her

that it was Furlong, his own father and the cause of her own ruin who had now murdered her niece. He knew she would blame herself in some way, as indeed he was beginning to blame himself for striking and humiliating Furlong. Had that fuelled his anger and prompted him to take out his revenge on poor Jane?

In the end, he simply said,

'They are saying it was Furlong mother.'

'Furlong! Oh no! But how? When? For goodness sake Michael, just tell me what happened!'

'I don't know the details. All we know is what is in this note sent by Aunt Margaret. Apparently, he met Jane in the woods on Benthall Edge and some sort of argument occurred. We can guess what that was about. Anyway, he struck her, and she stumbled off the path and down Benthall Edge, falling almost to the bottom before striking a tree stump which killed her instantly. As it happened the gamekeeper saw the whole thing, so Furlong's been arrested for her murder and taken to Much Wenlock.'

Abigail was stunned. So, he had attacked Jane as he had herself. Of course, Jane was older than she had been and rather more worldly wise, and so had no doubt resisted, which is why that monster had struck her. As Michael predicted, Abigail had already begun blaming herself.

'If only I'd told the Mistress or Master what he did to me. Maybe he could have been given his just desserts at the time and Jane may still be alive.'

'Mother you mustn't think like that. In any case,

it would only have been your word against his, and to put it bluntly, they wouldn't have taken the word of a scullery maid over that of the Under Butler, now would they?'

'Well, with the gamekeeper as a witness, he's not going to get away with this is he?'

'No, he certainly isn't. He'll hang for certain.'

'Oh Michael, how do you feel about that. He is your father after all, regardless of the circumstances of how you came to be.'

'Mother,' Michael pronounced with some force, 'I do not consider that monster to be my father, so don't worry on my account. In fact, I intend to go to the court to witness the trial, and the punishment for that matter. I want to be able to tell you that he is no more, and you need never worry about seeing him ever again.'

'And what about poor Arthur? I'm guessing the shock of Jane's death will have proved too much for his weakened body?'

'It would seem so Mother. Uncle Dick has ridden over there and when he gets back, we should know more. I expect the funerals will be in the next day or two.'

'What a tragic affair that will be, and no mistake,' said Abigail, 'I can't imagine what Liz is going through. I don't think she'll ever get over this.'

'I fear you're right mother, it's too much for anyone to bear, particularly given the manner of poor Jane's death.'

When Dick arrived at Banghams Wood he knocked on the cottage door with some trepidation. Jimmy opened it and was obviously pleased and somewhat relieved to see Dick standing there. He motioned for him to come in, thanking him for coming over and telling him that Elizabeth was upstairs. He quickly climbed the stairs and found her in the bedroom, seated beside the bodies of her husband and child. The room was cold as it must be until the day of the funeral, and Dick realised that he must get his sister downstairs, or she would catch her death. He was utterly shocked at her appearance. She looked up as he entered the room, but her eyes showed no hint of recognition. She was very obviously still in shock. Jimmy had followed him up and whispered,

'Uncle Dick, I can't get her to leave them. She should come down and get warm, and eat something, but has refused all food since yesterday.'

Dick knelt down beside his sister, putting his arm gently round her shoulder.

'Liz,' he said quietly, 'It's Dick. I'm come to see how you are. Will you come downstairs now, and warm yourself by the fire?'

She looked up again, and the sound of his voice, and the familiar lines of his face broke through her despair, and the light of recognition flickered in her eyes. She whispered his name and with a slight tilt of head indicated that she would go with him. With some effort, as she had been sitting for so long, she rose from the chair and gazing down at her beloved

Jane and Arthur lying under the sheets, she turned sadly away. Placing his hand under her elbow, Dick guided her to the stairs and down into the living room where he led her to the chair in front of the fire.

Ella Forester had brought some broth round earlier and Jimmy tried to persuade Elizabeth to eat something. At first, she waved it away with her hand. Eventually however, Dick managed to persuade her to take a little, telling her that she needed to keep her strength up for the days ahead. He didn't spell it out, but she knew he was thinking about the ordeal of the funerals which would soon have to be endured.

Not wishing to cause Elizabeth any more grief than was necessary, Dick motioned to Jimmy that he wanted to speak to him alone, and they went into the scullery. Assuming that his uncle wanted to know exactly what had happened. Jimmy, who was just about holding on to his emotions, said,

'I'm sorry Uncle Dick, I probably don't know much more than you do. We only know that Furlong met Jane on the path near the kissing gate and then struck her, and she fell off the path and down Benthall Edge until she hit a tree stump and her neck was broke.'

At this, Jimmy's voice faltered with emotion.

Dick placed a reassuring hand on his arm, then, when he had recovered somewhat, Jimmy went on to say they had brought Jane's body to the cottage. He hadn't been there, but Margaret had earlier come to warn them, thank goodness. Apparently when his father left his sick bed to find out what was going on, the sight of his daughter laid out on the table had been too much and he had collapsed into a terrible coughing fit. His lungs must have finally given out and although Aunt Margaret had managed to get him back upstairs into bed, when he arrived home an hour later, he found his father dead.

His emotion now took over and Jimmy's face contorted, his shoulders shook, and the tears fell. Dick threw his arms round the young man to console him as best he could but wondered to himself how anyone could deal with such a horrific double tragedy. When Jimmy had regained his composure they returned to sit awhile with Elizabeth. Dick felt there were no words to express his feelings and decided that he would just sit quietly with her for a while.

Eventually he spoke to Jimmy to ask him if there was anything he could do. Jimmy thought for a moment before saying,

'Well, I was wondering how I would let Joe and Will know about the funeral. I don't feel I can leave Ma here on her own with – you know...'

'No problem,' Dick said immediately, 'I'll ride over there before I leave for Bridgnorth.'

'Oh Uncle Dick, that would be a weight off my mind.'

At that, Dick picked up his coat before taking a sovereign out of his waistcoat pocket and pressing it into Jimmy's hand. Jimmy tried to refuse it but Dick insisted that it was the least he could do to help his sister at this terrible time. At least it would pay for the funeral, he said.

Jimmy would have rather refused it but he had to admit that there hadn't been much money around since his father had taken to his bed, and he had been worrying how he was going to pay for the funeral. He thanked Dick for his generosity, saying he wouldn't forget it.

'I know that lad, and if there's anything else, don't hesitate to ask me.'

Jimmy told him that the funerals were to be two days hence on the following Thursday at noon in Buildwas, and he hoped he and Aunt Margaret would come, and perhaps they would bring Aunt Abigail and Michael. Dick said that of course, they would all be there, and would meet them at the bridge. Jimmy told him that Ella and Rose had kindly offered to prepare the funeral meal. Dick said that he was sure that Margaret would insist on bringing something with them to help out with it in any case.

With that, Dick knelt down beside his sister, kissing her gently on the cheek and telling her that he would see her again in a couple of days, then he said his goodbyes to Jimmy, who thanked him again for coming. With one last smile at his sister, Dick took his leave. After riding the couple of miles over Buildwas bridge and along to Dale End to give the message about the funerals to Liz at Nailer's Row, Dick returned to the bridge to take the Bridgnorth road. He arrived just as dusk began to fall, going straight to Michael's house to tell his sister exactly what had happened. He knew she would be taking this badly, given her history with Furlong.

# Chapter 25

James Furlong was slumped on the floor in the corner of the very cell beneath Much Wenlock courtroom his son had occupied over ten years earlier. He wasn't the only occupant. Apart from the rats he was sharing it with a ruffian who looked as if he was no stranger to such a place. Furlong, of course, felt he should not be here at all. He truly believed he was innocent of any crime. It had been an accident. The stupid girl only had herself to blame. If she had taken more care, she wouldn't have slipped off the edge of the path. Curse that damn gamekeeper Sykes, he thought. If he hadn't been around, no one would ever have suspected he had anything to do with it.

Furlong seethed with indignation that he should have been thrown in here with such a person as this criminal, who was so obviously far beneath his station in life. How could he endure a whole week of this until the Assize hearing? He was sure he would be acquitted. He would convince the jury it was an accident. The girl wasn't around to say anything different, and in the end, it was only his word against Sykes's. He was an Under Butler, the jury were bound to take his word over that of a mere gamekeeper!

As he had been charged with murder, he was to be tried at the Assize. As it happened, the next one was due to be held in Much Wenlock in eight days' time, on the Monday of the following week, before a jury in the courtroom above. In the meantime, he determined to keep his head down and have nothing to do with his fellow prisoner. In such a confined space this proved harder to do than he had imagined. The ruffian amused himself by intimidating Furlong. Food was scarce and he always ended up sharing the scraps with the rats. There was nowhere to wash and the privvy was a bucket in one corner of the cell. With each passing day he felt more humiliated and even his natural arrogance began to desert him.

In Banghams Wood, the day of the funeral had been set for Thursday. It was early morning when Johnson turned up with the coffins. He had brought two apprentices with him and between them they wrapped the bodies in plain woollen shrouds as the law dictated, and placed them in their coffins. Elizabeth still could not believe that Arthur and Jane were gone. She sat staring into the fire as the coffins were brought down the stairs and carried out to the waiting cart. Margaret had arrived an hour before and had made sure that Jimmy and Elizabeth had warm drinks and some food inside them, to sustain them through the difficult hours ahead. When all was ready Jimmy gently took his stepmother's elbow and said,

'It's time Ma.'

Elizabeth looked up at him with a pitiful, disbelieving expression on her face, hesitating for a moment before struggling wearily to her feet Margaret threw her shawl around her shoulders and guided her out to the waiting cart. Now she couldn't avoid seeing the coffins and and her legs buckled. Jimmy put his arms under hers to support her. Johnson suggested that she and Margaret ride up on the front of the cart, while everyone else could walk behind. Margaret helped her up onto the cart then climbed up beside her. Elizabeth sat next to Johnson, steadfastly keeping her eyes to the front. As they were leaving Ella and Rose arrived to speak to Jimmy to reassure him that they would be setting out the funeral meal for when the family returned. He thanked them and said how he could never have managed all this without their help.

The weather that day was perfectly appropriate to the desperately sad occasion. One of those mists that seem more like low cloud had settled across the Gorge, shutting out the sun and making it feel as though a cold, damp blanket had been thrown across the world. The procession slowly made its way down the track and as they approached the bridge, Margaret could see Dick and Margaret waiting for them in their carriage, with Michael and Abigail seated behind. They all greeted each other solemnly then Dick manoeuvred the carriage in behind the cart and followed it over the bridge, turning to the left and heading towards Buildwas. Joe, Liz, Will and Betty were already there when they reached the church and Dorothy and John arrived with young Elizabeth shortly afterwards.

So it was, that the Bangham family once more gathered around an open grave in the Buildwas burial ground at Holy Trinity Church. As Joe surveyed the scene, he was thinking that it was sad that the only time he saw his siblings these days was at a funeral, and this one was of course desperately sad. Jane was too young to die, and in such a violent fashion, which in turn, had hastened the death of her father. As he looked around the family, he reflected how everyone was ageing, particularly, and understandably, Elizabeth. She looked weighed down with the burden of her grief. At that moment, Joe knew she would never get over the loss of the two people she loved the most.

After the coffins had been lowered into the grave, Arthur first, and then Jane, the vicar recited the usual words and they each in turn, starting with Elizabeth, threw handfuls of soil into the grave, and then turned slowly away and began to make their way back up to Banghams Wood. Now Elizabeth and Margaret rode with Dick and Margaret in their carriage, with the rest of the family walking behind. As they walked some way behind the rest, Michael spoke to Jimmy, saying how sorry he was for his loss. He also brought up the subject of Furlong's trial, saying that he intended to go. Jimmy said that for his father's sake, he also was determined to go to see justice done, for not only did he blame Furlong for his sister's death, but also indirectly for his father's. Michael said he had heard that the trial was to be before a jury on the following Monday and the two men agreed to meet and go to the Courtroom together.

When the funeral party arrived at the cottage, Ella and Rose had laid the table with refreshments and Margaret brought in a basketful of bread, cakes and ham to add to the rest of the food. None of them knew it, but this was to be the last time they would all be together in their family home. The siblings had all been born in this cottage, built by their grandfather with his bare hands. Their roots were here, but as with any family, their chosen pathways were diverging and the bonds that had held them together were loosening. No-one felt this more keenly than Elizabeth, who now felt utterly rudderless, and without the love of Arthur to tether her to reality, and Jane to give her life meaning, she was lost.

Of course, everyone was very attentive of Elizabeth and tried to bring her into the conversations about times gone by when they were young and their mother and father were around, but she felt completely detached and unable to relate to anything they were saying. It all seemed so meaningless. When the time came for them to leave her, one by one they assured her that they would be there if ever she needed anything. She allowed herself to be embraced by them in turn, managing a half smile and a nod in acknowledgement, but her heart was numb, the coldness of grief stifling all feeling.

Will and Betty had decided to go down the steps to

the river and across in Bert Rogers' coracle, as it was a shorter way to Dale Coppice than taking the track towards Buildwas. As Joe and Liz made their way back down to the bridge and home, they reflected on the day. They agreed it had been good to spend a little time with their daughter, Elizabeth. They saw precious little of her these days. Liz remarked how grown up she looked. Quite the little lady! Dorothy and John were doing a good job of educating her, and not only in reading and writing. Joe commented that she had a certain confidence about her, and her speech had become more cultivated.

Joe remarked that Michael in particular had looked troubled. He was very attentive to his mother and was obviously concerned at how all this had affected her. He supposed that Abigail might well blame herself for what happened to Jane, as Furlong had never been brought to book for raping her, and had been allowed to go on abusing women all these years, eventually leading to the murder of Jane. Michael had told him that he intended to see Furlong tried, and hopefully finished off once and for all. However, Furlong was still his father, and Joe wondered how he would deal with maybe seeing him hang. Liz agreed it was a lot for Michael to deal with but she felt sure that Dick would continue to support him as he had all along. Joe agreed, saying that his brother was a good man and had chosen his wife well. Margaret was as kind and generous as her husband. He suspected that Dick had helped Jimmy out with the cost of the funeral, always ready to share his good fortune with his family. Michael had also told him that Jimmy intended to meet him in Much Wenlock for the trial. He of course, also needed to see justice done and Furlong punished for the deaths of his sister, and also his father's sudden demise. Joe did wonder whether he and possibly Will, ought also to go to the trial, but on balance, he felt that those most directly involved, Michael and Jimmy, should be the ones to represent the family.

Joe's deepest concern however was reserved for Elizabeth. He told Liz that he was afraid she would not get over this. Margaret had said she would visit as often as she could, but everyone knew that would be no more than once a month as long as she was still working at the Hall. Of course, Margaret herself was looking much older and Joe wondered how much longer she would be able to carry on, but then where would she go? The thought struck him that maybe she would be able to go to live with Elizabeth and Jimmy in the family cottage, but of course, that would be up to Jimmy, who was now head of the household.

As they turned into Dale Road, Liz said she would call at Lorna Bailey's house to pick up the children while Joe went on home to light the fire. Lorna had kindly offered to have them while she and Joe attended the funeral. Joe had barely got the fire going when Nathaniel and Benjamin burst in. They were excited and seemed to have had a good day, playing in the brook with the Bailey children, and wanted to tell Joe all about it. To calm them down he told

Nathaniel to go out to the store to bring some coal for the fire. Liz came in carrying Anne in her arms. She was a pretty, if serious little girl with eyes that looked as though they had seen this world before. Nathaniel strode back in with the coal bucket. He would be ten years old next birthday and growing fast and Joe was thinking it would soon be time to find him an apprenticeship. He determined to speak to Mr Ford about it soon.

Dick and Margaret had just arrived home, having dropped Abigail and Michael off on the way. Elizabeth, Richard and Walter, who were all in their nightclothes came running as their parents entered the hallway. Nanny had allowed them to stay up until their parents arrived home but young Joseph had already been put to bed. After the sad day they had spent in the Gorge, Dick and Margaret were glad to see them, and to make a fuss of them before Nanny eventually put her foot down and ushered them all upstairs to bed.

Abigail was worried. She felt this tragic train of events may yet claim another victim if, as she suspected, Elizabeth was unable to deal with her loss. She had seemed somehow detached from everything and everyone. And then there was Michael. He seemed determined to go to Furlong's trial on the following Monday in Much Wenlock. She fervently wished he wouldn't go. She couldn't imagine how he was going to deal with seeing Furlong tried and possibly hung for Jane's murder. He was still his father and however much Michael assured her that he meant nothing to him, Abigail wasn't so sure that when it came down to it, he would be able to remain so detached.

Michael woke early on Monday morning and was riding towards Much Wenlock before eight o'clock. He found Jimmy outside the Guildhall. Michael cast a glance towards the cells beneath the Courtroom. He knew that place all too well and the memory of that dreadful night flooded back. He knew that was where Furlong would have spent the days since his arrest and he knew how desolate he would be feeling right now. With a supreme effort of will he pushed the thoughts out of his mind, knowing he would have enough to deal with this day without re-living the past, let alone feeling sorry for Furlong. He followed Jimmy up the stone steps outside the building and into the Court-room itself.

There was quite a hubbub as the twelve men of the jury took their seats to the right of the judges' bench. There were five judges, looking impressive in their gowns and wigs, the one in the centre seated a little higher than the rest. The jury was now sworn in one by one. Opposite the judges was a low balustrade behind which the public were permitted to stand to observe the proceedings. Having arrived early, Michael had met Jimmy outside the Guildhall and they had now secured a spot at the front of the crowd. They stood side by side, nervously waiting for the trial to begin. Of course for Michael, this was evoking memories of the day he himself had been brought into this courtroom, before being sent to Bridgnorth to be tried at the Assize. He knew that Furlong would be at that moment, climbing the stairs outside the rear door of the courtroom, to await the judge's instruction. All eyes were on the judges. Finally it came,

'Bring forth the prisoner, James Furlong.'

A hush now fell over the courtroom. Michael clenched his fists in anticipation. His stomach churned and he turned to watch Furlong being brought into the room. He was shocked at the sight of him. He had spent over a week in that ghastly rat-infested cell and had probably had little sleep, or food for that matter. He was hardly recognisable. To his surprise, and in spite of himself, for a fleeting moment Michael felt a little sorry for him, until he reminded himself that here was the man who had ruined his mother's life and murdered his cousin.

Furlong's feet were shackled, and his hands cuffed. He was led down the side of the courtroom, past the assembled spectators, to the dock where accused prisoners were required to stand, facing the jury, to the left of the judges' bench. Furlong stood with his head bent, looking at the floor. Not so arrogant now, thought Michael, but just at that moment, Furlong raised his head and as he did so, saw Michael standing at the front of the crowd. Their eyes met and once again Michael was struck by a feeling of recognition, as though he was looking at an older version of himself, and he sensed some of the fear Furlong was feeling. He dragged his eyes away and looked towards the jury. They were staring at the accused with some animosity. The story of how Furlong had cold-heartedly murdered an innocent young woman had obviously already reached their ears, and it looked as though they would take some convincing that he was innocent. Michael felt Jimmy tense beside him as he looked at the monster who had taken his lovely sister and loving father away from him and he looked as though he would gladly have jumped over the balustrade and throttled him there and then, if he hadn't believed the law would soon do it for him.

The judge spoke directly to Furlong, saying,

'James Furlong, you have been accused of the murder of Jane Green on Sunday, the twenty first day of September. How do you plead. Guilty or not guilty.'

Furlong did his best to stand tall, then declared in the loudest voice he could manage,

'Not guilty, Your Worship.'

The judge then asked that the witnesses, if there were any, be brought forward to give evidence.

In the event, there were only two witnesses, the main one being the gamekeeper Mr Sykes who now entered the courtroom and stood before the judges. He related the story in a way that left little doubt as to its veracity. As he told the court about the callous way the defendant had struck Jane so hard that she had tumbled off the path and fallen to her death, there were several shouts of 'string him up' until the judge rapped the desk with a gavel and called for silence in the court. However, as Mr Sykes went on to say that the defendant had callously walked away from the scene of the crime without even going to check whether poor Jane was still alive, further shouts rose up. Jimmy looked across at Furlong and could see him diminish before his eyes. His shoulders sagged as he listened to the damning testimony and heard the calls for him to be hung.

When Mr Sykes had finished his evidence, the Master from the Hall who was the Justice of the Peace was called forward and he corroborated the version of events which had just been described. He confirmed that he had arrived at the scene shortly afterwards and found the deceased lying dead with her neck broken, exactly as Mr Sykes had said, and had seen evidence that she had fallen from the path at the top of Benthall Edge before plunging to her death. At this there was more murmuring amongst the crowd, with more pleas for the murderer to be hung.

The judge once again demanded silence and then turned to the jury. As there were no more witnesses to be called, he instructed them to come to a decision as to whether the defendant was guilty or not guilty of the crime of murder. The jury had no need to retire. After forming a huddle and conversing for no more than two minutes, Michael observed them nodding to each other, and the foreman of the jury stood up.

The judge asked whether they had reached a verdict upon which they were all agreed. The foreman replied that they had. The judge looked across at Furlong who had turned a deathly white, then turned back to the foreman of the jury and asked the question,

'Do you find the defendant, James Furlong, guilty or not guilty of murder?'

The court was completely silent as everyone held their breath, waiting for the answer. When it came, it was loud and clear,

'Guilty, your Honour.'

Furlong hung on to the front of the dock to stop himself from sliding to the floor. Michael was surprised to find himself suddenly wanting to vomit. He now knew that before this day was out he would have to witness his own father being hung on the gallows which he had walked past as he had arrived that morning. Jimmy just hissed 'Yess!' through clenched teeth.

The judge turned to Furlong saying,

'You have been found guilty of a most heinous crime, the coldblooded murder of an innocent young woman. Do you have anything you wish to say to the court before I pass sentence?'

Furlong could produce no words in his own defence. In fact, he could utter no words at all, and simply shook his head at the judge.

'Very well then,' said the judge, who then turned to the judges to each side of him in turn, obviously seeking their opinions as to what the sentence should be, although there was in fact, little doubt. Finally, and slowly, he took the square of black cloth handed to him by the clerk and placed it on his head, before stating loudly,

'James Furlong, you have been found guilty by a

jury of your peers of the crime of murder and there is only one punishment to fit such a crime.'

He paused for a moment and Furlong looked terrified, shaking his head. The judge finally went on,

'You will be taken from here to the place of execution and there you will be hung by the neck until you are dead.'

A cheer went up in the room. Michael felt numb and Jimmy was relieved. Jane and his father would have their justice. Furlong himself looked horrified and clung to the front of the dock as the two court officers gripped him by his arms and then dragged him down the side of the courtroom to the door at the back. As they left the courtroom, everyone, including the jury, followed them out. They all knew that the punishment would be delivered immediately. The gallows had been prepared in readiness, as Furlong knew only too well, as he had heard them being built the day before. They were just behind the Guildhall, beside the church. A crowd had already gathered to watch the spectacle and now it was swollen by the people who had been in the courtroom, including Michael and Jimmy.

Furlong had to be dragged towards the steps of the gallows. He resisted at every step. He knew it was hopeless but his mind could not accept that within minutes he would be no more, and his body wanted to live, his legs refusing to carry him towards his end. The officers now removed the shackles round his ankles and the handcuffs, then tied his hands behind his back. Finally, they managed to get him up the steps to stand on a low stool in front of the trapdoor. He looked round wildly in a last vain attempt to find a saviour, and his eyes landed upon Michael, pleading for him to do something to save him. Michael could stand it no longer and looked away. Jimmy however, did not. He was determined to witness to the last moment, the end of this monster.

A hessian sack full of sand had been placed on the trapdoor. The noose, attached to it by a long rope thrown over the beam above, was placed round Furlong's neck. His eyes were wild and he was trembling. The final humiliation came as his bladder let its contents dribble down his trousers as he took his last desperate breaths. At a signal from the presiding judge, the hangman pulled the lever and the sandbag dropped through the trapdoor, yanking Furlong off his feet. The noose tightened around his neck, and to the cheers of the crowd, Furlong was swinging about wildly and kicking his legs for a full ten seconds before the life left him and he hung, still and silent. The crowd continued to cheer for some moments, but they too eventually fell silent and began to drift away. The spectacle was over, justice had been dispensed.

Michael felt empty but also relieved that this ordeal was over. He had come for his mother's sake, and now at last he could tell her that Furlong was no more and would never trouble her again. As for his own feelings, not surprisingly, he was somewhat confused. Whatever this man had done, he had still been responsible for his own existence. He knew he must consciously dismiss such thoughts from his mind. They could serve no purpose now. He must concentrate on his mother's feelings.

Jimmy on the other hand, was elated. He had felt nothing but hatred for this evil man and he was happy that he had gone forever. His duty done, he could now return to his stepmother to tell her that her grief had been avenged.

It took just a few hours before news of the hanging reached the Gorge and everyone was glad of it, especially Joe, Dorothy and Will, who was glad that finally the hangman had finished the job he started all those years ago. Of course, they had all felt Elizabeth's losses particularly keenly and hoped that Furlong's death may help her to find some closure.

Over the next few months they all, whenever they were able, visited Elizabeth to see how she was coping, but it was obvious that, as they had all suspected, she would never get over the events of that terrible day when Jane had been carried home and laid out on the table, and within minutes, her beloved Arthur had gone too. It was obvious to everyone that her health was declining. She wasn't eating properly, and hadn't had a good night's sleep since. In fact, Elizabeth survived less than twelve months. It was in early May 1739 that she was struck down by a particularly bad cold, which her weakened body could not fight. It turned to pneumonia and within a week she was dead.

# Chapter 26

After Elizabeth died, the Bangham family's roots in Banghams Wood withered away. The old family home had now passed to Jimmy Green and his descendants. Margaret no longer visited the cottage on her days off, partly because the steep pathway down to the wood was now too much for her. Indeed, it was only two years later that she accepted she would have to leave service, as she could barely even manage the stairs up to the attic where she slept. The Master was very fair and gave her a small annuity in view of her decades of service. However, it was not enough for her to live independently. She had resigned herself to going to Mine Spout until one day, Michael arrived at the Hall. He had heard from Fred that Margaret was to retire, and after he and his mother had discussed it, they decided to ask her to come to live with them. The business was doing well, and Dick, appreciating Michael's contribution to its success, had rewarded him with generous wage increases over the years. He could afford to rent a larger house, and he had already begun to look around for something suitable. Margaret was relieved and delighted, and in the Spring of 1742, left the Hall for the last time to live out the rest of her days peacefully in Bridgnorth with her sister.

Will and Betty had no more children. Although they would have loved a little girl, it never happened. They continued to live in Dale Coppice. George was apprenticed to a carpenter in Madeley, and eventually Walter joined Will, in the boring mill. The family's finances became a little easier and life was tolerable, although Will could never quite rid himself of the feeling of injustice that his life should be one of constant struggle just in order for his family to survive. In America, even though the tragedy he'd suffered had led him to return to the Gorge, he had nevertheless glimpsed that a different life could have been possible, if circumstances had been different. He realised that he might have created a better, freer life there, and more than once as the years passed, he wondered if he had given up on the New World a little too easily. As the Bangham boys grew, he often talked to them about the land of opportunity across the ocean, and he could see that Joe's Benjamin, in particular, always sat enthralled, looking at him with eyes shining, whenever he did. Usually, Liz would intervene to change the subject at this point, unwilling to allow young Ben's imagination to be fired with thoughts of leaving the Gorge to seek his fortune on the other side of the world.

Nathaniel had been apprenticed to the Coalbrookdale Company as a mould maker in the moulding shop near the upper furnace pool. Now thirteen, he was a bright young man and had settled in well to the world of work. Joe was proud of him. As for Joe himself, he had to admit that as the years went on, the system of working thirteen twelve hour days without a break was beginning to take its toll on his body. Fortunately, the furnace was just a short way up the valley from Nailer's Row and at least he was able to go home for half an hour or so, during breaks. There were worse jobs in the Gorge and worse men to work for than Mr Ford, and Joe knew it.

With the children growing up and off her hands, Liz was now earning some money, taking in washing from middle class households, round and about. While they could afford to pay a washerwoman, they weren't rich enough to afford live-in servants, and as the Works expanded, so did the demand for this service and Liz had no shortage of customers. Joe wasn't too happy about this. He felt that his wife shouldn't have to wash other people's dirty clothes, but Liz was adamant. She enjoyed the feeling of independence being able to contribute to the household budget gave her,

Recently she had become worried about Ann. She sometimes seemed to struggle to get her breath. This was worse when the wind blew from the north, channeling the fumes and smoke from the furnaces down the narrow valley towards the river, and Liz was sure something in the smoke was affecting her more than the rest of the family. Not that there was anything to be done about that of course. They couldn't move out of the valley unless they wanted to face destitution.

Joe's living was here, and here they must stay, for better or worse.

A small half-day school had recently been set up by Mr Ford, to offer some limited education to the children of his workers, and Nathaniel and Benjamin were now learning to read and write. Joe was delighted. Maybe his children would, after all, have an easier life than he had had.

Although the hours were long and the work hard, Joe was still proud of working for the Coalbrookdale Company. However, somewhere in the back of his mind, a feeling had begun to form. He hadn't quite managed to put a name to it, until, one day he had occasion to visit the Clerk's office, which was opposite Rosehill House, where the Ford family lived. Next door was Dale House where Mr Darby and his daughter Hannah had lived since his wife's death two years earlier. As he was leaving, he stood for a minute or two, looking up at the grandeur of the two buildings. As he watched, a carriage pulled up, drawn by two fine black horses, and Mr Darby climbed out, followed by Hannah. Although their clothes were simple, they were of good quality, Hannah looking particularly fine in her long grey dress with white lace collar with a black velvet cloak around her shoulders.

At that moment, something clicked in Joe's mind. He couldn't help comparing this young woman's appearance to his own daughter, Ann's, in her simple brown shift. He thought back to the early days of his time with the Darbys. When he joined, there were less than a dozen men employed by the company. Although old Mr Darby was the owner and manager of the business, he had never acted as though he was above his workmen. Rather, he seemed to like to be considered as one of them. As Joe observed old Mr Darby's son Abraham and Hannah alighting from the carriage and entering the front door of their fine home, he realised just how much had changed in those twenty seven years. While he had a a roof over his head and a family, in spite of working hard, his station in life had, if anything, become lower. He still barely earned enough to sustain the family, so much so that, to his eternal shame, his wife now had to take in washing to make ends meet. His sons, instead of being properly educated as young Abraham had been, must be content with half a day a week of learning, which he suspected was provided to offer more benefit to the Company, than to the children of their workers. He was forty five now, and he was beginning to realise that, however hard he worked, he would be unable to improve his standard of living.

He turned away, and as he walked back down the valley, with the roar of the furnaces and the sound of metal on metal ringing in his ears, the contrast between the vision of gentility he had just witnessed, and the sight of the mean cottages with grubby little children standing beside their mothers as they hung out their washing, or tended their vegetable plots was stark. So this is the truth of my life then, for all my hard work, I have risen no further than any of these poor souls, he thought. He now realised the feeling that had been forming in his mind was crystalising. It was resentment. For the first time, he acknowledged to himself that the life he had imagined when he made that journey across the Gorge all those years ago, his employment with the Coalbrookdale Company had not entirely lived up to the promise he had imagined. How could a man who had worked as hard as he had, for twenty seven years, now be so much worse off than the man who had employed him. While the Darbys had prospered, he had not. His life had become harder and there was no prospect of it becoming any easier. He would have to work until the day he died, or became too ill and weak to work, and had to go to the poorhouse.

As he now approached the new furnace once more, he realised he must put aside these thoughts and concentrate on the job in hand. The furnace was no place to be distracted. Men's lives depended on his attentiveness. However, when he returned home at the end of his shift, Liz noticed that there was a change in her husband. After twenty years of marriage she knew his every mood, and couldn't rest until she had found out what was troubling him. Liz realised that such thoughts may well bring danger to the family, and said so. She told him that they had to be content with what they had, a home, money coming in and four healthy children, and that he must dismiss these notions. Joe knew she was right. Harbouring discontent was no help to anyone if nothing could be done about it, and he determined to put it out of his mind, for the time being, at any rate.

That night however, as he lay beside Liz, waiting for sleep to come, his mind drifted back to a Christmas Day long ago in Banghams wood, when all the neighbours joined them in the cottage, his father at the head of the table and Elizabeth at the other end, with a roaring fire in the hearth, as much food as they could eat, and drink more than they could take, and for a while, he indulged in the memory. Life had seemed more simple then. They hadn't had much money, but then they didn't need much. They had their squatters' cottage with rights to remain there as long as they wished. They had the means to grow their own food, chickens in the yard and a hog fattening in its pen. They were able to make enough to live on using the resources around them, coppicing the woodland and building their clamps, and in the summer months could earn more, helping out at the farm up at the Hall. They made their own choices about what work they would do each day, and if they wanted a day off, they took it. How different, he mused, from his life now. Instead of being ruled by the seasons and the weather, it was ruled by the clock and the incessant demands of the furnace. Had he known what his life here would be like, would he still have made the same decision to leave the Wood, to be part of the changes that were surely coming? Maybe he would have taken the same decision sooner or later. The world was changing and whether he liked it or not, he was part of that world. Confounded by this inescapable logic, he turned over and drifted off to sleep.

After that, although he continued to work for the Coalbrookdale Company, it was never again to be with the same level of belief and commitment. All around now, his eyes were to be opened to the injustices, and not only within the ironworks. In many ways, the Darby's were one of the better employers in the area. In some of the coalmines he observed little children no older than six years old now being sent underground, to work long hours in the blackness with only a single candle to bring comfort. He saw the young women, forced to pick coal off the spoil heaps to sell to their betters or to bring warmth to their families in times of deprivation. He saw men and women, maimed or worse, leaving their families destitute and to be returned to their parishes, or sent to Mine Spout poorhouse to live out their miserable lives. He did tell himself that actually, his family was better off than most, working as he did, for the well respected Coalbrookdale Partners, but from time to time, the resentment resurfaced, as he observed the mine owners and ironmasters growing rich, while he and his family remained forever trapped in a life of drudgery.

Most of the time though, Liz and Joe were to concentrate on giving their children and each other as much love and care as they were able. Elizabeth became a schoolteacher and Ann stayed at home to look after Liz and Joe as they grew older. Nathaniel and Benjamin continued to work for the Company and were destined to be part of even bigger changes that would be coming to the Severn Gorge, and to the world; but that is another story.

# EPILOGUE

The Coalbrookdale Company continued to prosper for the next two centuries. The following years brought many innovations and improvements to iron production in the valley, and other ironworks were opened upin the district. Within fifteen years the first single span iron bridge was constructed across the River Severn, and became a wonder of the world, visited by travellers from across the globe, as it still is today. Over the next century, the first iron rails and steam driven trains facilitated the rapid spread of the railway system in Britain and throughout the Empire and parts for the first iron ship, the SS Great Britain, were cast in the Coalbrookdale Company works.

The technology developed in the Gorge spread around the country and then the world, and the unstoppable Industrial Revolution had begun.

For better, or worse, remains to be seen.

# ABOUT THE AUTHOR

Marilyn lives in Bedford with her husband. She loves to take the long look at her characters' lives. She is fascinated by the way differing personalities interact and how decisions taken with the best of intentions can cause effects that resonate down the generations. Marilyn has written two further books:

**Karma, A Mystery in Paris:** A story set largely in 1970's Paris when a fatal accident and chance discovery propel Adrienne on a quest to discover what happened to her mother when she disappeared from the family home ten years previously. The story she reveals spans three decades and has its roots in the Nazi occupation of the city during the 1940's and the evils perpetrated. The consequences of those events echo down the years and little by little we learn what happened to Janey and why she never came home. It is a story with many twists and turns, the shocking conclusion delivering a certain natural justice.

**Secrets and Lives:** When Joan gave her baby up for adoption in 1972, she could have had no idea what consequences would follow decades later. When her son, now a man, re-enters her life without warning, tragedy ensues. The life John was forced to lead has left its mark on him and even the love and acceptance of his half sister Sophie, living a comfortable life in Bath cannot undo the harm done.

Both books are available from all good online bookstores including Amazo, Kobo and Barnes and Noble, in ebook and paperback format.

Please visit her webpage at www.spellbrooktales.com for more information or email her at inbox@marilynfreeman.org.